"Think of the life you have lived until now as over and, as a dead man, see what's left as a bonus and live it according to Nature. Love the hand that fate deals you and play it as your own, for what could be more fitting?"

— MARCUS AURELIUS

勇気

SHIN OF THE RAVENFIN

by

Mark Jenkins

ALSO BY MARK JENKINS

Klickitat and other stories

Saving Schrödinger's Cat

Verglas

Rainshadow

Connect with Mark.

Please visit his website **MarkJenkinsBooks.com** and check out some interesting tidbits from this novel and his other works. While there, be sure to sign up for his newsletter **Pen & Puget Sound** for original content, updates, nature photography, and works from other authors.

Shin of the Ravenfin

ISBN 978-1-7352061-8-9 (paperback)

ISBN 978-1-7352061-9-6 (epub)

Shin of the Ravenfin is a work of fiction. Any resemblance to actual events or persons is entirely coincidental. Certain long-standing institutions, places, agencies, historical figures and facts, public figures and public offices are mentioned, but otherwise all of this story — and the characters involved — is wholly imaginary.

MarkJenkinsBooks.com

ACKNOWLEDGMENTS

I am deeply grateful to the editorial team for their work on this manuscript.

The gorgeous cover design & illustration were composed by the brilliant artist **Mark Thomas/Coverness.com**

Interior title art and formatting by Mark Jenkins.

A special thank you to Kotomi Yamamura for manuscript review, and to Thelma Jenkins for proofreading.

For Jo

1

"I will join you soon, my love," said Shin Takeda, and braced himself on the cabin table as he leaned forward to kiss his wife's photo. Gentle ocean swells rolled the 32-foot sailboat as he exited the cabin, naked, walked to the stern, and dove off.

The frigid salt water shocked him, taking away his breath.

Shin kicked to the surface and began swimming. Long arm pulls powered him through the waves.

The heat from his muscles built, and warded off the cold. Shin counted three hundred strokes before stopping and turning to look back. He panted to catch his breath in the bone-chilling waters as he scanned for his sailboat.

In light winds — and under full sail with her wheel tied off — the *Harumi* glided westward in the twilight. Shin had committed to this course, though, and knew he would never again see the sailboat that had been the source of so much joy for he and his wife.

His body heat fled. He shivered.

Shin's throat constricted and sobs wracked his chest. He stuttered, "Ayumi... why'd... you die?"

Treading water, he watched his boat sail straight and true in the rising moonlight, until it disappeared from view. Another round of shivering swept through him, and he clenched his jaw.

Bobbing in the indigo waves of the Strait of Juan de Fuca, Shin could see neither ship nor shore. Everything was as perfect as he'd imagined it to be.

He focused on the release soon to arrive — the absence of pain.

Shin sang a love song to Ayumi, recalling the first time they'd met, but his cold-slowed brain and tongue fumbled the lyrics.

He slurred more words, then gave up.

He floated on his back, weeping. Ocean swells bobbed him up and down.

The moon, near full, showed through a gap in the clouds. Shin searched for navigation points in the sky. Old mariner habits were hard to stifle.

As the hypothermia progressed, the paradoxical sensation of heat built within Shin's torso. It flowed out toward his limbs and settled his tremors. His muscles relaxed as if he were floating in a hot tub.

Bliss, he thought. *Ayumi, I will be with you.*

The moon grew brighter. Shin stared at it as he slipped underwater.

"Beautiful," he burbled, expelling the last air in his lungs.

His lips spasmed as he tried to smile. *So damn beautiful…*

Shin drifted deeper.

2

Shin opened his eyes and blinked at the bright white light in confusion. A staccato beeping noise pierced a background hiss which came from everywhere and nowhere.

His vision adjusted to the glare. He stared at fluorescent tubes in a tiled ceiling.

What... Where?

He sat up—

—the room spun around him as pain exploded in his skull. Shin gasped and collapsed back onto a cushioned surface, panting.

Even when the grip on his cranium eased, he remained motionless, afraid to move. His gaze darted as he tried to figure out his environment.

He lay on his back, flanked by chrome rails, like small train tracks. Something was on his face — this was the source of the hissing.

"What the hell," croaked Shin in a muffled, foreign voice.

As he reached up and pulled away the plastic oxygen mask, he noticed the IV tubing snaking into his arm beneath a gauze bandage.

The odor of the antiseptic used by corpsmen penetrated his nose.

Medevac, he concluded. *But where? What happened?*

The beeping grew more urgent.

"He's awake," said a voice. Shin heard a squeak of sneakers.

A hand squeezed his.

The beeping stopped.

"Everything's okay, Shin," said a woman's voice. "You're in the intensive care unit, and you're getting better."

He looked into her brown eyes and studied her oval face and angular nose, but didn't know who she was.

"I'm Mary, your nurse," she said, and smiled.

"What happened?" he said. "Where am I?"

"You were rescued on the north coastline of the Olympics, severely hypothermic, after an accident at sea. A Coast Guard team brought you here to Harborview in Seattle, and we've been caring for you."

Shin parsed the information, and tried to recall what had happened to him. There were fragments, but they made no sense. He remembered the cold of the ocean, the moon in the sky — then a strange voice... a black boat... a helicopter.

Jumbled images of his rescue, he assumed. *But I was six miles from shore when I—*

"How are you feeling?"

"I don't know," said Shin. He shivered. *Why am I alive?* His teeth clacked as the shudders intensified.

"You're cold." Mary got a blanket and spread it over him.

"Thank you," said Shin. "I think I'm fine."

Mary studied him with a look he'd seen before, in the nurses caring for his wife — a blend of open compassion and wariness.

The shivers passed. He turned his head away from her and looked through the sliding glass door at the nurses station. "How long have I been here?" he asked.

"You've been in the ICU for a week."

"A w-week," said Shin. The ceiling swam, and his head pounded again.

The damn beeping returned. He closed his eyes. After several breaths, the pain vanished.

Shin opened his eyes to see Mary depress a button on a machine. She turned to him as the alert silenced. "Your heart rate dropped very low," she said. "But it's been happening less as you've improved."

"What does it mean?" he asked.

"Dr. Brody will explain everything to you — when the critical care team makes their clinical rounds this afternoon."

"So, I just lie here until then?"

"Yes." Mary chuckled. "You rest for now and build up your strength, okay?"

"Okay."

Mary left and Shin was again alone in the plexiglass-enclosed bay. He was isolated in terms of human companionship, but not in the sense of quiet. A cacophony of beeps, whistles, voices, squeaks, bangs, and hisses echoed everywhere. Shin couldn't believe how loud it all was.

He closed his eyes but soon gave up on trying to get any sort of rest.

He opened his eyes and stared at the ceiling. His left hand grasped the toggle for the bed controls. Holding his breath, and bracing himself for another headache, he depressed the button to raise the head of the bed.

Gears whirled.

With the slow mechanical rise, more of his ICU environment was revealed. He released his thumb when the head of the bed was at 30 degrees, and studied his new surroundings.

He was in a rectangular plexiglass bay, with a solid white wall on one side and beige curtains on rails framing the rest. The curtains were pulled back and he studied the central nurses' station. It was crowded with computer workstations, stacks of paper, and electrical charging cradles. Even though the transparent door of his room was closed, he could still hear the hum and buzz of the machinery.

After looking over the various machines within his bay, some of which he knew, his attention landed on a white erasable board attached to the wall. There were words in neat blue lettering: *Shin Takeda, your nurse is Mary; today is April 14, 2006; Dr. Brody - ICU Team 2.* At the bottom of the board was a smiley face and the words *Good Friday.*

Seven days, Shin thought. *And every shift they've updated that board, even though I couldn't see it.*

Outside his bay was a hallway. On both sides of that central corridor were more bays like his. At the end were a set of double doors. Abruptly, they burst open, admitting a cluster of people wearing long and short white coats: an ICU team.

Shin recalled that there was a pecking order. The short coats trailing in the back were the medical students, the long coats in the center were the interns (physicians who'd just started their training program), and the long coats in the front were the residents and fellows (more senior physicians to the interns). And at the tip of the flock of white was the single attending physician, the faculty member who was ultimately responsible for all the life and death decisions of the team.

The white flock flowed behind the lead doctor like a wave of swans until they stopped at one of the bays.

Shin looked at the analog clock on the wall and watched the second hand sweep around.

His eyes unfocused. Snatches of shattered memory appeared, then fled. But there was a bit more clarity than before. A long zodiac boat, or a black torpedo, with white markings had lifted him through the waves. But where it had come from and how it had found him remained a mystery.

The more disturbing part, though, was the strange voice. Shin struggled to remember its words. The commands were harsh, angry, and—

A knock interrupted his reverie.

"Mr. Takeda, I'm Dr. Brody," said a man in a long, white coat, who was standing in front of Shin. The rest of the team of a dozen or so spilled out into the hallway. "How are you feeling today?"

"Confused."

"That's understandable," said Dr. Brody with a smile. "You've been through a lot. After you were airlifted to the hospital last week, your heart stopped in the ER. We shocked you back to life and put you on a breathing machine. You were comatose and on life support until two days ago. It was touch and go for a while, but you have made an amazing recovery."

The words *breathing machine* shot into Shin like bullets. He had come off that machine. But Ayumi had not. Her last days, as the cancer had overwhelmed her body, had been spent connected to one. Shin could still hear the hiss of the bellows as that machine had pumped air into Ayumi's emaciated body.

"I don't remember any of that," he said. Tears trickled onto his cheeks.

A young woman in a short white coat, stepped forward with a tissue in her hand. Shin looked into her eyes as he accepted it. She was Japanese. He bowed his head and wiped away the tears on his face.

She bowed in return, and rejoined her place in the midst of the white swans.

Dr. Brody then asked him a bunch of questions. Some were almost games, like counting backward from one hundred in sevens. Shin figured that these were designed to test his cognitive function. Next, the doctor used his stethoscope to listen to Shin's lungs and then his heart. He smiled at Shin as he folded his stethoscope into one of the large pockets in his clean, starched lab coat.

"Excellent," he said. "We were very concerned about your status, but tomorrow you'll be able to go to a regular floor room. And then probably home in a few days."

Two of the long coats smiled at each other. One reached out to put a hand on the other's shoulder. "It's a *save*," someone whispered.

Many smiled. Some grinned.

Dr. Brody cleared his throat, then turned his back on Shin to face his team. "Hush," he whispered. "Saves only happen in baseball and religion. By the grace of God, and your adherence to the protocols of resuscitation and critical care medicine, an individual has survived — but that doesn't make *you* saviors."

The smiles vanished.

Shin comprehended that he wasn't supposed to hear any of this, much less understand what Dr. Brody had said, but every word — even the whispered murmur of a nurse at the desk — seemed loud and clear.

Dr. Brody turned toward him. "Do you have any questions, Mr. Takeda?" he asked.

"Yes," said Shin. "I have headaches when I sit up, and Mary said my heart rate has been dropping very low sometimes. Will these go away?"

"Dysautonomia," interjected one of the long coats, stroking his beard.

"Yes," said Dr. Brody. "That's correct."

"Huh?" said Shin.

"What he's saying is that the shock of the hypothermia and subsequent cardiac arrest have induced a sort of disequilibrium into your autonomic nervous system. These are the systems that regulate blood pressure, heart rate, and other aspects of your physiology. The good news is that the monitors demonstrate fewer heart rate drops with each day. So, to answer your question — yes, I think all of these things will eventually go away."

"And my hearing?" asked Shin. "Everything's so damned loud."

"Hyperacusis," said the bearded long coat.

Shin cocked his head to the side. "What?"

The man stepped forward. "Your brain is rebooting itself, like a computer unplugged and replugged into a power source. Sometimes the senses, like your ears, register in excess. Your hearing isn't better, it's just your brain's misinterpretation of the sound your ears perceive. It will fade with time. You're lucky to be alive."

With that pronouncement, several in the flock extended their well wishes for Shin's future, and then the entire ICU team pivoted on their squeaky shoes and left.

3

Three days after his awakening in the ICU, Shin was discharged.

Sitting outside in a wheelchair, accompanied by a hospital aide, the chill marine air nipped his face. He adjusted the hospital blanket and waited for his friend to pick him up.

Shin opened the plastic bag, which contained his discharge paperwork, his watch, and a gift. He pulled out and examined the origami, which had been left for him at the nurses' station by the medical student from the ICU. He didn't know her name, but her thoughtfulness had lifted him from his dark funk. The cobalt-blue paper was folded into the shape of a whale, which signified compassion and solitude.

Tyler's truck rumbled into the sheltered semicircular driveway, pulling Shin from his musings.

The aide helped Shin rise from the wheelchair. The blanket dropped from Shin's shoulders, and the cold bit through the hospital scrubs and slippers they'd given him. He limped two steps toward the parked pickup before the world swam and he stopped.

Seconds later, his dizziness cleared. He became aware of Tyler the Texas yeti at his side. He helped Shin into an oversized maroon wool coat and appeared poised to sweep Shin up should he stumble.

Shin waved him off and completed the remaining steps to the truck. He pulled himself into the elevated cab, and stared through the windshield at misty Seattle. The truck's chassis groaned as Tyler slid his big frame into the driver's seat. Though thankful to be out of the hospital, Shin was nevertheless embarrassed. He'd created a mess, and he knew his friend had taken a day off work to help him.

"You're welcome," said Tyler, in his southern drawl, and started the engine.

"Uh, yeah," said Shin. "Thanks for picking me up." He kept his gaze fixed on the hazy outline of the skyscrapers.

The truck pulled away from the pick-up spot. Shin glanced in the mirror at Harborview as it receded behind them. He never wanted to see the inside of a hospital again. Too many people died there. His wife had died there.

After motoring along for a few blocks in the mist, the truck turned left and trundled down Columbia Street, toward the ferries. Somehow they caught every damned red light on the way.

As he stopped at a light at Third Avenue in the silent rain, Tyler turned on the wipers, which scraped and squealed as they blended dust and moisture together. He pulled on a lever and washer-fluid squirted onto the windshield, blurring the red traffic light into a series of rippled distortions.

When the view cleared, Shin spotted a ferry approaching Colman Dock. The ship's white double-decker structure stood out sharply against the gray sea and sky of Puget Sound, which merged into a uniform steel haze on the horizon.

The traffic light turned green. The truck coughed and the engine knocked as Tyler powered it forward. He drove the remaining few blocks to the dock's terminal. The truck passed under the State Route 99 viaduct, which thumped with traffic speeding overhead, and got in line with the other vehicles waiting for the ferry to finish disgorging its contents. Tyler killed the engine.

Shin rolled down his window.

"I hope they treated you well in there," said Tyler. He pushed his Mariners baseball cap back and scratched his red hair. "I was worried about you."

"Thank you," said Shin.

A series of red brake lights winked to life as the drivers in front of them started their engines. Exhaust fumes mixed with the salt-laden air.

Ahead, a Washington State Ferry worker in reflective yellow clothing directed traffic. Two columns of vehicles crept forward, then clanked over the hydraulic ramp and onto the metal deck of the MV *Puyallup*.

Tyler followed the hand signals as he drove onto the ferry. Once on deck, he stopped at the indicated spot.

He turned off the engine, glanced at Shin, and cleared his throat. "Let's go up top and grab a beer," he said, "or a sake, if they got any of those. I know you like them better."

"Thank you," said Shin.

"And while we're toasting the fact that you're still alive," said Tyler, "maybe you can freakin' stop saying 'thank you' and tell me what the hell happened to you out there."

AFTER BEING REMINDED to 'keep it in the galley' by the WSF worker who poured them two beers and took their cash, Shin and Tyler carried their plastic cups to a table at the edge of the galley confines, and sat down. Shin was about to thank Tyler for buying the beer, but thought better of it, lest he get scolded again. Instead, he nodded his head and raised the cup to his lips.

Tyler raised his cup in response, took a deep swallow, and then wiped a plaid sleeve across his red beard to clear the foam clinging there. The ferry shuddered as it powered away from the pier. Outside the window, white sparks arced and jumped from the tools of the welders in the adjacent naval shipyard.

"You want to tell me what happened?" said Tyler, locking eyes with Shin.

"I already told you on the phone. I fell off my boat. Got picked up by the Coast Guard."

Tyler leaned forward. "I call bullshit," he whispered.

"No, it's true," insisted Shin. "It seemed like a torpedo, but it must've been some type of Zodiac boat."

"No," said Tyler. "That isn't what I meant. You're a SEAL. You don't fall off a boat unless you want to."

"Ex-SEAL," said Shin.

"Don't play with me," said Tyler. His face darkened. He took another sip of beer, and continued, "You know *exactly* what I'm talking about. You told me you were doing better, man. Now this! You lied to me."

"I didn't."

"You did."

"What is this?" retorted Shin. "High school? Just leave me alone."

Shin regretted the words as soon as they left his lips. Tyler had done so much to help him after Ayumi died, and had just rescued him from the hospital. He didn't deserve this.

"If you can't keep your word," said Tyler, "a pact with a brother, then you're a man without honor."

Tyler's words hit Shin harder than if the giant had body slammed him to the metal deck. His face twitched. He wanted to rage at his friend, and the world — but instead lowered his head in shame. His shoulders shook, and his vision blurred with tears.

"You promised me you wouldn't kill yourself," said Tyler softly as he extended a huge paw onto Shin's neck and squeezed. "That you'd call me anytime, day or night, if your thoughts went dark. You're not the only person on this planet in pain. But if we can't trust each other, then I don't think I know you anymore. You guard me. I guard you. That's the agreement. Your suffering ain't any better than mine."

Shin's friend spoke the truth. It was a bitter reminder of how focused Shin had been on his own plight, neglecting others around him. Tyler had lost his left leg, below-the-knee, in Afghanistan and, during treatment overseas, gunmen had killed his family. His wife and daughter were slaughtered in a home invasion that netted the killers a thousand dollars in cash.

Shin pulled his gaze away from Tyler's prosthesis, and said, "I am sorry, my friend. I'm confused. I want to th—"

"Don't say *thank you*," interrupted Tyler. "Just uphold your word! As I do with you."

THE FERRY BUMPED into the slip at their destination, jostling Shin from his contemplation.

Tyler rose as the PA system squawked that they were at Bainbridge Island and it was time to disembark the vessel. He thumped toward the stairs leading to the car deck.

As Shin followed, he checked his watch. He'd done this trip home from the hospital, after visiting Ayumi, many times. All two hours of it.

It'd take twenty minutes to drive the length of the small island on Highway 305, cross the narrow two-lane bridge off of it and onto the Kitsap Peninsula. After an additional thirty minutes, traffic permitting, the truck would arrive at Highway 104, and the floating 1.5-mile bridge across Hood Canal which led to the Olympic Peninsula.

From there, if the articulating bridge wasn't closed due to a nuclear submarine on its way in or out of Bangor, it'd be an easy hour cruise to Sequim.

Shin wasn't looking forward to any of it — especially if the 104 bridge was closed for an hour or two — because he knew Tyler was going to hound him like a pit bull the whole way.

He climbed into Tyler's truck, shut the door, and sighed.

4

Twilight fell, and the dark trip back from Seattle in Tyler's truck felt like another spiritual death. *Another of the one hundred-and-eight torments in Buddhism,* he thought. *How many more must I endure before enlightenment?*

It might as well be a million. Nothing was the same. *Nothing* appeared to be at the end of his life's journey. He closed his eyes. His body swayed with the gentle rocking of the truck. Thankfully, at least for now, his buddy wasn't pressing him or digging for details.

Shin gave up on trying to nap. He was more wired than sleepy. Curiosity about the details of his rescue consumed his thoughts. He replayed it: freezing in the water as he watched the moon; burning heat; bliss as hypothermia shut down his brain — but then the voice!

What had it said?

The words were on the tip of his tongue, but he couldn't grasp them.

The tone of that voice in the water had been angry.

No. Not angry. Scolding.

Yes, he thought. *Like a mother to her child, too close to the hearth.*

Shin focused. He conjured a mental image of a mother, child, and flames. He opened his mouth to try to form a syllable tickling at the edge of his thoughts.

His head swam, and his heart rate plunged like it had in the ICU.

He didn't want to black out, so he clung to the words bobbing up in his mind as if they were a life raft.

"You," said Shin, panting out the word, followed by the others as they surfaced: "Don't. Belong. Here."

"You okay?"

His eyes snapped open.

"Huh?" said Shin. His heart rate returned to normal, and the dizziness receded.

"You were talking in your sleep."

"Oh," said Shin. "Weird dreams. I'm pretty wiped out."

"Sure, brother," said Tyler. "It's understandable."

The truck crested a hill. In the distance, a traffic light emerged from the dark forest.

The night sky opened above them as they left the trees and Tyler turned onto the Hood Canal bridge. The vibrations in the cab changed as the surface underneath switched from concrete to metal grating. Shin glanced at the surface of the sea zipping by, mere meters below.

The whine of the truck's tires on the steel grates grew, then began to pierce his skull like a dental drill. Shin plugged his ears with his fingertips — but the screeching wouldn't abate. His head pounded with the pain.

Too much—

The banshee vanished as Tyler's truck crossed back onto concrete at the opposite end of the bridge.

Shin panted and sank back into his seat with relief.

Tyler glanced at him. "Anything about your health I should know about?"

"Ugh," said Shin, as the headache faded and he could once again focus. "My hearing is more acute. Painful, actually. They said it'd get better with time."

"Gotcha, brother," said Tyler. "Have you home soon."

Shin nodded. But his thoughts were consumed with the words of that undersea voice.

IN THE DEEPENING TWILIGHT, gravel crunched underneath the tires as Tyler drove up the driveway. Shin surveyed his home — dark, quiet, and empty.

"Maybe it'd be good if I stayed here tonight, and sleep on the couch," said Tyler, after he killed the engine. "In case you need something."

Shin hesitated. His instinct was to say no — he had already disturbed his friend enough for one day — but it would be rude after all this. "Yes," he said. "I'd like that."

And truth be told, he didn't want to spend another night alone in this house.

He approached the front door, still wearing the green scrubs and slippers the hospital had given him and Tyler's huge maroon wool coat. Shin stopped at the threshold, bent down, and picked up a dead potted plant. The deer had eaten his rose bush. He fished out the house key from underneath.

"Kinda obvious spot, don't ya think?" said Tyler. "Maybe back in the day ya'll could get away with it, but everyone knows that trick now. Makes me wonder what else you're behind the times on."

The lock turned and the door creaked open. He hesitated. Within lay memories.

Shin stepped inside. It appeared undisturbed, though dustier than when he'd left it for what he thought was the last time. He turned to Tyler, and said, "Please come in. Let me get you something to drink and some food."

"Beer," said Tyler as he ascended the groaning stairs. "And yeah, I'm kinda hungry. But don't you need to crash?"

"No, I'm feeling better," said Shin. For the first time in months, dread hadn't gripped him when he'd crossed the threshold. A tiny flame of his emotional energy returned. "It's good to be home."

Though much of his memory of the incident at sea remained blank, he knew exactly what was in the fridge before he opened it. "Sapporo?"

"Not the best," said Tyler. "But it'll do."

Shin popped open two bottles, and held one out. His friend accepted it and they clinked the necks together. "Cheers," Shin said and took a sip. "Now to food."

He plugged in the Zojirushi cooker, then measured out water and rice. He closed the lid and punched a button.

"Rice," said Tyler. "Is that all you people know?"

"Texan wants some BBQ moo-cow," said Shin in a southern drawl.

Tyler slapped an enormous palm on his thigh, and chuckled. "Short people are so funny."

Shin opened the freezer drawer and pulled out a steak. "Wagyu beef," he said. "I got you covered. Now fire up that grill, Marine."

"Now we're talking," said Tyler. He slid open the glass patio-door and thunked out onto the deck toward the grill.

The sound of wind chimes, the smell of pine, and cold maritime air flowed inside. A breeze sighed in the tall evergreens.

Shin thought he heard music. He turned to look, but his wife's koto remained silent on the table.

He watched Tyler raise the lid of the barbecue grill, then twist on the propane tank underneath. Tyler stepped back and flicked a lit match at the grill. It whooshed in a golden flare, then settled into a glow. A smile creased Tyler's bearded face as he stared at the flames.

Two decades separated them, and they'd grown up worlds apart. Yet both had fought in foreign wars for their country. Both had survived those wars. And both had lost their families to circumstances out of their control.

"Hand me that steak," said Tyler, leaning in through the open patio door.

Camaraderie, and the warm buzz of the beer, chiseled away at Shin's armor.

AFTER DINNER, they sat down in the den. Shin lit a fire in the potbellied stove to ward off the April evening chill.

"I hope that was enough food for you," he said.

"Shoot, yeah," said Tyler. "Best steak I've had this year."

"You're just saying that because you cooked it."

"Well, I am damn good," said Tyler, and shrugged. "Hell, they won't even let you get a driver's license in Texas without knowing how to barbecue. If you wanna drive there's the written test, the road test, and the grill test." He laughed, drained his beer, wiped a sleeve across his beard. "But seriously, that was a fine cut of beef."

Shin bowed his head, then clenched his jaw as he thought about his own selfish actions. Had he been successful in his suicide, he wouldn't be having this moment with Tyler. Had he been successful, Tyler would be in pain, mourning the loss of another military buddy — and too many had taken their own lives.

"Got any more beer?" asked Tyler.

"Sadly, no," said Shin. "But I do have mizunara whisky from Japan."

Tyler's eyebrows climbed up his forehead. "Hell yeah!"

Shin rose, and retrieved the bottle and two shot glasses from the oak armoire. Tyler picked up the square-shaped whisky bottle and studied the label.

"I've only ever had a sip with Ayumi on special occasions, like our anniversary," said Shin. The mention of a merry time with his wife was bittersweet, but Tyler's presence kept Shin from ruminating on the pain.

"This bottle is over forty years old," exclaimed Tyler. "It must be priceless."

"Yes," said Shin. "It is very special. My grandfather gave it to us as a wedding gift, when he visited from Hokkaido."

"You sure it's okay to have some?"

"Yes," said Shin. "There are no more family rituals."

Tyler uncorked the bottle. He closed his eyes and leaned forward. His big chest expanded as he put his nose over the bottle and took in a long breath. "Sandalwood and tropical flowers," he said, and poured a splash into each of the two glasses. "I've never had it before."

Tyler held his glass up, inspecting it as he swirled the coppery liquid. "To Ayumi, Amy, and Cassandra," he said. "God rest their souls."

Shin raised his glass and clinked it against Tyler's. He wanted to scream. But instead, he said a silent wish for forgiveness and drank a sip of the fiery liquid.

"We can never forget them," said Tyler, and thunked his empty glass on the table. "Just as we *must* never forget their spiritual wish is for us to find happiness and meaning in our lives. I never got chance to say goodbye to Amy and Cassandra, but I feel them in my heart everyday. I know they want me to be happy."

Shin poured another round of whisky.

"I had months of saying goodbye," said Shin, his voice cracking. "It didn't make it easier."

Rivulets of tears streamed down Tyler's face, and disappeared within his beard. He raised his glass. "To us, brother. And to life."

Shin returned the salute.

For several minutes they said nothing, sipping whisky in the silence of the dark evening. A barred owl called: *who cooks for you, who cooks for you all.*

The distinctive sound brought back a memory. Sitting on the deck with Ayumi, years ago, Shin had mimicked the call of the nocturnal raptor — and the damn thing had flown right at them, perhaps thinking Shin was a rival. They'd bolted into the house and the owl had veered off from its attack.

"Are you sure it's okay for you to drink?" asked Tyler, interrupting his musings.

"I read my hospital discharge papers," said Shin. "Mizunara whisky was not mentioned."

Tyler giggled.

Shin steered the conversation back toward pain. Tyler had given him a sliver of hope and he wanted — needed — reassurance. "It's been three years since you lost your family," he said.

"Three years, three months and a day," said Tyler.

"Does it ever get better?"

"I told you before — yes!" said Tyler. "After you hit rock bottom, there's a spark you come across. And that spark tells you that here, right now, is the beauty and meaning of your new life. Not the life you asked for, but the one you got right now.

"That spark might be some random encounter, or finding God, or something you read in a book. But it lights you up, and *then* you understand a salient truth.

"The past remains unchanged. The present dictates the future. Because what happens *now* — right now — in every thought and action you control is all that matters."

SHIN SANK UNDER THE SURFACE. *Bright moonlight rippled the waves. He drifted deeper and deeper and the light above faded—*

He flinched as a large, black shape streamed past.

The fat torpedo vanished in the dark water.

Shin desperately wanted to breathe. He kicked toward the surface. A part of his mind knew he was dreaming but he was powerless to wake up. He tried to scream.

The object returned, slower this time. A flash of white, like a saddle, gleaned as it glided past just beyond reach.

Shin struggled upward but moved as if his limbs were fixed with lead weights. His chest was near to exploding. I need air!

The black shape came toward again — its third run.

It stopped and hovered, close enough to touch. Shin put a hand on the sleek body. He tried to communicate: I need air...

The shape twisted, nudged him, then pushed.

It pushed again, with more force.

A dark eye appeared, then blinked. A white teardrop shape next to it contrasted the black body like the Taoist symbol of yin-yang.

"You. Don't. Belong. Here!"

The words screeched like amplified nails on a chalkboard, and echoed in his mind.

Shin kicked harder, trying to move up and away—

A blow struck his backside, jolting through his spine. The creature propelled him upward.

The wavy moon grew brighter and brighter.

Shin burst through the surface, then collapsed onto his back, supported by the broad body of the creature.

He gagged and retched — and drew in ragged breaths of life-giving air.

A blast whooshed from a hole on top of the creature. Abruptly, Shin's platform surged forward, and he hooked his arm around a tall black fin to avoid falling off.

Dark waves slid past. Cold seawater cascaded over his numb body.

"Surface dweller," said the creature. "You don't belong here."

Shin hung on with hands of ice that were curled into claws from the cold. He prayed.

Surf roared in his ears.

"Go. Home," said the creature as it bucked and tossed like an angry bull.

Shin lost his grip as he was launched into the air—

And jerked awake. His heart thundered in his chest as if he'd been underwater for minutes. He panted to catch his breath.

Reassuring himself that he was alive and at home, Shin flipped on the nightstand light. He diverted his gaze from the empty space next to him that Ayumi used to occupy, and searched in the drawer of the nightstand for his journal.

His shaking hands closed on the leather-bound cover. He opened it to the bookmark and his scrambling fingers found a pen.

The ballpoint dragged and scraped as ink flowed across the page.

Shin became frantic as the dream ebbed from his consciousness. He scribbled faster, trying to capture every detail before it was gone. Even as tried to keep pace, he was astonished that more memories surfaced.

Shin wrote and wrote, then sketched until his left hand cramped. The pen fell to the floor, ending his manic scribbling.

He flipped and read through the pages, then stared at the final drawings.

"My God," he whispered.

$$5$$

In the morning, over breakfast, Shin was subjected to another round of questions from Tyler about his mental state and wanting details about how he'd survived. At some point during the inquisition, Shin decided he'd had enough. "Okay," he said. "I yield."

"Meaning what?" said Tyler.

"More pieces of the puzzle are falling into place, thanks to a weird dream I had last night," said Shin. He considered his next words with care. The dream had alarmed him — and he'd no idea of how Tyler would react. He decided to parse out limited snippets, and test the waters. "Want to hear it?"

"Yes," said Tyler. "Dreams are important." He forked in another mouthful of breakfast sausage, chewed, and swallowed. "Just talk through what you can recall."

Shin described, minus a few details, the dream of being carried to shore by some kind of large creature with white markings. "Perhaps there was a Coast Guard patrol in the area," he said, and chuckled to hide his nervousness, "and they sent a team to help me, which I misinterpreted as a creature." He cleared his throat, took another sip of tea, and studied Tyler.

Tyler's eyes were closed. His jaw moved in slow motion as he set down the fork and chewed the last mouthful of his breakfast. His plate

— full of scrambled eggs, sausage, cheese, bacon, and biscuits only minutes ago — had been cleaned.

What's he thinking? Shin wondered, and clenched his teeth. He stood to clear their plates from the table. The wall clocked ticked off the seconds as he stalked toward the kitchen.

I should never have told him about the dream, thought Shin, thankful he hadn't mentioned the journal notes or the drawings. He plunked the dishes into the sink.

"A creature," said Tyler. "Interesting."

The utterance, flat and emotionless, wasn't a surprise. Shin had expected a dismissal.

Flipping on the faucet and grabbing the liquid soap, he began scrubbing. "I told you it was a strange dream," he said. "But you said to talk through what I could recall. You said it might be important. So I did. Now I'm sorry for mentioning it.

"To parrot the words of the neurologist in the ICU, my dying brain cells generated a story. Apparently, it's common in near-death survivors — a bright star or Jesus or a whale or something. I dreamt a story last night, but it's just a damn dream."

"No," said Tyler. "It's real."

Shin turned off the faucet, dried his hands, and turned. "It's not real. There couldn't have been a creature."

"So how'd you get to shore?" asked Tyler.

"Coast Guard found me, I guess. Medevaced. That's what they told me in the hospital."

"Wrong," said Tyler. He rose from the table. "The truth is that a couple, enjoying a romantic wine and dine campfire on the beach, called 911 after witnessing your pale ass flip up onto shore. The EMTs and Coast Guard helicopter came after that. It's in the local papers, and all over the internet."

Shin squeezed his eyes shut. His head swam. *It can't be true*, he thought.

"Though we can conjecture as to the degree," continued Tyler. "I'm pretty sure you ruined that couple's evening. You should probably find them and thank them. However, the thing I really want to know is how far away from shore you were when you jumped."

Shin's eyes snapped open. He hesitated, but saw no reason to hide anything anymore. "Six miles."

"And yet you made it to shore. How'd that happen?"

"Has the *Harumi* been found yet?" asked Shin, guiding the topic toward his boat, and away from the conclusions spooling up in his mind.

"No," said Tyler. "Your ship is lost at sea — or hath been splintered upon the rocks, as the ancient mariners say."

"Bummer."

"Stop it!" said Tyler. "I see it in your eyes. You know *exactly* what happened. Tell me the truth, brother."

I heard it speak, thought Shin. He closed his eyes. *But that's impossible.*

His heart thundered in his chest. "Orca," he whispered.

"I couldn't hear you," said Tyler.

"Orca," said Shin. He lifted his head, looked into Tyler's eyes, and his voice rose in volume. "An *orca* saved me."

"Holy crap!" said Tyler.

Shin wanted to retract the statement, but it was too late.

"Now you understand," said Tyler. "It wasn't a boat full of Coasties who just happened to be ten klicks from shore on a search and rescue training mission and randomly found you. Or a mysterious black torpedo controlled by Poseidon."

"I never said that," said Shin. The verbal challenge left him reeling. *No need for ridicule*, he thought, as the heat built in his face. "I was confused... *am* confused."

"Honest statement," said Tyler, scratching his beard. "But you are one lucky dude. Wow! An orca carried you and then chucked you onto shore. Anyone else out there in that strait would be dead, but you're not."

"Maybe we should drop it," said Shin. "You don't believe me, and I don't either. So we agree. There's nothing else to say."

"But it's the truth."

"Huh?"

"Dude, you're alive," said Tyler. "Rescued by a freakin' orca. Stop being so dense. There's a reason for this."

Shin blinked. "You believe that an orca rescued me?"

"Yes!" said Tyler. "Nothing else works, brother. Your dreams, no matter how weird, are the truth."

"It gets weirder," said Shin.

Tyler cocked his head to the side. "Yeah?"

"The orca spoke."

"Spoke?"

"Yes," said Shin. As he recounted the killer whale's guttural words, he watched Tyler for his reaction.

The Texan remained as impassive as one of the Sasquatch effigies that dotted so many of Washington state's highways, marking coffee stands, motels, and tourist traps.

After a protracted silence, Tyler grunted. "Profound," he said. "There's a purpose to this."

"What?"

"You said your hearing had become more acute," said Tyler, "and now you're deaf."

"I know enough about the underwater world," retorted Shin, "from my time in subs and scuba, to understand that there's no way I could comprehend their language. Whales. Dolphins. Whatever. Some of their communication frequencies are beyond our scale of hearing anyway."

"And yet," said Tyler, raising his hedgerow eyebrows. "Here we are. There *is* a reason for this."

"You've been reading existential philosophy again, haven't you? There isn't any deeper meaning to what happened to me. I tried to off myself and failed." *What is he driving at?*

"There is meaning," insisted Tyler. He shook his shaggy head from side to side, and a smile split his face as he added, "And that's why you're gonna figure this out, right? Go back there. I know you."

"Yes," said Shin, surprising himself. *Am I so transparent?* he thought. *Not a word said and he knows that I have to go back.*

Still grinning, Tyler said, "Right on, brother. You've always been a seeker of truth. But as I see it, you've got several problems." He held up a big closed fist, and opened one finger at a time as he ticked them off. "One, no boat. Two, no acoustics gear. And three, no idea of how to find the orca that saved you."

"Pretty good summary," said Shin, staring at the floor.

"And that's exactly why you need my help," said Tyler. "We've got a lot of work to do."

6

During the next week, Shin developed a new routine. At 5 a.m., he rose, drank tea, and then practiced a breathing and stretching ritual. This was followed by pushups, a short trail run, and a shower. Breakfast was spent with his laptop as he scoured the internet for information about killer whales: *Orcinus orca*

One day, while browsing a website dedicated to the scientific study of cetaceans, he'd discovered a series of hydrophone recordings of orcas. As he waited for them to download, his hopes rose at the prospect that maybe it wasn't just one killer whale he could understand, but all of them. The excitement was short lived, however, as all he could comprehend were squeals, squelches, and pops — the same as any other human would hear. He also tried humpback whales, and dolphins. The songs and calls were intriguing but he could make no sense of them.

Not wanting to dwell on the setback, he'd refocused his efforts on learning as much as he could about the species.

Diving in to every detail he could find on the internet, he'd learned about their habitat, physiology, and their social structure. The term 'pod' referred to a group of orcas who travelled and hunted together, led by a matriarch. Pods comprised fifteen to forty or more orcas, and there were several resident pods which transited the waters where he'd been rescued.

Though it was fascinating to study the *whats* and *whys* of these marine mammals, Shin was much more interested in learning *where* and *how* to find them — especially the *one*. Last night in bed, in a why-didn't-I-think-of-this-sooner moment, he'd concluded that the best way to find orcas in the area was to contact the people who followed them.

And that's where he resumed his research this morning.

Shin bookmarked several organizations of whale conservationists and amateur enthusiasts who traced the movements of the various pods in the Pacific Northwest. In addition to websites, he found several social media groups on a variety of platforms. Shin joined what groups he could, and applied to the ones he couldn't yet access.

He scanned through old postings, and was soon immersed in sightings and photos.

This is incredible, he thought as he zoomed in on a picture of an orca breaching the waves. Its white belly, and its saddle and eye patches were bold accents on the jet-black body. Although he didn't know if this was the orca he sought, goosebumps raised on his arms; collectively, these postings were a treasure trove of observations and GPS data.

His head started to throb. He closed the laptop, surprised to see it was now afternoon, and rose to fix himself a sandwich.

After a brief nap, he was back at the computer. He had been accepted to a few of the online groups, and he cycled through the acknowledgment checkboxes, clicking *yes* on each one: *I certify my awareness of the Marine Mammal Protection Act and the four-hundred yard distance I must keep my boat from all whales. I acknowledge that I must never approach, harass, or touch a whale.*

Reading the word *boat* hammered a dark wedge into his emotions. The loss of the *Harumi* was huge. Even if he could figure out which pod he had encountered, and specifically which orca had spoken to him, without a ship he could never hope to get within several miles.

Bile rose in his throat. *Idiot*, he castigated himself. He'd permanently lost the *Harumi*. His times at sea with his wife had formed joyous memories, and sailing had been the one of the few things that had kept him sane after Ayumi had died — until it had depressed him into a bottomless quagmire.

And now he was shipless.

He paced back and forth to try to halt the burn rising in his guts. *I'm a failure.*

He stopped. And yelled.

Shin hurled each wrathful word like a stone, until his throat was ragged and he ran out of breath.

After the last syllable echoed off the walls, Shin heard the strings of the koto vibrating.

His gaze snapped to the instrument resting on its stand in the den, dusty and untouched. He scanned for what might have disturbed it. The windows were all closed — so it hadn't been the wind or an errant bird or insect. He was truly alone.

Shin tilted his head to listen to the koto. *A harmonic*, he realized. He focused on the soothing sound until it faded to silence.

Strange, he thought. *Did my shouting vibrate the strings?*

Given the exposure to firearms in his military career, more acute hearing was the last thing he had expected in life. Sympathetic strings, vibrating in response to a voice, would be difficult for anyone to hear.

Another manifestation of hyperacusis, a hallucination in the acoustic center of my brain, he thought. *Or is it real?*

Shin tried to recount his stream of raw anger. What words had he said? In what order?

To hell with life. Screw my life. I hate my life!

Yes, he thought, *that was correct.*

He padded to the koto, and screamed the words again.

Beautiful notes resonated from the strings. A smile twitched Shin's face, and he leaned closer to the koto. He'd unlocked the sound puzzle. The final word was the key.

Shin stood directly above the thirteen-string, polished wooden frame of the koto, and yelled, "Life!"

The instrument resonated in a pleasant harmony, like a chord from a pop music love song.

My God, he thought. *Such a lovely sound from one word.* He put his hand out and lowered it to mute the strings. His throat tightened, and tears blurred his vision.

Shin staggered to the couch and sat down. He collapsed on his back, and sobbed.

―――――――

THE PHONE JARRED SHIN AWAKE. He looked at his watch as he picked it up: 7 p.m.

"Checking in," said Tyler.

"Right on time, my friend," Shin said. He wiped away the crusts on his eyes, and opened up his laptop. "How was work?"

"Usual. Dull. Boring."

As Tyler described his day, Shin scanned through the social media groups he'd been accepted to and began reading the posts in detail.

Tyler wound down his recount of his workday with a story about a forklift collision that sent a man to the hospital. Then he said, "So, what'd you find out today?"

Shin continued scanning through the posts on the internet as he filled Tyler in on the various groups that followed the main orca pods. He stopped mid-sentence, and reread the time stamps of the messages from Orca Network. The hairs on his forearms tingled. "Oh my God," he exclaimed.

"What?" said Tyler.

Shin's hand trembled as he wrote down the numbers on a scratch pad. His thoughts leapt. He made several calculations in his head. "I think I know which pod it was," he said, the words tumbling out.

"How?"

"Observers post sightings with pictures that are date, time, and GPS tagged. The pods in the Salish Sea are well known. I cross-referenced the sightings of each against the day I was rescued."

"But it was at night," said Tyler. "Surely, no smart person tries to spot black killer whales in the dark."

"No," said Shin. "These are confirmed daylight sightings from the days before and after I jumped."

"I see you've strayed from *I fell off my boat*," said Tyler, "and arrived firmly on *jumped*. Good for you, brother."

Shin drew in a sharp breath. Last week, he would have hung up.

"Yep," he admitted. "But can I finish telling the jarhead how flippin' cool this is?"

Laughter erupted from his cell phone. "Sure."

"M-pod transited into the Strait, headed east on the morning of April 7," said Shin. "Two days later, it was spotted near Port Townsend, arcing south into Puget Sound. During the same time period, J-pod was far south, near Vashon Island. And K and L were hunting salmon up north of the San Juans."

"Okay," said Tyler. "So, you believe it was a member of M-pod?"

"Yep."

"But which one? And how do you know it was part of the M-pod and not a transient orca?"

"I don't," said Shin. He glanced at the large map with color-coded pushpins that he'd tacked up on the wall. "And there's no way to figure it out except to find them and listen."

"You're gonna put yourself in the path of M-pod," said Tyler. "Get underwater and see... hear, for yourself. Go down in a wetsuit, to scope it out."

"Yes, exactly," said Shin, smiling at his friend's insight. "I need to get re-certified and buy some scuba gear. But I can solve this mystery. Underwater is like home to me." His gaze shifted, and landed on Ayumi's koto. Shin recalled her smile as she'd played. The walls of the empty house began to close in on him.

"Supposing you get all the timing down just so," said Tyler. "A magic carpet drops your butt in precisely the right spot — smack dab in the center of M-Pod's predicted path. But this time the killer whales are hungry, and there you are, a juicy neoprene-covered meat snack. Have you thought of that?"

"I could've been killed before," argued Shin. "And there's never been a recorded orca attack on humans in the wild."

"I could say that it's because dead people don't talk much," said Tyler. "However, I'll stop nagging and give you some advice you already know. A solo dive ain't smart."

"I'm not going deep," said Shin, hoping to head off any further objections. "Just a shallow dive to listen to them."

"But you'll need someone to man a boat topside," said Tyler. "Keep a secure line and flag the area as a dive site."

"Yes. That's technically true but—"

"I'll captain the ship," interrupted Tyler.

"Huh?" said Shin. "You hate the open water, and you don't even have a boat."

"True," said Tyler, "but I know of a slick ride for sale."

7

Shin depressed the red starter button. The 150-hp Yamaha engine on the rigid inflatable boat rumbled to life. The 20-foot Zodiac was a bit weathered. UV exposure had hazed the plexiglass windscreen and scorched most of the paint, but the inflatable skirt had recently been redone. Shin wondered at the condition of the parts he couldn't see, and made a mental note to conduct a full inspection.

Standing behind the wheel, he eased on the throttle, and waved at Tyler and the owner on the dock as he skimmed out of the harbor on a test ride.

On the horizon, the rising sun stained the fast-moving clouds with streaks of gold and rust. The wind churned up small whitecaps in the steel-blue sea.

Once beyond the confines of the protective boulders of the harbor, Shin opened the throttle a touch. The ocean morphed from reflective glass to light chop and then to swells as the RIB powered into the strait.

It got rougher.

Spindrift blew off the bow. Shin smiled.

He balanced and flexed his legs to accommodate the g-forces as the Zodiac crested and crashed again. The RIB brought back memories of hundreds of hours of SEAL training and the close teamwork he'd first experienced in a boat like this. He recalled all too well his pounding heart and cottonmouth when he'd been deployed into combat.

The boat was tossed into the air by a wave.

Rocking down into the nadir, it climbed the next.

At the top, when the balance felt right, Shin yawed the craft 180 degrees, and throttled to full. The engine roared, and he rode the large surge back toward the harbor.

Hell yeah, he thought as the nimble craft responded to his commands.

Returning to the mouth of the harbor, Shin throttled back the engine, and puttered toward the dock. He looked over his shoulder, remembering the last time he'd been out in the strait.

Tyler waved at him. As Shin pulled up, the boat's owner joined Tyler to help secure the lines.

"Used for scuba and sightseeing," said the white-bearded man as he tied off the boat. His stick-thin arms were mottled with sun exposure and faded tattoos — and stuck out like a scarecrow's limbs from the round torso that swelled to spill over his shorts. "She's been well cared for, but it's time to pack up the business and go." He appeared on the verge of saying more, but halted. "Whatcha think?"

"She'll do," said Shin, muting his excitement. *She's fantastic*, he thought.

"I'm also selling some scuba gear," said the owner, squinting in the sunlight reflecting off the water. "Your friend here says you're a diver."

"Aye," said Shin. "That I am. Let's take a look at that gear."

———

SHIN DIDN'T HAVE enough money in his savings account to purchase the boat, much less the scuba gear he also needed, so he gave the owner a hundred bucks to hold the boat until the end of the week. He'd have to raid his retirement account.

Shin said goodbye to Tyler in the marina parking lot. As he drove home, an analytical part of his mind rebelled at the idea of spending cash like a drunken sailor on shore leave. However, another voice said that he was pursuing a deeper truth, one that mattered.

You'd be dead without that orca, he concluded. *Money is meaningless.*

At home, he opened his laptop and perused his social media feeds for orca updates. He took notes, then pressed more colored pushpins into the map on the wall. From each pin dangled a tiny note with the date and time of the sighting.

Shin stepped back and took in the scope of the oceanic range of the local resident orca pods on the map, then thought about the transient orcas Tyler had mentioned. Though they looked the same, resident orcas and transient orcas were far apart in behavior. Residents travelled in large multi-family pods and ate only fish. Transients travelled in small groups, usually consisting of a mother and her sons, and preferred eating other marine mammals like seals and porpoises.

Though he'd flagged the location of M-pod, it didn't exclude the possibility that it was a transient orca. He sighed. There were far fewer sightings of transients, and their paths less predictable, which would make finding the right orca much harder.

Nothing I can do about it, he thought, and turned his back to the map. *Except buy that boat, then go and find out.*

Shin logged into his retirement account. He was surprised it had grown so much in the two years since he'd stopped checking. His Navy pension was sufficient for living expenses, but he'd put aside this nest egg so that he and Ayumi could do all the fun things in life that retired couples did: travel, sail, and explore new hobbies and horizons. He'd cracked into it before, to purchase the *Harumi*.

But the purpose for that money had turned to ash with Ayumi's sickness and death, and he hadn't been able to look at it until now.

After answering an endless series of IRS questions about taxes and the consequences of his withdrawal, Shin requested a check for a quarter of the balance.

8

The next month passed in a blur. Every day was filled from dawn until well into the night.

Shin added swimming to his physical routine of running and aikido. On good weather days, he trained with his scuba gear and the Zodiac boat which was now berthed in the John Wayne Marina in Sequim Bay, in the same slip that his sailboat *Harumi* had once occupied. On bad weather days, he ran the forested trails near home.

In any small marina, people knew each other and liked to talk. Sequim was no exception. Some, who probably wanted to avoid uncomfortable topics like spousal death, asked Shin about the technical transition from sail to power. A few wanted to hear the details about his accident in the Strait, and opined about what a miracle it was that he was alive. One guy, who probably scored near the bottom of the emotional intelligence scale, asked Shin what life was like after losing both his wife and his sailboat.

Most people, however, left him alone.

In the evenings, he searched the internet, and filled his notebook with details on orcas, and plotted how he would arrive in front of M-pod and greet them.

Tonight marked the eve of Shin's attempted interdiction into the path of the pod. After he turned out the bedside lamp, despite the darkness and the quiet, his mind would not still. *What ifs*, occupied his thoughts.

<hr>

IN THE SILVERY glow of dawn, the engine's low rumbles echoed off the rocks of the protective jetty as Shin and Tyler glided out of the harbor on the *New Harumi*. The sulfurous smells of low tide hung in the cold air, and seagulls called mournfully as they gyrated and hunted for breakfast in the intertidal zone. Shin imagined he could hear the clicks and clacks of crabs scurrying over the stones.

Once clear of the harbor, Shin advanced the throttle to the one-quarter position. The four cylinder engine growled and propelled the craft at a steady 8 knots. The sky brightened, casting the high cirrus clouds in pinks and purples.

Tyler was bundled up in cold-weather gear and a life-vest, seated on the "throne" — the large padded-chair just in front of the open cockpit. His height and broad back would have obscured Shin's vision had Shin not been standing.

The giant sat motionless, red beard blowing in the wind. Shin knew his friend didn't like the sea, and hoped he wasn't too miserable.

Keeping the *New Harumi* at an even throttle, Shin eased the craft into the gentle rolls of the Strait of Juan de Fuca. He verified the target GPS coordinates on the display, then glanced at the sea and sky. Today's forecast promised calm in the morning, but in the early afternoon the winds would increase with the arrival of the next Pacific front, and by the evening there'd be gales. Hopefully, he'd have them safely back to shore long before then.

M-pod had been sighted traveling this way late yesterday, but Shin had no internet feed to check for any dawn sightings today.

He glanced over his shoulder at the scuba gear stowed aft. He'd done a thorough inspection last night, and again this morning as he'd loaded it onboard. But there was always the inescapable sense that something had been overlooked or left behind.

Far on the horizon, five cargo ships crept like gargantuan beetles, hulls glinting in the rising sun. The mountainous islands north of the strait appeared as a smudged charcoal line in the marine mist rising off the frigid water.

Shin zipped up his jacket.

Thirty minutes later, he killed the throttle and the RIB settled into the low rolls of the Strait. He stepped astern, and began donning his scuba gear.

The bundled yeti stood. "Here?"

"Yep," said Shin. "Just watch the boat, and tug the line if you need me."

AT FIVE METERS below the surface, Shin adjusted his ballast to halt his descent. Hovering at a neutral buoyancy, he turned in place to survey the space surrounding him. The water was far from Caribbean-clear, but neither was it Mekong-Delta-murky. He'd done a handful of underwater missions in Vietnam and he'd hated every single one. The brown water was filled with sewage and was so opaque that he couldn't see his hand at the end of his arm.

Currently, though he couldn't see much beyond fifteen feet, the reason for this dive was acoustics, and even the darkest of waters carried sound just fine. He knew the orcas' echolocation abilities could spot him well in advance of a collision. A collision wouldn't hurt them, of course, but being struck by a multi-ton killer whale would end his experiment quickly.

If I'm lucky, I'll hear them from far enough away, Shin thought, *and get the hell up to the surface and completely avoid the risk of a physical encounter.*

He exhaled. Bubbles streamed upward. The regulator hissed with his inhalation.

Conscious of the noise, Shin slowed his breathing cycles. He was drifting, not swimming, and didn't need as much air. Though amped up with the excitement, Shin willed his respiration slower, and his heart rate responded.

He heard the screws of a large motorboat. How far off, he didn't know, but the dropping pitch of the Doppler effect told him it was moving away from his position.

Shin scanned his environment. Rhythmic waves passed across the electric blue surface above. Below, the depths darkened to squid ink. The weather and currents were holding so far.

After checking his watch, and calculating his air supply, Shin descended to twenty meters.

He readjusted his buoyancy and then relaxed his muscles. Holding the line to the boat above, he drifted in the current. He could ascertain the flow by holding out one arm and sensing the spin on his body

There was nothing to do but wait. He couldn't communicate with Tyler on the surface.

A school of salmon streamed past, beaked mouths and silver scales flickering in the ephemeral daylight that filtered down to this depth.

A faint, deep rumble passed through the water. Shin held his breath.

It repeated, and after several seconds, the pulsating regularity of the sound identified it as man-made. One of the large cargo ships he'd seen earlier, perhaps. Though the water was cold — 48 °F — the wetsuit was keeping him comfortable enough. He hadn't shivered yet.

His mind wandered as he waited.

Shin gazed up through the sun dappled water, and recalled the moonlight shining through the surface. The back of his neck tingled at the memory. On that night, he'd been warm, numb, and on the verge of ecstasy.

He wondered if that's what Ayumi had experienced when she'd drawn her last breath.

Shin's chest bucked and he sobbed.

Don't, he scolded himself, and pushed down the thoughts of Ayumi's death. *Pay attention to where you are now!*

He checked his watch and was surprised to see that he had only five minutes of dive time left. He examined his pressure gauge. At 2,000 psi he had plenty of air remaining, which was odd. He wondered if the gauge had malfunctioned. Shin had calculated for a one-hour dive and expected to be down to 200 psi by now.

Regardless, it was time to head up. Though Shin wanted to stay under, if he was even ten seconds late to the top, Tyler would begin hauling him up on the line.

Shin broke through the surface, spat out the mouthpiece, and pulled back his mask. "I'm back."

"I can see that," said Tyler. "Hear anything?"

"Nope, just cargo ships." Holding onto the side of the boat, Shin took in the calm surface waters and weather. He rechecked his pressure gauge. "See anything?"

Tyler shook his head. "No whale blow or dorsal fins up here."

"I got plenty of air," said Shin, "so I'm going back down."

"What?" said Tyler. "You said you'd only have enough air for an hour. Are you sure?"

By way of an answer, Shin held up the gauge for Tyler's inspection, and said, "Wasn't born yesterday."

Tyler frowned. "How? Is it broken?"

"Slowed my breathing," said Shin. "Anyway, if you're cool with it, I'm going under for another thirty minutes. Mark the time now." He secured his mask, then caught the briefest nod from Tyler before disappearing under the surface.

Shin adjusted his buoyancy, and descended. Drifting as before, he held onto the line and reexamined his surroundings. There wasn't much to see. He strained his ears but detected only the faint throb of a cargo ship.

Halfway through his second time allotment, Shin's bladder was near to bursting. He released it into his wetsuit, the warm pee spreading across his thighs.

With five minutes left, he shrugged and thought, *It's not happening*.

On a whim motivated by frustration, he removed his mouthpiece and yelled, "Where are you?"

The garbled syllables faded in the wash of bubbles streaming toward the surface. He replaced his mouthpiece, and admonished himself for the impulsive act. Communications during scuba dives were limited to hand signals and writing slates for the very good reason that attempting to talk or shout was futile; no one could understand you.

Giving up, he headed topside with slow sweeps of his flippers.

"We hear you," said a voice that screeched like tires on asphalt. Shin startled. The words triggered his memory like a key opening a lock. *My God*, he thought. *It's an orca!*

"We're coming," said another voice.

Shin spun to face the direction of the voices but could see nothing. The skin on his torso buzzed, like he'd leaned against a vibrating clothes dryer. *Did they just scan me?* he wondered. His heart pounded.

"Surface-dweller in the water," called a third voice.

Astounded, Shin listened to the speakers approaching. Each voice was distinct, and as more joined in Shin guessed there were well over a dozen individuals. He squinted, straining to spot them.

"But surface-dwellers can't talk."

"This one can."

"Mothersong, are you sure it's the surface-dweller that's talking?"

"I'm staring right at it, Boomer."

Emerging from the shadows, headed straight toward Shin was the sleek head — black on top, white on the bottom — of an orca. He shook and grappled with the instinctual drive to flee as the gigantic killer whale approached.

Shin drew in a quick breath and then spat out his mouthpiece. "Friend," he blurted in a mass of bubbles.

The huge creature ghosted closer. Shin stared at the pair of white eye patches. He pressed the mouthpiece back in his mouth, and panted like a steam locomotive. The enormous nose stopped a few feet away. The mouth opened, revealing rows of gleaming white teeth longer than Shin's fingers.

"See, I told you," said the creature.

More orcas appeared and surrounded him. Never had Shin felt so dwarfed, helpless, and insignificant.

"Mothersong, is this the one?"

"Yes, Spyhopper."

Mothersong twisted. A large eye appeared in Shin's face, and blinked at him. "How are you talking?" she asked. "We know your kind. You have hurt us before but you have never spoken."

Stunned by the orca conversations around him, Shin forgot to breathe.

Recovering his wits, he inhaled. Shin wanted to respond, but realized he only had a few syllables to expend with each ejaculation of breath. He pointed to himself and removed his mouthpiece. "I, Shin," he blurted.

"Shin?" said another orca, drifting closer and showing his teeth. "Like the crunchy flipper-bone of a seal."

Squeaks and chirrups erupted from the orcas surrounding Shin. *Laughter*, he thought, *and a joke about eating me.* His pulse pounded in his ears.

"Shush," said Mothersong. "Do not alarm the surface-dweller."

The line tugged, and Shin realized he was overdue. *But I can't leave now — this is fantastic.*

He looked up for the dark shape of the RIB-hull above, but couldn't see it.

Three orcas sped upward to where he imagined the boat to be. There was a splashing noise. Two orcas streamed down past Shin, leaving long bubble trails. He hoped Tyler was okay — and wasn't freaking out.

Shin's gaze returned to Mothersong only feet away.

"I remember you," she said.

This can't be real, thought Shin. The line tugged again, more urgently this time.

Shin sucked in a partial breath—

He tried to inhale again but received no more air. Shin held up his pressure gauge. Zero. Empty.

Dammit, he thought. *Why now!*

Shin placed a cautious hand on Mothersong's head. "Sorry," he blurted with his remaining breath, then thrashed his flippers to swim upward.

His chest bucked, and his arms and thighs burned as his body ached for air. The blue surface rippled, now just five meters away.

"Come back," said Mothersong.

Shin stopped swimming and spun to look below.

Flickering lines formed in the periphery of his vision, and stormed inward, graying his sight into a jagged fuzz. Though he longed to stay, the instinct to breathe overpowered all other considerations. He sprinted for the surface.

Shin burst through the water and clung to the boat as his lungs blasted like bellows.

The boat tilted as Tyler lurched over toward him. "I thought you were dead," Tyler shouted. "And that I was next!"

The gray phantoms relinquished their grip on Shin's vision.

Shin looked at Tyler, whose wild eyes were darting about, and said, "It's good… I'm okay."

He drew in a deep breath, then stuck his head back underwater. "I will come back," he burbled.

"We will listen for you then," said Mothersong, her voice now faint. "Talking Shin of the surface-dwellers."

Shin trembled. Soon was shaking too much to get into the Zodiac without Tyler's help.

The Texan's large arms hauled Shin into the boat where he collapsed on the deck. He stared at the blue sky, his mind abuzz. His thoughts alternated between recalling the details of what had just happened, and calming himself so that it didn't overwhelm him.

As he unbuckled the tank and stripped off his fins and weight-belt, Shin struggled to articulate anything from the swirling vortex of his thoughts.

Tyler spoke first. "They circled the boat," he said, words tumbling out. "Blowing — and watching me. I could see their eyes. Jesus Christ, what happened down there? I've never seen so many killer whales before."

Shin wanted to shout, cry, and dance all at the same time. A wave tingled along his neck and flowed into his extremities. "Unbelievable," he said, in a voice that sounded detached and alien.

"That you're alive?" said Tyler, starting the boat's engine. "That's for damn sure."

"No," said Shin. He sat up and gazed at the orcas, surfacing to breathe as they graced away. Their breath-spray hung in the air, then drifted down in slow-motion clouds. "I talked, t-they talked. And we… understood each other."

9

In the nightmare, Shin's throat filled with rubber cement, slowly suffocating him. He tried to speak, then scream for help, but could make no sound. Frantic to breathe, his fingers reached into his mouth and tugged — and tore out chunks of the taffy, plastic substance.

But no matter how feverishly he pulled the plastic out, more clogs formed. It was an endless silk-scarfs-from-the-mouth trick gone fatally wrong. Unable to yank them out fast enough, the magician was losing the race and choking to death as the polymers hardened in his airway.

Shin's body writhed and jerked—

He woke up panting, and drenched in sweat.

As the dream eased its grip and his thundering heart settled, Shin stared at the dark ceiling.

He wasn't ready to get up, so he closed his eyes. But his mind swirled through the events of yesterday, and attempting to fall back asleep was as fruitful as trying to catch a hummingbird with one hand.

I communicated with orcas, he thought. *Not one, but the whole damn pod!*

Last night, he'd been so giddy with adrenaline that the events of the day had seemed as if he'd watched an intense movie. But in the pre-dawn hours of today, he knew the truth of his experience — and reality settled in. It was an unwanted gift, for certain, but one with which he must contend.

The room brightened to slate gray with the dawn. Shin arose from bed.

The birds started their routine. As he made tea, he listened to their songs. Sparrows, robins, and chickadees. He identified their tweets and calls, and named the songbirds in his mind.

Shin sat down at the breakfast table with a bowl of oatmeal and a pot of tea, and read through his notes from last night. He'd stayed up until well past midnight journaling every detail of his encounter with the orcas.

Mothersong, the one who had saved him, was the matriarch and the leader of M-pod. Boomer and Spyhopper were large males. Regarding the dozens of others, Shin held only vague memories.

There had been several high-pitched voices, like sopranos in an orchestra, which he imagined were the calves. The majority of voices, though, ran a swath from contralto to bass. The facet that intrigued him the most was the dynamic of their conversations.

Sometimes there had been group chat, in which everyone communicated at once. But at other times, only a single orca or a pair had spoken.

From his research, Shin knew there was a strong social structure within an orca pod, but to witness it aurally was astonishing. He wondered if there were signals to orchestrate orca conversations, perhaps distinct from the frequencies they used for scanning: he recalled the vibrations on his chest. Shin mused about their language, and its structure and hierarchy.

The spoon trembled and dribbled oatmeal onto the table.

Shin set it down.

I can't believe I'm contemplating an orca codex, he thought. His forearms tingled, and he looked up from his journal to see the hairs standing on end. *I ought to consult a marine biologist.*

Shin chuckled at the idea of describing his perspective on orca-language syntax to a group of cetologists who'd studied the creatures all of their professional lives.

No one would listen.

He shrugged and returned to his journal. He penned notes in the margins, then used a yellow highlighter to mark the most important. By the time he'd finished, the songbirds of the morning had yielded space to the arguing crows of the afternoon.

His stomach growled, reminding him of the lunch that was long past due.

At 3 p.m., Shin hastily assembled and then devoured, a Swiss cheese, tomato, and mustard sandwich.

He returned to his notes, and opened up his laptop to catch up on the feed from the whale-watching groups. His pulse quickened, as he followed a link to a hydrophone recording of M-pod — from only two days ago!

He clicked on the file. His chair squeaked as he slid forward to watch the download progress bar.

At 53%, it stalled… and then crept forward.

The chair groaned as he rocked back and forth, glancing between the ticking wall clock and the glacial progress bar. He read the GPS tag for the file, then rose to pin the course of M-pod on his wall map.

The orcas were recorded in northern Puget Sound, just one day before he'd dove to meet them.

At 57%, he wanted to hurl the laptop off the back porch, toward the murder of crows currently harassing a raccoon in a Bigleaf maple.

The bar jumped and lurched as the download resumed. Shin leaned forward.

His mouth went dry as it hit 99% and then finished.

Shin turned on his hi-fi system. He opened the file, and a trembling mouse pointer hit the play icon.

Amplified through the speakers were the squeals, squelches, chirps, and pops common to every killer whale recording Shin had ever heard. He couldn't understand a single garbled word.

Shin ground his teeth in frustration. He'd heard M-pod with his own ears! *Why is this happening?*

Underwater, the talk within the pod had been as plain as a sunrise. But the recording he'd just listened to — of the *exact* same creatures he'd encountered — was gibberish.

Shin double-checked the data on the recording to verify that this was indeed M-pod. *What's different?* he wondered. *Why can't I hear them?*

He probed the differences. The sound he'd just heard had been recorded at a distance, from a boat with a hydrophone.

But Shin had been ten meters below and right next to the orcas, who'd surrounded him.

Compared to air, sound travels four times faster in water and carries greater energy. From his SEAL days, Shin knew how devastating even the smallest of underwater detonations could be.

And whales didn't hear the same way that humans did. Sound waves struck their bodies and were relayed to their neural-acoustic centers by their skeleton and other specialized tissues. Cetaceans possessed a hyper-acute antenna made of their own flesh and bone.

I didn't hear them with my ears, Shin realized. *I heard them with my body.*

The epiphany energized him. He paced around the kitchen, his mind soaring.

His near-death experience had altered him in ways beyond the hyperacusis and dysautonomia diagnoses of the ICU doctors.

And it's more than heightened perception, he thought. *The orcas can understand me, too.*

10

Mothersong crested the surface, blew, and drew in another breath.

She dove.

Behind, the Ravenfin fanned out in a diamond shape and kept to the even, steady pace she'd prescribed. The feeding fields wouldn't coalesce until late in this light cycle, when the sky began to darken. There was ample time.

She'd clicked out quarter-tempo, and they had all settled into a leisurely cycle of shallow dives. It conserved energy, and guided the timing of hunt.

From underneath, she watched her grandson Boomer rise to breathe. The gentle giant was seldom far from her side, and always alert to protect the clan.

One of the cows, Melody, who was the most recent in the clan to give birth to a healthy child — a feat less common these days — called for her calf Oddpatches to stay close. Though he'd ceased nursing, and there was no danger at present, Oddpatches was the youngest and most vulnerable of the clan, and if they weren't careful, he could become ensnared in surface-dweller trash and drown, or be struck by the hardened-shells and whirling-blades of their vessels. Though the calf yearned to explore, Melody rightly kept him at the center of the clan's flexible formation.

The Ravenfin loved this pace. They socialized and spoke of the journey behind as well as the one ahead. The teenagers, full of energy, chittered.

Mothersong smiled at the banter, but kept her echolocation focused on the array of valleys and ridges below as she led.

A buzz sounded through the clan.

Two young males had challenged each other to *skytime* — a game of who could leap into the air and achieve the greatest horizontal distance. The rules were simple: a big bull floated on the surface as the judge, and the remainder of the clan, watching and spy-hopping, served as witnesses. Taking turns, each competitor must breach the water from behind the judge's fluke and were scored by how far along his body they went before crashing back in.

Mothersong clicked her approval, chuckling as she recalled her youth.

The competitors lined up for their runs. The clan burbled with chants as the anticipation built.

The first, Wavedancer, powered his fluke into a sweeping, strong surge, breached the surface of the water, and landed in front of the dorsal fin of Boomer, who was serving as judge.

A good score. The clan cheered.

Then Jumper sped upward. A year older and larger than his competitor, he had earned his name due to his ability in this discipline. No one in the clan could beat the young bull.

Deep fluke-sweeps accelerated Jumper, and his long body sped and broke the surface.

Mothersong rolled her torso to watch him arc in the air. He was so high, he seemed to hang there.

When he crashed back into the water, he was well past Boomer's eye patches, and almost beyond his nose!

Cheers and chirps of celebration burst out. A high score and victory.

Afterward, Wavedancer and Jumper swam next to each other. For several breath cycles, they chatted about *next-time*, and who would actually make a better bull for a sexy young cow.

A faint, deep-pitched sound swept through the Ravenfin. All chatter stopped.

The foreign noise repeated, and then settled into the familiar, pulsating *wob-wob* of a behemoth surface-dweller vessel.

Mothersong cursed. Even if it wasn't a fishing vessel out for the same catch as the clan (and she'd seen the surface-dwellers manipulate their huge nets before), its presence could drive off the schools of salmon they hunted. The harsh, unnatural sounds disrupted navigation and communications. A proper hunt required timing and coordination, which was difficult if no one could speak or hear.

She listened to the throb of the surface behemoth — and determined it was moving away. Nevertheless, the interruption had altered her timing and she needed to recalculate.

Deciding upon a new course, Mothersong clicked her instructions. The clan members repeated and relayed them.

She dove hard, then swept to the left. Driving her fluke, she went deeper.

Detecting a temperature change, she halted her descent and echo-scanned the terrain below.

Three small grooves in a starfish pattern lead the way, she recalled. The teachings of her mother had helped her find the fertile valley before. She hummed the rhyme as she looked for the signs.

A narrow slit in the seabed emerged, then intersected two others. *There,* she thought.

She scanned far ahead and was rewarded by a giant swirling sphere of tiny, dancing echo-patterns. The size and rhythm suggested a huge school of Chinook salmon.

"Food," Mothersong called. "Favorite fish-valley ahead."

She ascended to breathe, then dove again.

Mothersong clicked out instructions for a *triangle hunt,* and the orcas split into three teams. The plan was swift and, if done right, would yield full bellies for all.

When close to the salmon, two of the teams would dive and then speed upward, flanking the school in a V shape and forcing them toward the surface. The third team would power through the center channel with mouths open and flukes slapping the water to stun the fish.

When executed properly, an attack on an average-sized school could yield them enough food for a decent meal. With luck, a precision strike on a large school could provide a feast that kept their bellies full for a day. Mothersong hoped for the latter. This would be their last chance to eat before dark, and earlier hunts had been wanting. All were hungry and tired.

The orcas approached the edge of the school. Mothersong slowed her center team and watched the flanking teams dive. Huntress and Sounder called out instructions to their wings. Nervous talk filled the water. Boasts were exchanged.

The prey couldn't hear the orcas, and would remain oblivious to the hunters — right up until the moment the trap sprung.

The flanking teams surged upward. Silvery fish swirled in tighter and tighter circles as they fled upward and away from the ascending orcas that closed on them like the pincers of a crab.

A frothing mass churned the surface. The fish were trapped. Mothersong's group sped into the central pool of fish, smacking their flukes and feasting. The delicious taste of salmon blood and guts saturated the water.

When Mothersong's team had completed its run, the next team swept across the killing field. Then a third group took their turn.

It was a large school, and the teams had pulled off a superb hunt. The vast majority of the salmon had escaped, as they always did and would replenish their losses. Individual orcas swam through and swallowed the bobbing remains.

The salmon, scattered by the orca assault, regrouped, and swam away. The school — minus one in ten of its former membership — had survived, but the clan had scored a big feast and would sleep with full bellies tonight.

Mothersong would soon lead them to their resting spot for the evening but, for now, she listened to their banter as they wallowed in satiated happiness.

Melody began a rhyme-song, recounting their travels this day, to teach her calf Oddpatches. The traditional tool began with what had just happened and worked backward. It was designed to assimilate sensation, vocabulary, and memory into a young one.

Melody recounted the tale, ending at the beginning with the surface-dweller who spoke.

Oddpatches started the song, and others joined in the telling. Melody signaled her approval.

Mothersong listened to them as they started the song for a third time, and thought about the strange encounter with Talking-Shin. In the near hundred years of her life, she'd never encountered a surface-dweller who could talk. And though his speech was as garbled and simplistic as a new-born calf, it was communication. Before this, she hadn't realized that surface-dwellers were intelligent.

What does it mean? she wondered. *He said he'd return. But will he bring more of his kind?*

Her thoughts turned dark. The water suddenly felt cold.

Will they begin hunting us again, as they did in my youth?

11

"No," said Shin, rolling his eyes. This was the third time Tyler had insisted on the idea. "It's not a miracle, or a gift from God."

"Who are you to decide that?" said Tyler. "I'm sorry, but did I miss your coronation as emperor of the universe?"

Shin sighed. Every time their conversation took a metaphysical or spiritual aspect, it drilled into his skull like a visit to the dentist. He glanced around the Bell and Whistle. On this warm Sunday afternoon, the pub was as deserted as the streets outside.

Port Angeles had seen busier times back in her youth in the early 1900s, when the town had been a major shipping hub. Now the remnants of eateries, antique stores, and sundries clung to shore like weathered driftwood.

"I think you should tell people about it," insisted Tyler.

"Tell them what?" said Shin. He thunked down his beer glass on the table, earning a brief glance from the bartender. "That Ishmael can put his head underneath the waves and understand whales. Is that what I should say?"

"Did you ever hunt whales?"

"No!" said Shin. "Of course not."

"Then you ain't no Captain Ahab," said Tyler. He grinned, his red beard bristling.

"Oh my God," said Shin with mounting frustration. "Can you just drop the Moby Dick crap?"

"You brought it up."

At a loss for words, Shin gazed out through the open windows.

He'd seldom visited the Bell and Whistle, but had always enjoyed the view of the water from its perch on the pier. The blue ocean sparkled in the bright sunlight — and the cool, salty air breezing in through the windows carried the melody of wind-chimes and the soft clangs of halyards.

Shin took a sip of beer, and looked at his friend. "Sorry, Tyler," he said. "I know you're trying to help. But I'm confused as to *why* this has happened to me."

"It's a gift," said Tyler. "Don't question it. Follow it, brother."

"But where?"

"Wherever it leads you. Stop overthinking. You know what needs to happen. And face it, you've got the time."

Truth, thought Shin.

He had all the time in world. And he wasn't just excited, he was consumed. For the first time since Ayumi's diagnosis, treatment, and death, his spirit was alive. Mothersong and M-pod had rekindled a fire.

Shin reached into his backpack and retrieved his notebook. He opened it to his notes from last night, glanced at Tyler, and said, "You're right. Want to see what's next?"

"You bet."

"Underwater comm system with mic and speakers." Shin showed Tyler the schematics for the modification to his scuba rig. "With the full face mask I'll be able to speak without having to remove my mouthpiece, to shout two or three syllables at a time."

Tyler picked up the notebook. His eyes darted across the pages as he flipped through them. A smile lit his face. "This is cool," he said. "Hydro-speakers to broadcast your voice. But I still don't get how the orcas can understand *you*. When they were circling the boat, bobbing and staring at me, I said 'Shoo' and 'Go away' but they didn't seem to understand shit!" Tyler's expression went blank, as if he were struggling with a thought. After a few seconds, he added, "So in addition to understanding orcas, you must also be speaking their tongue underwater.

Woah, that's a blessed gift, brother." Tyler beamed like a Cheshire Cat perched on top of a Sasquatch.

Shin glanced around to make sure no one was eavesdropping, but the pub remained empty of other patrons, and the bartender appeared engrossed in the want ads in the newspaper.

"When you gonna try out that new gear to talk with M-pod? You gotta keep that channel flowing, brother!"

"I need to order this stuff," said Shin, with a shrug. "Put it together, and test it out. But next time the pod sweeps through, I hope to be ready — though I have no idea when that might be."

Tyler raised his glass. "I'll be there with you, brother."

Shin returned the salute, and drained his beer.

Seagulls cried and circled above the deserted pier where a busker performed a mic-check: "Testing. One, two..."

He strummed a few chords and fine-tuned his guitar. Then he launched into song: a grunge-ballad of love and lost opportunities, once popular in the nineties.

Optimistic, thought Shin. *Maybe a seagull will drop him a clam.*

12

The timing hadn't worked out. The pod was due right in the middle of Tyler's workday. Nevertheless, Shin headed out in the *New Harumi*, intending to dive alone. This violated a prime safety rule, but there wasn't much he could do about it; bringing a third person into the loop about his orca communications was out of the question.

Once beyond the harbor, he steered the boat into open water and aimed for a cluster of shoals and rocky islets. He couldn't know M-pod's route, but this was a place where he could anchor the boat and get underwater.

He'd brought three compressed air tanks this time, as he intended to stay down as long as necessary to find the pod, or they him.

Ahead lay the shoal. He slowed the boat. Drifting in, he beached it, set the anchor and rechecked the tidal log.

"MOTHERSONG," Shin called below the surface. "Mothersong."

He could hear himself broadcasting through the new scuba sound system, loud and clear. But a question remained: could the orcas hear him as before? He'd no idea if the strange factors of orca-human communication required that he burble into the ocean with air from his lips in order to be understood.

He hoped not, but he'd hooked up a buddy regulator up to the air-tanks just in case. If needed, he could rip the fancy sound helmet off his face and grab the backup mouthpiece to breathe, and continue talking as he did before, in gasping syllables.

Shin adjusted his buoyancy and hovered, listening for a reply. The three compressed-air tanks on his back dragged in the water, as hydrodynamic as a piano.

The tidal flows were in his favor. The nadir would bottom out in ninety minutes, which meant he was going to drift out, then drift back in with the change of tide.

He'd GPS-tagged the mooring spot of the *New Harumi*, but if he'd miscalculated his drift, getting back was going to be a pain in the ass.

Shin checked his dive watch: twenty meters.

He rotated in place to survey the dark water. The flourishing algae blooms and bull kelp on the surface had claimed much of the sunlight, leaving little penetrating below. The gloom, and his isolation from humanity and safety, unnerved his resolve.

Shin heard the faint sounds of a large screw in the distance.

Solo-diving in the Strait wasn't the brightest strategy, but at least he was deep enough to not have to worry about getting run over by a cargo ship or an aircraft carrier. Even without a major catastrophe, a small underwater mishap could quickly escalate. He maintained vigilance.

"Mothersong," he called. "This is Shin." His face mask fogged with the vocalization, not that it mattered much in the murky light. Still, it was irritating. He reached up to clear it.

"Murderer," said a deep voice.

Startled, Shin pivoted to locate the source of the sound.

"Capturing and killing is evil!"

A huge object struck Shin's ribcage from the side, jarring him. He spun away from the painful impact.

The black and white body of a large orca swam away.

"Boomer. Stop!" said an orca.

Shin recognized Mothersong's voice.

"They are hunting us again," said Boomer. "And it's because of Talking-Shin."

"No. No," panted Shin, fogging the mask further. "It's not true."

A black shape appeared in the corner of his vision. He spun—

—and flinched at the nose of Boomer mere feet from his head. The mouth opened, revealing rows of pointed teeth.

"Boomer," commanded Mothersong. "This is not our way."

Boomer's jaw closed. He turned aside and dragged his body along Shin's torso, inflicting more pain to Shin's ribs. "I curse the day you saved this surface-dweller, Mothersong."

There was a series of disapproving clicks and harsh mutterings. Shin now realized that dozens of orcas were present. Until this moment, they had been silent, unnoticed in the shadows.

He wasn't sure if the orcas' reproach was directed at Boomer's words, or Shin's existence.

His throat constricted. "Let me help," he said. "Give me a chance."

He recognized Mothersong's patches as she appeared next to him. Shin placed a hand on her pectoral fin. "Please," he said.

"Are you injured?" asked Mothersong.

"No," lied Shin. A sharp pain persisted in his chest from the collision, and he hoped it wasn't more serious than a bruise. A collapsed lung while diving could be fatal on the ascent.

The pod drifted in around them, and Mothersong said, "Shin is protected by the Ravenfin, and I will not harm him."

All the orcas repeated the words, including Boomer. Shin was certain he would remember that deep voice until his dying day. "T-thank you," he said.

"Talking-Shin doesn't know our ways," said an orca. "He is like a calf."

"Yes, Melody," said Mothersong. "He is speaking better than before, so maybe he is a young one."

Trembling, Shin wondered what had happened to get the pod so upset. Boomer had called him a murderer. He wasn't sure if it was his turn to speak, and part of him was terrified of intruding, but he had offered help. "My people are forbidden to hunt you," he said. "Has someone in the pod been killed?"

If someone is hunting orcas in this region, he thought, *there'll be hell to pay. I'll make sure of it.*

"No." The word was uttered by several orcas.

"Not our clan," said Mothersong. "Another. Far away. Tell him."

Tension crept back into Shin's neck as Boomer's rumbling bass voice spoke. "This morning, I went deep to listen in the sound channel. I heard the screams of a mother calling for her calf, and warnings from a clan. *Hunted. Captured. Killed.*

"I do not know which clan, or where, only that their language was strange. I have never heard it before, but some words are known to all. The channel carries messages from far away. From places we have never visited. But the meaning is clear — and surface-dwellers *must* be the cause."

Mothersong lowed a long, mournful sound. One of pain.

Murmurs and groans of sadness echoed from the pod.

Shin thought about Boomer's teeth and powerful jaws, and shuddered. An orca bite is the most powerful on Earth, and one he hoped to avoid. He couldn't blame them for their anger, though. He knew the history of the orca hunts in Puget Sound. Acid rose in his throat at the thought of the human cruelty. But that practice had been halted decades ago.

However, someone was harming and capturing orcas.

"I will hunt those surface-dwellers," said Shin, "and make them stop!"

The promise left his mouth before he had processed what might be involved.

The angst of M-pod was as obvious as the North Star on a cloudless night, but Shin didn't know exactly what was happening to the other pod. He didn't know where they were. But he did know that if people were hunting orcas, he would put a stop to it.

M-pod trusted him, and these noble creatures were tormented by knowledge of the suffering of distant kin. Tears flowed into the stubble on Shin's face, and his throat tightened.

The more Shin thought about it, the angrier he became. He was certain that *hunting* the hunters was the right decision — no matter the obstacle.

I will find them.

13

After a fitful sleep in which he was tormented by dreams of terrorists kidnapping children, Shin spent the morning and afternoon searching every rabbit hole on the internet. He sent out scores of emails to organizations and people he didn't know. He was determined to find those responsible for inflicting pain on the orcas. But for now, he'd done all he could and there was nothing more to do than wait.

Shin marched into the bedroom and pushed the four-post queen bed aside. Dust-motes swirled in the beams of evergreen-filtered sunlight dappling on the cherrywood floor.

Shin knelt. His fingers found the edge of a floorboard, and he pried up a two-square-foot rectangle to expose a cavity underneath. Fishing inside, he pulled out a mahogany strongbox.

This was part of a ritual performed each year. It was Shin's time to put aside thoughts of the present and future, and to touch the past.

He carried the box over to the bed and set it down. It was constructed using the art of sashimono, which utilized neither metal fasteners or glue, and had been a marriage gift from an uncle in Osaka.

Shin closed his eyes and whispered a Buddhist prayer for forgiveness, acceptance, and mercy. His index fingers found and pressed the recessed seam on the back. It clicked and the lid released.

He lifted the top and placed it to the side.

The strongbox contained memories of his past life, from before he'd met Ayumi.

Shin unfolded a cloth cover to expose the top layer. He lifted out a framed black-and-white photograph, taken in 1942 at the Manzanar internment camp in the California desert. In the picture, his mother, Natsumi, smiled and held the infant Shin in her arms. His father, Kaito, stood close. But even the graininess of the old photo couldn't hide the shame etched into his face. Being ripped from their island home in Puget Sound and taken to a camp surrounded by barbed wire and guards, with no ocean in sight, for the *crime* of being Japanese-American, had taken an enormous toll on his parents.

Three decades later, not long after Shin's return from Vietnam, his father had died. Natsumi had told Shin that Kaito had waited until he knew his son was safe.

Teardrops fell onto the glass. Shin wiped them away, and carefully folded the picture back into its protective cloth, and set it aside.

Underneath the photo lay the makiri of his ancestors. His father had given him this knife when Shin had graduated from his SEAL training.

All the Ainu people — each and every one — carry a makiri for fishing, woodcarving, and self-defense, Kaito had said. *And this blade has been in our family for generations. It has seen both calm seas and conflicts in Manchuria and Korea. If steel could talk, can you imagine what this makiri would say? Now it is yours, Shin, my son. Honor your ancestors, and the blade will never fail you.*

Shin picked up the weapon. The back of his neck tingled as he recalled the times he'd carried it into combat.

The weathered wood of the hilt and scabbard were magnolia, and had darkened to a deep rust color with the passage of time. An ocean motif was carved along the length. Beginning at the tip of the scabbard, the flowing water rose in larger crests toward the hilt, where the whorls crashed upon a shore.

The intricate carving was more than decorative. The channels and grooves provided the otherwise smooth wood a surface that wouldn't slip when wet (or bloodied).

Shin gripped the hilt. The blade slid free, silent as a butterfly's wings, as he drew it out.

Six inches of Japanese forged steel curved gently to the tip of the single-edged knife. Shin tested the balance. The tang extended deep into the hilt, and gave the weapon a center of mass that complimented the rotation of the human wrist. The dynamic sphere of aikido amplified the close quarters lethality of this weapon.

He bowed his head and whispered a prayer for the lives he had taken.

In the last layer of the strongbox was a plank of Western redcedar onto which his military insignia, patches, and medals were affixed, and a transparent plastic bag, which contained his Mk 22 service pistol and silencer (and two thirteen-round clips of 9mm ammunition). In Vietnam, SEALs called the beloved weapon the 'Hush Puppy'.

Shin had abandoned violence decades ago — and he would never go back — but he inspected and cleaned the weapon nonetheless. The worn silver ridge-tips on the black handgrips showed the firearm's age, but he'd cared for it well enough, and the oiled-action cycled with as much noise as a stamp being licked.

He set it down. And braced himself.

Touching these relics from the Vietnam War always triggered memories. Some dark and dreaded. Some cherished.

One recollection would forever burn in his mind. And though there'd been days he'd wished to expunge it, to never relive it again, there'd been other times when recalling it had generated within him the fearless tenacity of a blast furnace.

His platoon knew about the event; they'd been there. The base had talked about it for several days — until the gristmill of war had ground several of their own soldiers into corpses, and hearts and minds had returned to despair.

Shin had never told this story to another human ear, even his wife, though he'd recited it privately to himself every year.

Now, life had upended him: Ayumi was dead. He'd been told that things would be different, and that over time he would adapt. But *different* didn't approach the reality of the emotional tsunami that had rent him apart.

But, as Tyler had said, Shin needed to change course. Maybe uncorking this memory and committing it to paper before age befuddled him or his heart stopped was a step toward salvation; to once again aim his compass at true north.

He picked up his journal and, not knowing where to start, wrote:

April 1970.

Emerging from the fogging stench of smoke in the jungle, barefoot and naked, a screaming child ran toward me. She couldn't have been much more than five years old. Without thinking, I slung my shotgun and scooped her up. She wasn't bleeding, but she was terrified.

I wrapped her in a poncho and held her. Fabio, our corpsman, gave her sips of water from his canteen, and checked her for injuries with the same care as he did for all of us.

Fabio was a saint, God rest his soul.

Her cries settled and stopped. We joined the tail end of the platoon as it moved along the trail.

Around the next bend, we found her village. It had been laid to waste. Men, women, and children lay on the ground where they'd been gunned down. Or lay roasting in the smoldering embers of the burned-down hooches like forgotten meat on a grill.

To this day, I can't get that smell out of my mind. Burning human flesh.

Mercifully, the child had fallen asleep in my arms, though her tiny fists hadn't relaxed their fierce grasp on my fatigues.

I squatted to inspect one of the many shell casings littering the scene. 7-62. Kalashnikov.

We were supposed to meet a local, who'd guide us to a spot where we'd wait to ambush a VC sampan convoy moving down the canal with guns and ammunition. But the Viet Cong had visited the village first, and were probably still out there laying their own ambush for us.

Mission over, we needed to get the hell out. My commander, Mike, gave me the eye. There were ten VC-infested kilometers to hump to the patrol boat waiting to extract us, and we had to move fast. But there was no way I was setting that girl down to this fate.

However, it went against standing orders to carry her. If the girl had cried out at the wrong time, the whole platoon could've been slaughtered.

We scurried back, alert for any attack that might spring up from the mangrove swamps. But though she stirred, the child remained silent in my arms the whole way.

After the gunboats took us back to our ramshackle military base on the Mekong, I handed the girl over to a nurse at the medical station. Though we'd failed at the mission objectives, we'd all come back alive and uninjured. And that was always a win for everyone.

For weeks, I sweated about a reprimand for my actions — or a demotion, or worse.

One gloomy day, I responded to a summons by the base commanding officer. He was a torqued-up discipline type of guy. Fair, but he never gave an inch. I dragged my sorry ass through the downpour and boot-sucking mud over to the circus tent, as we used to call it. In reality, it was a pockmarked two-story hotel in the center of the small city of My Tho, that had been converted into an HQ with barracks for ground-pounders, plus a mess hall, and medical facilities.

I found the CO's office. The door was open. I entered and saluted.

In front of me, sitting on the CO's desk, was a nurse in fatigues — and in her lap was a little girl, giggling and playing with a doll. Healthy, clean, clothed, and with her hair in pigtails, I barely recognized her.

I took a few steps toward her, and she leapt into my arms. Her intense brown eyes locked on my face, and I knew she remembered me.

Thùy, was her name. She'd been well cared for, and the nurse said they were arranging for a foster family back in the States. My eyes blurred and I was speechless for a while. I don't know how long I held her, but it seemed like only a minute before I was waving goodbye.

As they left, my entire platoon — as well as the base CO, corpsmen, and a whole bunch of pretty nurses — came storming in like it was D-Day. They dragged me over to the officers' mess, which us non-coms were forbidden to enter. To my surprise, the CO waved everyone inside, where we were treated to as much steak and lobster as we could eat. For the rest of the night, I was surrounded by laughter, beers, bear hugs, and tears.

I never did see Thùy again, but I hope she's living a good life. God knows she deserves it.

SHIN REPACKED the strongbox and stowed it. The soft cuff of his plaid shirt was damp from the number of times he'd wiped his eyes.

It was his past, and when he'd walked away from being a warrior, Shin had put away the knife and pistol, retrieving them only once a year for inspection, maintenance — and introspection.

But holding the makiri today, and his commitment to stop the orca hunters, had made him realize that he was balancing on the edge of a broken vow.

No, said a voice in his head. *It's not combat. When you find them, you reason with them.*

Another voice chimed in. *And if they won't stop?*

14

Mothersong's dream disturbed her but did not rouse her to full consciousness. She rose to the surface to breathe. Sensing no danger she swam slowly in a circle and surveyed the clan with her left eye.

Like her, they were sleeping, with one eye open — to breathe, scan, and slowly swim on autopilot while one hemisphere of the brain slept. After a period of time, the brain sides, and eyes, switched. The rhythmic back-and-forth flows were the neurological tides that enabled the mind to achieve full restorative sleep.

Mothersong's left eyelid grew heavy. Between the time it closed, and the right one opened, her nightmare leapt the gap into the other side of her mind. Her fluke twitched, as the horror from her youth replayed:

Mechanical screeches, spears that jabbed, and blasts that rendered her deaf drove the Ravenfin into the harbor's narrow confines. The clan members probed and called and searched for an escape — but the vessels, booms, and spears struck anyone who challenged. Even the largest bulls were turned back. More explosions. Nets dropped. The young one, Whistler screamed and screamed as he was dragged away...

Tension coursed throughout her body, and the nightmare shook Mothersong fully awake. As the dark dream's tentacles released their grip, her attention swept through the clan. But their quiet and peaceful movements reassured her they were still asleep, and there were no immediate threats in the area. She cast her senses further out, but heard only the distant rumble of a surface-vessel. Her anxiety faded.

She flexed and stretched her muscles, and pondered the dream. Driven by her memories of that terrible day in the past, the phantom had disturbed her sleep many times before. It was a story that everyone in the clan knew. She made certain of it. The navigation points of the ridges and valleys that led to the cursed harbor were imprinted into the memories of all the adults, even those who were born long after the trauma of that surface-dweller hunt. Mothersong told the warning tale from her youth whenever the clan passed by the channels that led to that evil area, so that no member would ever venture in there again.

That her nightmare had surfaced now was an ill omen. She thought of Talking-Shin, and the distant calls of alarm that Boomer had reported from the sound channel. Other than her torments in the dream world, she had long been free of that form of worry. But if the surface-dwellers had indeed started hunting orcas again, then the phantoms of the past might become the grim reality of the present and future. It was her job to protect and guide the Ravenfin, and she needed to know.

Boomer seemed certain of what he'd heard, but he was two generations younger and didn't have her experience with the languages of the clans, nor the foreign utterances of other species. He may have misheard.

She knew the pips and squeaks of the porpoises, the strange dialects of their sister clans in the sea, and the mellifluous songs of the gargantuan deep-whales who visited places far away.

The harsh pressures in the depths near the sound channel were too much for almost everyone in the clan except Boomer and Deepdive — and sometimes even they were turned back by the crushing weight of the ocean.

She had rarely gone that deep, but the thought that she must go and listen for herself grew with the same insistence as the red dawn brightening the surface above.

As the Ravenfin woke and stirred, the thought of journeying to the sound channel — and the cold dread of what she might hear down there — weighed on her heart.

15

"Shit," exclaimed Shin as he read the email. "I found them!"

The kettle's low whistle rose to a gentle scream, and he stood from the table to shut it off. Dawn warmed the kitchen as Shin poured a pot of tea and stormed back to the laptop to reread the communication.

```
TO: Shin Takeda
FROM: M.T. Salvatore, Chief Liaison, Cetacean
Preservation International. Basel, CH.
DATE: 26 June 2006
Thank you for contacting CPI and being part of
the effort to stop the inhumane practice of
hunting and capturing cetaceans. Collaboration
will enable us all to move forward and end these
practices. We are a tax-exempt, nonviolent advo-
cacy group and your donations will help us.
In response to your inquiry, we can confirm that
in the Sea of Okhotsk, Chinese ships are coordi-
nating within Russian territory to bring live
cetaceans to their burgeoning aquarium entertain-
ment complexes.
In the hunt for their prey, dozens of small fast
boats are dispatched from larger vessels, flagged
```

as benign fishing or cargo ships. The fast boats
herd a pod into a shallow harbor by dropping
explosive grenades underwater. Once the hunters
have trapped the pod, they look for their desired
specimens.
When the young ones are netted, the pod reacts.
The hunters' boats are rammed but the guns,
harpoons, and explosives are too much for the
pod. Sometimes pod members are killed. The event
is so traumatic that even some of the 'safely
captured' young die in transport.
In the past five years, the hunter-ships have
captured dozens of dolphins, killer and Beluga
whales. Those marine mammals will, until their
deaths, be isolated and tormented by the loss of
their family. The pod will mourn the loss of
their member, and will forever avoid the harbor
where the capture occurred.
My number is below. Please contact me directly
with any advice I can provide to help you on your
quest.
Sincerely, MTS

Shin opened a web browser and called up a map of the Sea of
Okhotsk.

Boxed in by Russian territory, it was framed by the Kamchatka
Peninsula to the east, Sakhalin Island to the west, and the mainland to
the north, and it occupied roughly 100,000 square kilometers. The
Kuril chain to the south was a long spine of fifty volcanic islands,
sloping to the southwest with the tip ending at Hokkaido, Japan's
northernmost island. Shin knew from his father that their Ainu ancestors had once populated Hokkaido, Sakhalin Island, and the Kuril
chain, all of which had been swallowed up by Japan centuries ago.
But everything north of Hokkaido was Russian territory at present.
The area possessed a long history of conflict between Japan and
Russia.

After pouring more tea, Shin grabbed a banana and a granola bar and returned to his laptop to research more about the region.

In 1945, during the six days between the Hiroshima and Nagasaki atomic bombings, the Soviets had claimed all of the Kuril chain and Sakhalin Island, scooped up any Japanese they found, and deposited them on Hokkaido. In 1956, under international pressure, Soviet Russia signed an agreement to relinquish everything within Japan's territorial waters back to Japan. But as of 2006 — despite the collapse of the old Soviet regime and the emergence of a new Russia — nothing had changed.

Shin had relatives in Sapporo, Hokkaido's largest city, and though the Sea of Okhotsk was officially off limits, he wondered if his cousins might know someone who knew of a backdoor way to access it. In every port he'd ever visited, there was always someone who worked outside the rules. With discreet inquiries, he might locate a fisherman or a shipping 'importer' who could provide useful information, though he definitely wanted to steer clear of any entanglements with the Japanese mafia, the Yakuza.

He must find the ships hunting the whales and convince them to stop — but the more he thought about it, the more hopeless it seemed. He didn't have a plan.

Shin closed the laptop and stared into space, wondering if there was a way to pull this off without getting shot or arrested.

The wind chimes and birds sang in the gentle breeze outside as his mind struggled with obstacles that rose to the surface like sea monsters. His mood darkened as he named them:

First, Shin was *nisei* — born in the US to first-generation immigrants from Japan. And despite his proficiency in Japanese, his accent and status would stand out like a sore thumb. He knew only the barest facts about Japanese social customs; in the hierarchical society of Japan, he would forever be an outsider.

Two, he would be without a boat. The fanciful idea of zooming toward the Chinese ships and catching them in the act with a video camera seemed foolish. He could rent or charter a boat, but illegally sailing into Russian territorial waters was a fool's errand.

Three, joining a militant wing of a whale conservationist group, and convincing them of the importance of his mission, also seemed far-fetched. Organizations such as Greenpeace had successfully intervened in whale hunts, but they weren't exactly welcome in Japan, and would probably balk at operating in the Sea of Okhotsk where the Russians would sink them, shrug, and claim it was an accident.

Tired of dives into emptiness, Shin stood and paced about the house.

After an hour of wandering like a caged tiger, he arrived at a conclusion. *The only way I'm going to solve this is to go over there and figure something out on the fly. I won't know until I see it — but I've got to go.*

Shin hadn't kept up with his extended family and didn't participate in social media (other than to follow the whale watchers). He turned to the dusty old Rolodex on his desk and began thumbing through the yellowed cards.

Seeing the names of relatives and acquaintances, both here and overseas, brought back memories. Some faces he could barely recall, and some were deceased. But some were as fresh as the morning's sunrise.

His fingers stopped at a card and pulled it out.

After ten minutes, Shin had extracted six more cards of relatives in Japan. He sorted through the stack. One of them, Daichi Iwasaki, caught his attention. He remembered the son of his mother's younger sister, having met him on a trip to Sapporo twenty years ago.

The faded card contained a phone number, but no other details. Shin didn't know if it was still the correct number, but picked up his cell phone and dialed.

16

S hin walked up the sun-bleached wooden steps to the bar and grill overlooking the John Wayne Marina. Locating Tyler within wasn't difficult. Sitting at a corner table, dressed in surfer shorts and a Hawaiian shirt, the bushy ex-Marine was as subtle as a Wookiee in a nail salon.

"Hey, little brother," said Tyler as Shin approached. He stood and they hugged.

"Good to see you," said Shin.

It was a hot, dusty July afternoon and the ceiling fans were on, and all the windows were open, wafting in fishy scents from the marina and an occasional cool breeze.

Sequim lay in the rain shadow: a place where the mountains of the Olympic Peninsula wrung out almost all the moisture from the Pacific fronts crossing over them. Though there were rainforests only a hundred miles away, here it was bone dry.

The waitress came over and fanned herself with a plastic menu as she took their drink order.

"What's new?" Shin asked Tyler. "You look like you just came from the set of a California surf movie."

"Been stand-up paddle boarding," said Tyler. He tapped his prosthesis. "Testing out a new foot attachment. The balance and feel can never be the same as what was, but this one rocks."

"Cool," said Shin with a smile. He wished he had a quarter of the resilience that Tyler possessed. Not only did his friend *not* enjoy open water, but he was pushing his comfort zone: conquering fear by rejecting it.

The waitress arrived with their drinks: an amber ale and a dark lager. They ordered a plate of nachos.

"You said you had some news," said Tyler. "You figure out a way to stop those bastards on the other side of the ocean?"

"Yes," said Shin. He swallowed a sip of his lager. "I'm going to Japan." He described the rough outline of what he hoped to achieve and how.

"That's your plan?" said Tyler, after Shin had finished. "You're going to fly to Sapporo, set up shop in your cousin's house, and with the help of a bootlegger or an advocacy group, convince the Chinese to *please* stop hunting killer whales. Are you out of your freakin' mind?"

"Well, there are still a few details to nail down," admitted Shin.

"Ya think?"

"I'll learn more when I get there," said Shin. "My cousin was excited about the prospect of helping, and said he had some connections and—"

"Yakuza," interrupted Tyler. "You wanna stay away from those guys. They'll slice you up like sushi."

Shin rolled his eyes. "I have no intention of getting into anything dangerous."

"Naïveté is one hell of a drug."

"Listen," argued Shin. "I'm going there with my eyes wide open. I'm taking charge of my destiny and doing something worthwhile. You said that after hitting rock bottom I would find a spark of meaning — a calling, or something — and here it is!"

"Yep, you're right," agreed Tyler. "But that doesn't mean doing dumb shit. The kind of people you're up against ain't gonna say, 'Oh golly-gee, we'd hadn't considered this perspective before. Maybe we should just stop.' No, dumbass, they'll shoot first — this is suicide by confrontation with a group who will object to your attempted interruption of their gravy train with bullets."

Tyler's words stung.

"Don't throw that in my face," said Shin, raising his voice. "This is *me*. Alive and thinking clearly. Living with meaning and purpose."

"Your plan still sucks," said Tyler. "Did you talk to your whale friends? The human ones, I mean. It seems like a coordinated campaign by Greenpeace and others might make the killer whale hunters stop."

Shin nodded. "Yes, I reached out to CPI, the Freedom Whale Friends, and Orcas International, and learned that there's activity to pressure the owners of the main Chinese-flagged ship suspected of being the command post for the hunts — as well as the Russian government in whose territorial waters the ships are operating."

"And?" said Tyler.

Their plate of nachos — full of melted cheddar cheese, sliced jalapeños, sour cream, and fresh guacamole — was delivered. Shin waited for the waitress to leave before he continued. "The Chinese holding company said they only sponsor fishing safaris, and the Russians said to check with the Chinese. Both denied that there was killer-whale hunting or captures occurring in the Sea of Okhotsk."

"Pretty classic circular bullshit," said Tyler, smirking. He scooped up a loaded tortilla chip, popped it in his mouth, and crunched loudly.

"I agree," said Shin.

Tyler took a swig of his ale. "But with more pressure, and time, they should be able to get the Chinese to stop, right? You could add your voice to theirs and be a keyboard warrior from here. No need to travel to Japan."

"There isn't time," said Shin. "Every day that passes is critical. The Chinese aren't hunting right now, but that could change. Their command-post ship, the *Zheng Yi*, went into port last week in Shanghai, and—"

"Wait," said Tyler. "How do you know that?"

"The CPI told me the ship's name over the phone when I called them. There's a website that tracks real-time vessel traffic based on the Automatic Identification System transponder. All large vessels are required by international law to have AIS — it's a satellite monitored safety network to prevent collisions at sea."

"Hmm." Tyler scratched his beard. "But what's to stop them from turning it off?"

Shin grinned. "You've always had a good tactical mind. Yes. That's exactly what they do. Go dark while they do their bad stuff and then pop up innocently, somewhere else, later."

"Damn."

"And if someone files a report, accusing a huge trawler of illegal fishing or a cargo ship of dumping waste, they'll just claim it was an electrical problem with the AIS and they were never in the questioned waters," said Shin. "It's a smuggler's game — carried out on the seven seas for centuries. In this case, unless the Russians do something to stop them, the *Zheng Yi* and its flotilla of small fast boats can operate with impunity. And with all their radar sites and military outposts in the Kurils, Kamchatka, and Sakhalin, the Russians must know what's going on. So, they're clearly in on it."

Tyler frowned. He reached for more nachos, and Shin realized he'd better start eating before the Texan ate them all. For a few minutes, they munched without speaking.

Tyler licked his fingers, belched, and said, "This place still has the best Mexican food you can get in the Olympics."

Shin chuckled. The peninsula was larger than several countries in Europe, and one state in the US, but few people lived in the waning towns and hamlets scattered along the narrow coastline rim bordering the impenetrable mountainous interior.

"There are... what, two restaurants?" he said.

"Three. And they're all much better than anything on the mainland in Seattle. Nowhere near Houston-good, you understand, but I like this place." Tyler flagged down the waitress and ordered a plate of salmon tacos.

After she left, Tyler leaned forward and whispered, "Little brother, what're you *really* gonna do?"

"Fly out there and reason with them."

Tyler burst out laughing. "You already said that — and I still ain't buying it."

"I'm very persuasive."

"You can't go in there alone," said Tyler. He tilted his grizzly head to the side. "Think back to your time in 'Nam. It was always a team effort, right? Same with me. There were no loose cannons because that shit got you and your squad hammered."

"True. But I'm not going into a firefight. I'm just going to talk. Besides, I have a team. I have cousins in Hokkaido, and *you* are going to check on my house and boat."

Tyler narrowed his eyes. "I am?"

"Yes." Shin steepled his fingers and bobbed his head in a brief bow. "And I greatly appreciate your offer to serve as home base."

"Like a dandelion in a hurricane," huffed Tyler. "I guess you done made up your mind to scatter."

17

Two mornings later, Shin drove down to the John Wayne Marina.

He hauled his scuba gear aboard the *New Harumi*, and cast off. The internet contained rumors that M-pod was in northern Puget Sound and may be headed toward the San Juans, but the sightings were days old and hundreds of miles away. It was possible the orcas could turn west into the Strait, in which case Shin had a chance to talk to them again.

Shin had spent most of yesterday preparing. He'd adjusted the gain and cranked up the volume on his acoustic gear. If he could broadcast far enough, M-pod might hear him and come.

He puttered the RIB through the harbor, which was a calm mirror to the placid blue sky.

Shin wasn't sure if Mothersong would understand all of what he had to say, but he didn't want to disappear overseas without telling her what he'd learned and what he was going to do. He didn't know if orcas worried or not, but if he vanished after their communication breakthrough, Mothersong might be concerned.

The matriarch and the pod had accepted him, and Shin respected this trust.

As he steered his boat toward the mouth of the harbor, he thought, *No one can truly understand what I've witnessed of these sentient souls.*

A half-hour later, he moored his boat on a tiny islet, and was soon underwater.

"Mothersong," Shin called, and waited. After five minutes, he went up.

For the next three hours, he repeated the same ritual. Every fifteen minutes, he donned his mask, dove to ten meters and rebroadcast his message, then listened for five minutes before returning topside.

The once bright afternoon sun had transformed into a golden lozenge, with rays that pierced the gathering dark clouds like swords. Shin knew he must soon swim back to his boat.

He dove under for another attempt.

After Shin broadcast his message, he glanced at his watch, then calmed his breathing and hung limp. The heartbeat pulsing in his ears slowed.

Focusing on his auditory senses, he closed his eyes. Shin fantasized about what it must be like to be an orca, to be the apex predator in the ocean. He wondered if—

A screeching echo jolted him from his musing. "W-we are c-coming."

Shin's heart rate soared. *They're here.*

His body buzzed with the scans of the approaching orcas.

M-pod arrived and gathered around Shin. Chills swept his spine, as their majestic presence again struck him. Mothersong approached him.

"Mothersong," he said. "I found the hunters. I will force them to stop when I get there."

"You are going to battle the other surface-dwellers?" said Mothersong. "Your own kind."

"Yes," said Shin. "If I must."

"Where are they?"

"A place far away," said Shin. He struggled to think of a way to explain, but everything about this interaction was foreign. The orcas knew nothing of maps, GPS navigation, or international boundaries. He was at the blind end of a communication cul-de-sac. Species to species, there was little commonality in their experiences of the world, especially as related to land masses and air travel.

"Tell us how to *hurt* the surface-dweller vessels," said Boomer. "You have ridden one. Teach us."

The request spun him. He had a flashback to Vietnam where he'd taught Montagnards how to booby-trap the trails the Viet Cong used. Most of the young men that Shin had trained hadn't even begun shaving yet, but they were quick learners and possessed a fierce desire to kill the enemy.

Shin never imagined that one day he would find himself in the role of instructing orcas to take on humans.

"I will," he said, and held out his arm. "Can you pull me along? There's much I can tell you about surface-dwellers and our boats — and there's a place where I can show you."

The marina would be the ideal location to point out different craft and describe to the orcas how they might disable them, but they would need to be secretive. Several large orcas cruising into a sheltered marina would arouse a lot of interest, if not outright panic. However, if they were smart about it, the group of orcas could hang out at the periphery and stay underwater while Shin conducted his tutelage.

Boomer swept toward him, and Shin flinched, recalling the earlier encounter.

"I will help you," said Boomer. "Grab."

Shin grasped both hands around the proffered pectoral fin. The paddle-shaped appendage was two meters in length and over a meter in width. It was like clinging to a giant's arm. Shin could feel the strong muscles and bones beneath his grip: an X-ray would reveal the exact same bone structures as a human's arm — humerus, ulna, radius, metacarpals. But any sort of analysis of comparative anatomy fell to the wayside as the ten-ton orca accelerated.

Whoa!

Shin squeezed Boomer's pectoral fin like he'd grip the handlebars on a motorcycle going too fast. The rushing water threatened to rip the mask from his face. For several seconds, just trying to hang on consumed all of his focus.

Soon, though, Shin had adapted to the sudden burst of speed. He took in his immediate surroundings. From his perch on the pec-fin,

Shin's head was just behind Boomer's left eye. The eye rotated to study him: its pupil was U-shaped, and resembled the hull of a ship.

Shin looked over his shoulder. The majority of M-pod had stayed behind, but several orcas swam alongside Boomer. Shin learned their names: Pouncer, Flukethumper, and Spyhopper were all young and strong.

Incredible, thought Shin. *This is the most thrilling experience I've ever had!*

"Where are we going?" asked Boomer.

Shin opened his mouth, but then paused. They probably didn't know the word *marina*. He released one arm from Boomer's pectoral fin and pointed. Boomer's eye blinked and he turned his torso in the direction that Shin had identified.

Shin began, "We must be stealthy as we approach—"

Boomer's bass chuckle cut him off. "Yes, we know," he said. "Rest places for surface-dweller vessels are harbors we avoid."

"Too many of you," agreed Pouncer. "Lines that snare, foul water, and blades that cut."

"The fish are sickly," added Flukethumper. "Your vessels just sit and leave waste in the water."

Boomer slowed, and rose to the surface. As they glided, Shin glimpsed the marina lights. Though he'd seen these exact lights hundreds of times before, he knew he'd never look at them the same way again.

The red sky deepened. Dusk would soon be here. They stopped at the jetty guarding the entrance to the harbor. Shin looked at the orcas' tall dorsal fins, which resembled four black sails. They were sure to attract attention.

At the moment, no boats were entering or leaving, but he didn't want to risk being spotted. "Let's stay underwater," he said. "Stealth and quiet. Follow me."

He submerged and led them through the narrow channel into the harbor.

"Is that as fast as you can swim?" asked Pouncer.

"Yes," answered Shin.

"You're very slow," said Flukethumper. "Even with those fake-fins on your feet. I've seen dead seals move faster."

"Yes, I know," said Shin. "But I'm much quicker on land than you."

Boomer chuckled.

Shin poked his head up to get his bearings. The outermost pier was a hundred meters distant. It was the smallest in the marina, and out of the way. A dozen small vessels were moored there: dinghies, sailboats, and speedboats. It would be perfect for his needs. Thankfully, it was mid-week, and with the approaching darkness, the pier was deserted.

The instructions were hypothetical, Shin reminded himself. No boats should be damaged. But because orcas and humans didn't have shared technical language, the task would be impossible without some kind of hands-on demonstration.

"Here," whispered Shin, and they rose to the surface as silent and invisible as driftwood.

Boomer whispered to his companions. They all angled their bodies so that only their heads were visible above the surface.

Shin dipped below, and tagged a rudder with his hand. "A rudder is how they steer," he said. "If you bite it off, they are directionless. But you must always stay away from the spinning—"

"We know about the blades," said Pouncer.

"Yes," said Shin. "Propellers are dangerous. But not all boats have them." He drifted over to a 16-foot sailboat and touched its white hull. "Some use the wind to move across the water."

"We know that too," said Boomer. "The sound is as different from blades as the sun is from the moon — and when the wind dies, they sag and stop. It's part of a rhyme we teach young calves about the world. What to avoid, and how to stay out of danger."

A few weeks ago, this revelation would have stunned Shin — but now it felt like just another dip in the pool.

"The small inflatables with outboard motors," he continued, pointing one out, "have no rudders. But you can go airborne, land on it, and it will drown."

"Ahh," said Spyhopper.

"You can punch them from below as well," said Pouncer.

"Yes," answered Shin. A boat this size — regardless of whether its hull was wood, fiberglass, or inflatable — would be blown apart by an orca.

He answered each subsequent question tossed by the orcas, to the best of his abilities.

When they were through, four orcas and one human left the marina as peaceful as they'd found it.

As they travelled back to where they'd met, Shin asked, "I'm curious. How you are named?"

"What do you mean?" rumbled Boomer.

"Why are you called Boomer?"

"Hmm," said Boomer. "As soon as a calf is born, the mother calls out her own name first— and when the calf swims to her side and repeats it back, she then tells the newborn what its name is."

"This is not the only name the calf will have in its lifetime," added Spyhopper. "At different stages, the orca will get different names. I was once known as 'Warbler', because I had a funny voice. Today, I am called 'Spyhopper' because I can balance on my fluke, push my head high above the surface, and spy things far away. Names are earned."

Each disclosure about orca society, roiled Shin anew. He'd read every scientific article he could get his hands on and combed through scores of websites and social media posts, but his conversations with orcas blew all of that out of the water. Humanity had only glimpsed the surface, and had no inkling of the depth of intelligence and social structure that orcas possessed.

"Why are you called Shin?" asked Spyhopper.

"My parents gave me the name," said Shin. "It means genuine."

"Ahh," said Boomer. "A good name. And true."

The murmurs of approval from the other orcas made Shin choke up.

The longer this conversation went on, the more he wanted to cancel his trip overseas. There was so much more to learn here. He could stay, continue to socialize with M-pod, and one day write it all down.

But he wasn't an author, and no one would believe it. And he'd made a promise to Mothersong and the pod.

Boomer stopped swimming and surfaced. "This is where we met."

Shin checked his GPS and was startled by Boomer's precision.

"May you have a safe journey," said Boomer. "We will listen for you."

"And I will listen for you," Shin echoed the parting words.

The orcas disappeared and Shin swam the remaining distance to the *New Harumi*, still beached on the tiny islet. It was low tide and the boat was a higher than he'd left it seven hours ago.

After thirty minutes of tugging and heaving, he managed to wrestle it back into the water.

As Shin motored back, a sense of urgency took hold of him. He wanted to get to Japan, stop the hunting, and get back here as quickly as possible. The desire to be with M-pod was like nothing he'd ever experienced before.

Shin puttered into the marina, and moored the *New Harumi* in her slip.

As he walked along the pier, passing the other boats, he couldn't help but feel a twinge of remorse at having taught orcas how to disable or sink them.

M-pod wouldn't assault innocent ships, of course. And all he'd done was to show them the right place to apply their primitive tools to maximum effect. Boomer and his clan-mates could propel their multi-ton bodies through the water at over 30 knots, and bite with 19,000 psi. They weren't defenseless.

But humans who were morally bankrupt enough to torment and capture orcas wouldn't think twice about blowing them away, using weapons that Mothersong couldn't even imagine. In any human-orca conflict, the warfare would be asymmetric. And if Shin had given the pod a false sense of power or confidence, then they'd be the ones paying the price for his hubris.

18

Mothersong told Boomer of her plan to dive to the sound channel. He tried to dissuade her, but she clicked a confident reproach: "I will do it — and I will be safe." Truth be told, her spine felt like a jellyfish. "If Shin is traveling to help the other clan, I wish to listen to their words myself."

"We'll go together," said Boomer. "You will not be alone."

Mothersong chirped an acknowledgment, thankful that her grandson would be with her. She told the clan that Huntress would be in charge while she was gone. If all went well, Mothersong and Boomer would reunite with the Ravenfin tonight or tomorrow morning.

The depth was too shallow for the sound channel here. So, after bidding the clan goodbye, Mothersong and Boomer swam west toward the opening of the strait, beyond which the waters of the ocean plunged into the depths where the giant squid and unusual-looking fish lived.

It would take a half-day to reach a point where their probing scans would show the steep cliff that dropped off into the Abyss. Out of sight of land, they would need to use both the vibrating-currents and echolocation to keep them on course.

Vibrating-currents, like the flow of the tides and the ocean water, were invisible. One sensed them with the body. Ocean flow pushed against the skin or deflected a fin, revealing the force of the moving water. Vibrating-currents produced a faint sensation on the scalp, like brushing against a long strand of bull kelp. It was weak and could be ignored, if desired, but *where* the vibrating-current tingled on the head informed the orca of the direction it swam: north, south, east, or west — as well as up from down. Unlike the tides, vibrating-currents didn't change.

Mothersong and Boomer chatted. There were no natural ocean predators here, or anywhere, to concern them, but they must watch for *unnatural* dangers. Surface-dweller nets or lines could ensnare them, injuring or drowning them, and a collision with a vessel could break a spine or slice them open with whirling blades.

Boomer, ever protective, gave her tips about deep diving. Most of these she already knew, but Mothersong listened and asked questions because what they were going to do was indeed dangerous. Neither of them mentioned the death of Brokenfin, who'd drowned a year ago, but Mothersong was certain it was on Boomer's mind.

Brokenfin and Boomer had been protégés of Deepdive. That old bull had taught the enthusiastic young males everything he knew about the art and craft of probing the depths.

One fateful day, Brokenfin had ventured out solo and hadn't returned. The clan had scattered to dive and search.

They found his limp body drifting upward, without a mark on him.

The clan had stuck by Brokenfin's side for two days — but it was clear he was dead. Mothersong remembered the mourning wails as if she'd heard them only yesterday.

As she mulled the tragedy, Boomer continued his instructions. "The most important thing is to blow small bubbles all the way down," he said. "And if the deep presses too hard on your chest, blow out more."

"I am familiar with that detail, but thank you for reminding me," said Mothersong. "I wonder if—"

She was interrupted by the sudden chatter of many small voices, directly in front and headed in their direction. Talking in a rapid high pitch, they chirped and joked in the language of dolphins.

As Mothersong breached to breathe and gain sight above the water, she spied sleek white-sided bodies cresting and jumping.

Back under the waves, she scanned the group. Over two dozen dolphins were traveling east, from the open ocean. Whether they'd just dined upon, or were in search of, the small fish they loved was unknown. They veered to avoid the orcas.

Mothersong knew a few words in dolphin. She pitched her voice high and squeaked, "Friends."

Three dolphins broke from the group and headed toward them.

Strange, thought Mothersong. Though she'd called out her best greeting, dolphins always steered a wide path around orcas, and never approached. Boomer was larger than two dozen of them combined.

"We have guests," rumbled Boomer.

"Yes," she replied. "They must know we only eat fish."

Boomer chuckled. "From all of our talking, I think they knew it a half-tide ago."

Mothersong laughed at Boomer's exaggeration, but acknowledged the truth he told. The tribes of orcas who ate seals, porpoises, and other whales always hunted in silence, because their prey could hear them.

Fish couldn't hear Mothersong's clan, so they were unaware of the orca chatter referring to them as 'yummies' or the battle-plans being called out.

Evidently, the dolphins had heard Boomer and Mothersong a while ago, and decided that the two orcas didn't present a danger.

The scouting group of three dolphins were now halfway across.

"Try not to frighten them, Boomer."

As the dolphins closed in, Mothersong said, "Hello."

They stopped dead in the water and chattered so fast that Mothersong couldn't pick out any words.

Then, one approached her. The dolphin swam slowly, then tilted its head and turned to face her. She held still. The dolphin appeared more curious than afraid.

Mothersong's skin pricked with the vibrations of the dolphin's scan. "Friends," she repeated in their language.

The dolphin darted off, and with two quick strokes of its fluke it joined the other two. All three jabbered.

They began to swim away, but the first one stopped and spun. "Hello. Friends," it squeaked. Then it hurried to catch up with the others.

Remarkable, thought Mothersong, and contemplated the ancient stories of a matriarch who could talk fluently with other species.

"What did it say?" asked Boomer.

"'Hello' — and it agreed we were friends," she said.

"Ah," said Boomer. "I can't fathom how you speak so many languages. It must take forever to learn them."

"I only understand a few words," said Mothersong. "But that's the beauty of a long life. I've had ages of listening and learning. However, dolphins are such babblers it's tough to understand anything they say."

Boomer rumbled a laugh.

The sky was shrouded by dark clouds, and the sun invisible, but Mothersong's internal clock said it was past midday. Prickles of the vibrating-current on her head confirmed her westward direction, and the seafloor reflected familiar echoes. This corridor led to the deep ocean.

Mothersong couldn't imagine that the surface-dweller Shin had been responsible for the terror-calls that Boomer had heard. But she knew his kind were.

He is strange, she thought. But puzzling out what Talking-Shin meant to the Ravenfin was as elusive to her as hunting minnows in shallow water.

Yet there must be some reason that Talking-Shin had appeared — and spoken. It represented opportunity, and in orca legend, opportunity offered survival.

The Ravenfin were withering and without drastic change, would one day vanish — and that future was something no matriarch could endure.

19

Distracted, Shin missed the pun Tyler had just flung at him. He stopped trying to squeeze his suitcase closed and gave Tyler the briefest of smiles to indicate the Texan's presence was appreciated, though perhaps not his jokes.

Tomorrow morning Shin would be on a flight to Sapporo. He'd spent the day packing, unpacking, and repacking. Though he had always prided himself on knowing the importance of organizing and traveling light, he'd never managed to pull it off.

Tonight, he'd hoped to relax with Tyler, but his mind frothed and churned with the last-minute details that kept popping up.

He'd given up on the idea of taking his scuba gear and decided it'd have to be shipped. His fins, regulator, wetsuit, specialized mask, and sound equipment were neatly organized in a cardboard box. Time hadn't allowed him to attempt communications with pods other than Mothersong's in Puget Sound, so he didn't know if he could understand the orcas in the waters around Japan — but he had every intention of trying. He could rent compressed air tanks there, but having familiar gear, and his customized comms set, was crucial.

Shin hefted the box and deposited it on the table in front of Tyler. "I really should have figured this out earlier," he said, "but can you mail this to me in Hokkaido?" He pointed out the address written neatly with a black Sharpie. "Airmail, otherwise it'll arrive months after I leave Japan."

"Sure," said Tyler. "When do you need it? If it's next-day air, I might need to sell my truck to cover the costs."

Shin chuckled. "If it can get there in a week, that should give me enough time to get a lay of the land. And I got you covered on the cost."

Tyler took a sip of Shiner Bock. He'd brought over a six-pack of the Texas beer to celebrate the eve of Shin's journey. The beer wasn't sold anywhere west of the Rio Grande, but Tyler had bartered with a quartermaster at a military base in San Antonio to arrange for a delivery of this special treat.

To Shin, it was just beer.

"You know," said Tyler, pointing to the beer bottle, "it's amazing what you can get moved around when you know the right people."

"Cool story," agreed Shin, hoping he wasn't about to hear it again. "One more favor to ask?"

"Shoot," said Tyler.

"Be right back." Shin retreated to the bedroom, pulled out the strongbox from its hide-hole underneath the floorboards, and carried it back to the living room. He set it down. "Please watch over this, too."

Tyler's eyebrows raised. "What's in the footlocker?"

"The past." Shin demonstrated the mechanism to open it. "Family photos, medals, and my service pistol. Since you're watching the place, I wanted you to know about the firearm."

"Appreciate that," said Tyler. His face clouded. "But what *are* you taking? Tell me you're not dumb enough to go there unarmed."

"Just this," said Shin, holding up the sheathed makiri. "It's been in my family for generations and is within Japanese law."

Tyler shrugged. "A nice knife to have at your side," he said. "But what you gonna do if shit goes sideways — use your kung fu and cartwheel along the gunwales of the Chinese ship doing the stabby-thing?"

"No." Shin sighed. "It's aikido I practice. And violence is not the way."

"It's cool," said Tyler. "You don't have to go all Bruce Lee on me. I'm just watching out for you."

"I know you are," said Shin. "It's both reassuring and frightening."

If the Texan had registered the jab, he ignored it.

"You know what I think?" Tyler took a swig of Shiner. "You should shoot those sons of bitches."

"What?" exclaimed Shin, staring at his friend. "Nonviolence! I just finished saying—"

"You misunderstand," interrupted Tyler. "Hire a boat. Get yourself a good camera with a long lens — and *bang*! Catch 'em in the act. Upload those puppies to the internet, and they got nowhere to hide after you exposed 'em. That'll shut their ass down."

It wasn't a bad idea. Shin had done multiple internet searches but hadn't found anything on the *Zheng Yi*. International exposure would draw attention.

"Good point," he said. "I'll see if I can make that happen."

"See." Tyler tapped a finger to his head. "That's why I'm the brains and you're the brawn."

"Right," muttered Shin. "Just what I was thinking."

Tyler stood and hefted the box containing the scuba gear. He chuckled. "Dang, that's gonna leave a mark on your bank account. Good thing you're not shipping your boat."

20

The turbine engines of the Boeing 767 spooled up, vibrating the fuselage with a cascade of power. The pilot released the brakes. The craft crept forward, then accelerated along the Sea-Tac runway.

As the airliner lifted into the air, Shin pressed his forehead against the oval window and watched the ground recede.

The plane banked and soon he was able to see Puget Sound where sun-cast diamonds flashed from the emerald waters beneath the skyscrapers of Seattle.

The flight from Sea-Tac to Tokyo would take roughly eleven hours. Then he'd have to change planes for the hour and a half flight to Sapporo, where his cousin had promised to pick him up at the airport.

As the plane gained altitude, he craned his neck to look for the coastline of the Olympic Peninsula and his home, but it soon became impossible due to the clouds blossoming up from the mountains like mushrooms.

When the airliner's ascent had reached the seatbelt-off point, Shin extracted his laptop from his messenger bag. WiFi internet connection in-flight was new.

Shin swiped his credit card through the pay-slot of the entertainment system fused into the back of the seat in front of him. After a few minutes, he was able to connect to the WiFi, and called up the AIS website on his laptop.

And waited.

The data download was as fast as a frozen waterfall. Shin glanced up at the beige ceiling of the winged tube hurtling through the sky. Flying was something he only did if there were no other reasonable transportation options available. It'd been a decade since his feet had boarded an aircraft.

Shin stared out through the window. His gaze drifted up, and he studied the bottom of the dark cloud deck the plane was climbing toward.

The plane bucked, and a chorus of *oohs* spread though the aisle. It lurched again and for a fraction of a second Shin was weightless. His mouth went dry.

An urgent chime sounded and the *fasten your seatbelt* sign lit up. The oval window next to him darkened as the aircraft entered the clouds. He slammed the laptop closed, stowed it, and his hands clutched the armrests, fingertips digging into the vinyl.

The PA system squelched. The captain came online and, between jerking shudders of the aircraft, announced that they were "Experiencing some turbulence."

Understatement, thought Shin and wondered at the wisdom of his decision to travel to Japan.

Memories of helicopter crashes in Vietnam surged forward. Shin tightened his grip on the armrests. *Don't think about it,* he coached himself, but it was too late. He'd escaped from all three of the mishaps with his life and no permanent injuries, but some of the crew and passengers hadn't been so lucky.

The third crash had been the worst. After the fuselage of the Huey had rolled and crunched to a stop, he'd crawled out from the twisted metal with a section of his back filleted open, and second-degree burns on his calves from the fire spreading through the cabin. The helicopter had come to its final stop against the side of a bunker and the pilot had been impaled. The image of his green helmeted form slumped forward with a bloodied railroad timber erupting from his torso had been forever burned into Shin's mind.

The medics had patched Shin up, and the two weeks he'd spent in the hospital had consumed him with worry about his brothers in arms in the jungle. All Shin could do was lie on his side and fret away his time, praying that his absence wasn't jeopardizing their lives.

Reuniting with his team and seeing that they were okay had brought tears to his eyes, just as it did now as he remembered their faces. He wiped at his eyes.

"Are you alright?" asked the woman seated next to him.

"Yes," said Shin. He was trembling; he realized he must look ill. "Just don't like flying."

Sunlight streamed in the window, and the craft stopped shaking. Shin looked down at the tops of the cloud layer from which they'd emerged, and breathed out a long sigh.

He turned back to the woman. "Thank you," he said. "I'm better now." She smiled and picked up her book, one of the Steven King *Dark Tower* novels, and resumed reading.

Shin gave up on the idea of getting any further work done on the laptop, and browsed through the inflight entertainment system.

The third *Matrix* movie was playing. Though he'd already seen it, dark sci-fi fit his mood.

THE FLIGHT ATTENDANT tapped Shin's shoulder, waking him, and asked him to return his seat to the upright position. Twenty minutes later, the JAL 767 bounced and then settled onto the runway. As the seatbelt dug into his lap with the roaring deceleration of the plane, Shin glanced through the window. Moisture beaded and flowed, blurring the airport — but the big lettering on the main terminal left no question. He was in Tokyo.

After deplaning and picking up his luggage, he shuffled along with the rest of the passengers toward customs. He stood in line for less than ten minutes before two white-gloved customs officers arrived at his side. In English, they asked him to surrender his passport and pick up his luggage.

They escorted him along a corridor and arrived at a side room, guarded by two more customs agents, both of whom were armed.

Inside the room, they instructed Shin to place his suitcases on a metal table and then sit on a low stool in the center of the room.

One of the officers began to ask questions — the purpose of his visit, destinations, and so on — while the other two opened his luggage, and began rifling through it, placing everything they'd extracted into neat, tidy rows on the surface of the polished steel table.

"And what is this doing in your possession?" asked one of the officers, holding up Shin's Ainu knife in his white-gloved hand. "It's a restricted item for entry to Japan."

"It is the makiri of my ancestors," responded Shin in Japanese. "I'm bringing it home to the burial place of my grandfather in Hokkaido."

Two officers withdrew to a corner with the makiri and conferred, while inspecting it. The third stood ten feet away, in front of Shin, hands on his hips like a drill sergeant, and stared at him. A tightly coiled white wire lead from his radio to an earpiece, and a 38 revolver was holstered at his hip.

Shin was certain that he wasn't meant to hear the conversation of the two examining the makiri, and kept his face a mask as he listened to their words. They measured and discussed the length of the blade, then agreed it was permissible. "Hai," said one, pointing out that Shin had properly declared it on his customs form, while the other admired the construction and markings, and stated that it appeared genuine.

Shin heard the crackle of the radio of the man guarding him, and his acute hearing brought him the words from the earpiece: "The passport for Shin Takeda checks out. There are no outstanding warrants, and he is not on an international watch list."

The customs officer didn't take his eyes off Shin as he replied, "Understood."

The other two officers stepped forward. One announced that nothing illegal had been found.

"Welcome to Japan," said the white-gloved customs agent with the 38, and gave a cursory bow before directing Shin to please repack his belongings and carry on.

Shin glanced at his watch. An hour had been wasted in customs, but, thankfully, he had a two-hour window for his connection.

THE FLIGHT to Sapporo took an hour and a half, and was packed full with people. Unlike American airports, though, the passenger boarding and disembarking process was orderly and polite. No one tried to stuff a too-large suitcase into an overhead bin, or held up the aisle while sorting and repacking their things, or clubbed a seated passenger with a swinging carry-on.

As Shin strolled down the passenger boarding ramp, he thought about how the US might be improved by adopting a few Japanese customs — perhaps not the rigid social hierarchy, but certainly the politeness and cleanliness.

After exiting airport security, Shin walked toward the baggage claim area, passing dozens of people holding up neatly lettered placards. He paused to look for his name amongst the Kanji, but couldn't find it and moved on.

After arriving at the baggage claim area, he waited. Daichi had been polite and welcoming during their phone call, but Shin knew next to nothing about his relative other than he was in IT and lived on the northern tip of Hokkaido. He scanned the clean, orderly space — which was teeming with throngs of people yet somehow not chaotic — hoping to see a sign that read *Shin*.

There were dozens of placards — a few in English, but most in Kanji or Katakana. His name was not amongst them.

Shin paced along the central corridor. He and Daichi had spoken in Japanese and, though Shin was fluent, it was possible he'd misunderstood his cousin's instructions. He set down his messenger bag and suitcase, and checked his watch. It was 4 p.m., but his jet-lagged body told him it must be 4 a.m. — three days in the future, and without sleep.

"Shin," said a man emerging from the masses. He bowed. "I'm Daichi."

"Daichi!" said Shin. He returned his cousin's bow. "It is a pleasure to see you."

As they shook hands, Shin wondered how his cousin had spotted him amongst the crowds. *Do I stick out like an American tourist wearing a cowboy hat?*

"Here, let me help you with your bag," said Daichi. He bent and picked up Shin's suitcase, then motioned him forward. "This way. It's just over five hours drive to Wakkanai, so I recommend visiting the men's room before we go."

"Okay," said Shin. "That's a long way. I hope I haven't inconvenienced you. I could've taken a train."

"It is no trouble," answered Daichi. "Fumi and I are excited to have you stay with us."

Outside the airport, dark onyx clouds scurried across the summer sky. Unlike in Tokyo, it wasn't raining. The air carried the marine tang of salt and seaweed, similar to home, but it smelled different in a way that Shin couldn't identify.

Daichi led him to his vehicle, a sleek new model Acura.

After stowing Shin's luggage, Daichi drove them out of the airport complex. Though his eyes felt like sandpaper and his head a punching bag, Shin observed the intricacies of the complex traffic flow. He recalled that everything in Japan had an order and a place, and as long as that was respected, there existed a peaceful society.

On the winding road headed north along the western edge of Hokkaido, the valleys and hillsides inland to the east rolled with fields of green. Off to the west, small islands and islets erupted from the slate-gray sea like dark teeth. Olive green vegetation clung to their lower slopes, hacking out an existence in the aftermath of the tectonic violence of the Pacific Ring of Fire.

The sun's golden rays backlit the white crests and spindrift of the waves crashing onto the umber, rocky shore. Mere feet above the sea, a V-shaped flock of cormorants streaked southward, their stubby wings beating with fervor. Though heavy and underpowered in the air, the seabirds were exceptional divers for fish, and Shin had often seen them streak past his sailboat.

The ochre northern valley of Hokkaido opened up in a series of long, slow pulses of light as dark clouds competed with the sun. The Sea of Japan shifted between blue and indigo.

Shin wondered what Mothersong would think, if she could experience this vantage point of her world.

SHIN BECAME aware that the vehicle had stopped. His chin was resting on his chest, and now he looked up, unaware of how long he'd been dozing. In front of the car's headlights stood a gated metal fence topped by a short A-shaped roof.

"We have arrived," said Daichi. He depressed a button on the Acura's console and the gate rolled to the side, revealing a warmly-lit house with a sloped, tiled roof — the curve of which was steepest at the top and shallowed out to the eaves. Traditional Japanese windows, a veranda, and woodwork complemented the roof.

Daichi pulled into the carport, and killed the engine. Small lights sparkled along a path through an immaculate garden.

"I agreed to host you," said Daichi, turning toward Shin, "not due to a familial obligation, but because I am intrigued by the purpose of your visit. You wish to stop the people who are capturing the young of the *shachi* for display in zoos."

"Yes," said Shin. *Shachi* was the Japanese word for killer whales.

"You understand that the waters in question are not within the territorial jurisdiction of the government of Japan?"

There was an edge to the question. Shin felt off-balance. "I'm not here to cause conflict," he said, "I just want to talk to them."

"Yes," said Daichi. "That's what you said on the phone call. I'm making sure. I know of your past life in the US special forces and I have no wish to embroil my family in vigilante justice conflicts. Are we clear?"

"Clear as a bell," answered Shin, taken aback. He couldn't recall ever telling Daichi about his days as a SEAL.

"I'll take that as a *yes*," said Daichi. "Also, I would appreciate you not speaking of this topic in front of Fumi."

"Understood," said Shin.

"Excellent," said Daichi. "We are in agreement." He opened the driver's door, stepped out and beckoned Shin, smiling broadly. "Come, cousin. Welcome to my humble home."

Shin shouldered his bag and followed Daichi, who was carrying his suitcase, along the path. Mists flowed around them and gravel crunched underfoot as they walked through the garden toward the front of the house. The trimmed bonsai trees, interconnected ponds, and chunks of volcanic rock comprising the garden depicted in miniature the land they had just driven through.

The conversation in the carport weighed as heavily on his mind as the jet-lag. *Daichi's flipped like a switch*, thought Shin. *Friendly cousin to interrogator and back.*

"I believe Fumi is asleep," said Daichi, unlocking the door.

Inside the threshold, Shin's baggage was set down, and they removed their shoes.

Daichi said, "I'll show you to your room in a minute, but first let's toast your long journey."

Shin followed his cousin into the small kitchen. Daichi uncorked a bottle of nigori sake and poured the milky liquid into two porcelain cups. Shin accepted the proffered cup and studied its decorative motif. Rolling waves of cerulean blue extended toward a white rim where two black-and-white whales, one on each side of the cup, blew delicate lines of silver spray.

"The *shachi* are such beautiful beings," said Daichi, studying him. He raised his cup and switched to English: "*Cheers*, isn't it? Or is it *bottoms up?*"

"They're both good," said Shin.

"Ah," said Daichi, lowering his cup. "Such a strange language. The phrases are so different, yet mean the same thing."

"Yes," agreed Shin.

"I know another toast," said Daichi. "An American one."

Though the fatigue of travel clouded Shin's mind, he couldn't escape the feeling Daichi was toying with him. He smiled and waited.

"Good hunting," announced Daichi. He lifted his cup and drank.

Here's to mixed messages, thought Shin as he raised his drink. "Good hunting," he responded.

21

Mothersong bobbed on the surface next to Boomer, breathing deeply. They'd each done a shallow dive to scan the depths below and to sense the current and water temperature. In a moment they would plunge deep, and were now stocking up on as much oxygen as their tissues could carry.

"Ready?" rumbled Boomer.

"Yes," she said.

He arched his spine and dove. She followed.

Mothersong matched Boomer's strong pace, and side by side, the grandson and matriarch descended straight down.

A school of tuna parted and darted around them as the light grew dimmer and the water colder.

As they exited the bottom of the school, the pressure began to mount on Mothersong's chest. Boomer released a few bubbles and she did the same.

The pair of orcas dove deeper and deeper. The light vanished and it became as dark as squid ink. Mothersong tried to echo-locate the sea floor, but it remained fuzzy and far away, as if they'd made no progress at all.

Had they been in the deepest sections of Puget Sound, she and Boomer would have already hit bottom. But the depths here were indeterminable. The only signal to tell them if they'd gone far enough was whale song.

Mothersong dribbled out bubbles to lessen the pressure, but the force squeezing her body mounted. She imagined being rolled and crushed by a surface-dweller behemoth.

They kept silent, listening for the sound channel, as they continued downward. Though her eyes could no longer see Boomer in the darkness, Mothersong knew he was there, next to her.

Mothersong's heart pounded in her skull. She counted the heartbeats to distract herself from the crushing grip. The counting helped her mind dampen internal noise from the external signal she was straining to perceive.

It's too much, she thought, but stayed on her course.

The faint, dull rise and fall of a song tickled her hearing. Within ten beats of her heart, the sound became as sharp as a tooth. She leveled off her dive to listen.

"Here," clicked Boomer in his softest voice.

Mothersong hung motionless. The pain squeezing her body grew and she would need to go up for air soon, but she listened as the waves of sound in the long-distance channel washed over her.

Wooooo-arrrrrr.

The song was made by the gigantic whales that probed the depths. Though she understood little of their language, she was startled at the words *threat, hunted, surface-dweller, pain,* spoken in orca root-tongue.

This is what Boomer heard, she thought. The root spanned the languages and dialects of the orca clans and tribes. The deep-whales must have picked up the distress calls from orcas far away and woven them into their songs.

There is more, she realized. Words from dolphin, white whale, gray whale, and other species were buried in the mournful deep-whale signal. Mothersong searched her mind for the wisdom to extract them.

She hungered for air, but she couldn't tear herself away from the song. Images formed in her mind, and an icy cold crept through her bones. The demons from her youth had resurfaced.

"Up," she cried. "I must go up."

Mothersong dashed toward the surface.

She heard Boomer grunt, "Following."

Her body screamed for air as she powered upward.

Gray dots and blobs appeared and clouded her echolocation, and grew until she was completely blind. If there were surface-dweller vessels above, she would be unable to sense them to avoid a collision.

Gravity and the vibrating-currents told her which way was up, and she hammered her fluke with all the energy she had left to make it to the top. Her fluke-muscles cramped; she slowed down. There was no thought of how far she needed to go, only the instinct that if she didn't breathe soon she never would again.

Her consciousness began to fade. The deep Abyss — the final resting place — tugged her mind downward.

22

Shin slept late, and it was almost noon when he dragged his jet-lagged body out from under the covers of the futon on the tatami-mat floor. He shuffled into the small kitchen, massaging the back of his neck to try to break the vise-grip centered there. His hosts had left him a note explaining they'd gone to work and to make himself comfortable, and they'd be home at 6 p.m. for dinner. On the margin was written the password for the household WiFi, which was a lengthy hexadecimal character string.

Shin's body and mind were not in synch, and he wasn't hungry. Tea, however, was a priority, and hopefully it would chase away some of the cobwebs clogging his mind. He spent a few minutes searching for ingredients, then sprinkled tea leaves into an infuser and dispensed boiling water from the electric hot water pot. While the tea steeped, he retrieved his laptop, and set it up on the dining-room table.

Last night, he hadn't appreciated that the house was perched high on a hillside overlooking the sea, but in daylight it was impossible to miss the spectacular view. He unlocked the sliding glass door and stepped out on the balcony, into a brisk wind. A kilometer away and a hundred meters below, white caps in the slate-gray sea foamed and crashed on the rocky shore. The sigh of the waves and the breeze merged into a pleasant murmur that would have lulled him back to sleep had he not been standing.

Back inside, Shin poured a cup of tea and sat down with his laptop. It took him two tries to enter the WiFi password correctly; it was obvious that Daichi was a great deal more security-conscious than Shin, who merely used his first name and his date of birth, 1942. He hadn't asked Daichi which company he worked for, or what his wife did, which were topics to explore this evening.

He pulled up his email, then opened the AIS tracking website. The *Zheng Yi* wasn't visible, which meant it was either still in port in Shanghai or had slipped out and was now running dark. Shin sipped tea as he scanned through the cached historical data from the last week. Not finding any evidence of it leaving, he concluded that the ship was still in port and hadn't left during his marathon travel session yesterday.

The tension in his neck eased.

He turned to search for the whereabouts of M-pod back home. He found some recent postings of them in southern Puget Sound, thousands of miles from where he was now. Shin hoped they were enjoying good hunting, and weren't being hampered by the noises of cargo ships, tankers, and tugs.

Returning to regional geography, Shin called up the maritime maps displaying the commercial lanes surrounding Japan. He studied the islands and waterways and tried to deduce the route that the *Zheng Yi* would take on its journey from Shanghai to the Sea of Okhotsk.

After sailing east from Shanghai into the East China Sea, there were two options. One, head northeast through the Korea Strait, into the Sea of Japan, and then squirt through the narrow and shallow La Pérouse Strait (a Frenchman had named this after himself but the Japanese referred to it as the Sōya Strait), which separated the northern tip of Hokkaido and Sakhalin Island. Or, two, continue easterly into international waters and then bend north around the eastern edge of Japan and enter via island fenestrations in the Kuril chain — a longer trek.

The route taken would have been obvious if the cached AIS data had extended backward more than seven days. Unfortunately it didn't, but perhaps Shin could puzzle it out.

The *Zheng Yi* was the hunter command-and-control ship, and tended the smaller and faster boats which were used to corral a pod in a harbor and capture a young one. Shin was hunting the ambushers. Just like during his time in Vietnam, intel was of paramount importance.

The logistics and mission parameters of their cetacean hunt would determine the ship's chosen route. To determine that, Shin needed to find every single attribute he could about the *Zheng Yi*: range, engines, displacement, speed, crew, and cargo capacity, plus where it was built, and any sort of modifications. Additionally, if it had to refuel or call on a port during its excursions, he wanted to know where.

Feeling confident about his strategy, he dove into the task.

However, after an hour of searching, he'd located nothing — not even a picture of the damn ship. His stomach grumbled and he rose to look in the fridge.

Within it, Shin found a plate of *wanpaku* sandwiches, topped by a toothpick bearing a tiny American flag. He smiled at his hosts' thoughtfulness, then wolfed down the sliced carrots, deli chicken, Sakura cheese, and red cabbage wedged between squares of Japanese milk bread. He washed it all down with a tart lemon Ramune soda.

Satiated, he returned to the problem of the invisible ship.

Two hours later, a headache again gripped his neck like a vise.

"Why is there not even a single flippin' photo?" Shin asked his laptop in frustration. So far, he hadn't come up with even a byte of additional information on the ship. The more he thought about that fact, the more it bothered him.

He'd found the holding company's website, but it was bare bones and hadn't been updated this century. The last entry was from 1998, which promised *exciting, exclusive, executive fishing safaris*. But the website contained no contact or booking number, and no pictures of said 'fishing safaris'.

Worse, the entire internet was vacant as far as the *Zheng Yi* was concerned. There were a few search engine hits detailing the early 1800s exploits of a pirate couple, Zheng Yi and his wife Zheng Yi Sao.

Shin read them.

In their heyday, the swashbuckling duo had ruled the waves with four hundred pirate ships, and had successfully tormented the Portuguese armada, the East India Company, and the Qing dynasty.

Presumably, the financier-owners of the current *Zheng Yi* had had a good chuckle in the boardroom at the naming.

Undeterred, Shin continued his search, but found nothing of use.

It made zero sense. There were no blogs featuring photos of intoxicated business executives hoisting up large dead fish. Nor scenes of telephone-pole length rods, bent over in arcs, during an epic struggle of man versus fish. Every marketing department on the planet would've insisted upon at least a couple of those, and certainly some client would have plastered them all over his social media feed.

But there was nothing, anywhere. The *Zheng Yi* was a ghost ship.

Shin had imagined that the operators had chartered fishing trips as cover, and at other times they hunted and captured cetaceans for whomever paid the bills. But if they did run fishing safaris, they catered to a group of people who didn't like photography — which could be gang-bosses, politicians, actors, or musicians.

Considering how dark the ship was, it might be involved in an array of illicit activities. Shin's mood soured further as he considered the possibilities. Maybe the *Zheng Yi* was involved in human trafficking, smuggling, or illegal weapons/technology transfer.

Deep doo-doo, he thought.

Tyler had been right to warn him about approaching the ship's owners directly. Shin wondered how the CPI had learned about the clandestine whale kidnapping — and why it had been revealed to him in a phone call.

A grinding noise attracted his attention, and he went to the window. The outer gate was sliding open along its metal tracks.

Daichi's Acura rolled forward, gravel crunching under the tires. There was a passenger in the front.

Shin closed his laptop and then bounded to the front door to greet his hosts.

This was the first time he'd met Fumi, and as they exchanged pleasantries, he was struck by her height (nearly as tall as Shin, who was 5'8") and her green eyes. Both features were unusual in Japan.

"Thank you for the sandwiches," said Shin. "They were delicious."

"I'm glad you enjoyed them," said Fumi.

"How was your day, cousin?" asked Daichi.

"I'm jet-lagged, but feeling better," answered Shin. "I spent the afternoon researching..." He let his words trail off, remembering at the last second that he wasn't supposed to talk about the orcas or what he was here to do.

"Researching what?" asked Fumi. She turned to hang her sweater on a peg. Shin caught a stern glare from Daichi.

"Um... things about the seas, straits, and islands," he said, recovering. "Like, I had no idea that Russia owns a bunch of islands that used to be part of Japan, and..." He hunted for a way out of the conversation, aware he was babbling. "And won't give them back. Some of the islands are only a couple of miles off the coast of Hokkaido."

"Yes," said Fumi, as she walked toward the kitchen. "It isn't something for polite company to discuss."

Shin felt Daichi's hand squeeze his shoulder, and turned to see his cousin's eyebrows lift halfway up his forehead.

"Let me get Shin a drink," said Daichi. He raised a finger to his lips to indicate that Shin should stop talking. "And we'll sit on the patio. When will dinner be ready?"

"About seven," called Fumi. "I hope sashimi and rice is okay with Shin."

Shin nodded, and Daichi answered for him, "Yes."

Daichi guided Shin by the elbow to the porch, opened the sliding glass door, and ushered him out. "Be right back," he said, and slid the door closed.

The chill in the air was accentuated by the marine breeze, but the spotlight of the golden sun dipping westward warmed Shin as he sat in a deck chair and brooded. He hadn't been here twenty-four hours and he'd already managed to irk his hosts. He was no closer to finding the information he needed on the ship, and had no functional plan to interdict the hunters.

It's time to pull the plug on this, he thought, *and go home.*

THE PATIO DOOR SLID OPEN, halting Shin's ruminations. He looked up from staring at his feet.

Daichi stepped out onto the deck with two beer bottles in hand. "I hope Kirin is okay," he said, holding out one of the bottles.

"Thanks," said Shin.

Daichi clinked his bottle with Shin's, and drank. He turned to the wind-churned waters, and stepped toward the railing.

"I wish to show you something," said Daichi, and pointed.

Shin stood and joined him. He raised his hand to block the sun's bronze-fire reflection in the sea, and followed his cousin's gesture to a jagged island off the coast, dominated by a central volcano. The perfect conical shape reminded him of Mount Fuji and Mount St. Helens, prior to her pyroclastic tantrum in 1980.

"Only Mount Fuji has a more beautiful shape," said Daichi, as if reading Shin's mind. "That is Rishiri Island. Great skiing in winter, by the way. Behind it is Rebun island, but it's difficult to see from here." Daichi took a sip of beer. "There's been an interesting discovery there."

Shin waited for his host to continue, and wondered about the most polite way possible to tell him he was changing plans to head back home.

"Ancients living on that island," said Daichi, "held a funerary right for an orca."

Shin's gaze flicked between Daichi and the volcanic island.

"It's true," said Daichi. "Thousands of years ago. It is thought to be an Ainu tribute to Rep-un-Kumay, the orca god. He is sometimes depicted as a mischievous man with a harpoon who casts his kill onto the shore to feed villagers — and sometimes as a huge and fearsome *shachi*. It is even said that some Ainu could commune with orcas, who would then help the small boats on their hunts for gray whales."

The bottle of Kirin slipped from Shin's hand, and spun slowly before smashing on the rocks twenty meters below the deck.

"You didn't like it?" asked Daichi.

"I... am so sorry," said Shin, embarrassed. "It was delicious. I'm just clumsy."

"Be right back," said Daichi, and disappeared inside the house.

Shin sat down in a deck chair and ran his fingers through his hair. *Commune with orcas*, was what his cousin had said. *Was it something my ancestors a thousand years ago could do?*

The patio door slid open and Daichi popped back out with a fresh bottle of Kirin, which he passed to Shin.

Daichi sat down, and cleared his throat. "According to another legend," he said, "a giant spider named Yaushikep once descended from the mountains and terrorized the villages. People prayed for divine intervention, and Rep-un-Kumay answered the call. He pulled the spider into the bay and changed it into a giant octopus named Akkorokamui.

"Apparently, the sea monster still lives in Uchiura Bay, eating wayward boats — but I guess it's good that it's no longer a giant land-spider eating people."

Daichi's recitation of the legend was so deadpan that Shin studied him for signs of jest. Finding not so much as a twitch of the lip, he wondered if he'd misinterpreted the intent of the conversation. *I'm fluent in Japanese*, he thought, *but Daichi's true meaning is buried within complexities. He could be encouraging me, or he could be telling me to go to hell.*

"We should visit Rishiri," said Daichi. "There's a ferry, but I have a boat." He pointed down to the marina, nestled within the rocky, volcanic coastline. "If you'd like, we can go this weekend. Fumi will be visiting her mother in Okinawa for the next two weeks — and my work is changing directions a bit, so I'll have some free time to spend with you."

"Yes, I'd like that," said Shin. *Definitely encouraging me*, he thought.

"You should take Shin to the Onsen Dome," said Fumi as they sat around the low dinner table in the living room.

Midway through chewing the salmon nigiri he'd just deposited on his tongue, Shin raised his eyebrows. He began to speak, but the wasabi mustard lit up his palate with the subtlety of a flamethrower. He coughed and sneezed. His eyes watered.

"Yes," agreed Daichi.

When Shin could speak again, he asked, "What's the Onsen Dome?"

"A natural hot-spring bathhouse, not far from here," said Daichi. "Do you have any tattoos?"

"What?"

Daichi repeated the question in English.

"No," said Shin. "I have no tattoos."

"That's unusual for American ex-military," said Fumi.

"I guess it is," said Shin. The sense that he was being interrogated returned. "But I don't understand why you're asking."

"No one with a tattoo is permitted inside the bath house," said Daichi, and looked at his wife.

"Oh," said Shin, embarrassed he'd forgotten about the strict policies within Japanese bathhouses. There were so many customs and rules. He was certain to commit a major *faux pas* at some point. Shin finished his cup of sake and set it down.

"We understand that many in America get tattoos," said Fumi. "But why didn't you?" She poured more sake into his cup.

Though Fumi's question highlighted his *nisei* lineage — it was one he'd never been asked before.

Shin thought through his reply. "In Vietnam," he began, "guys were getting an anchor or a dagger, a skull or a rose, or a name to remind them of someone special. Perhaps to reinforce their status as badass or survivor. I was in my twenties and cherished the companionship of my squad, but I thought, why bother? I might be dead tomorrow. Ink isn't going to help me.

"And now decades later, it's popular to look as if you've had an industrial accident in a printing press. But I still think, why bother? No one other than you truly cares about the inked scars and joys of your life, nor your aspirations. Why must you telegraph with obscure hieroglyphics?

"However, I do believe something about tattoos," Shin continued, now feeling the full weight of the sake. He'd forgotten the Japanese custom that a guest's empty cup must always be filled. "One day, in keeping with the full circle of Buddhism, only righteous warriors will be unmarked."

Fumi laughed.

Daichi looked at Shin over his cup, his face expressionless.

23

Bursting through the surface, Mothersong blew out the little air she had left in her lungs, and dragged in a deep inhalation. Her muscles cramped and spasmed. She was as powerless as driftwood.

But as she continued to breathe, the gray fuzz clouding her senses faded, and control over her body returned. She became aware of Boomer next to her, thrashing the waters.

"Mothersong. Mothersong!" he blared. "Mothersong?"

When speech was again possible, she said, "I am alive. Exhausted. Must breathe and rest." She wallowed on the surface as she recovered.

"I should have never taken you that deep," said Boomer.

"I'm glad... you did," she answered, but the aches in her body, and the slow return of her mental faculties, told her it had been too deep a journey. "I will never forget the cries."

Images flooded her mind. She began to shudder.

"We must go back to the clan," said Boomer. "Can you travel?"

"Yes," said Mothersong. Her thoughts flittered toward worry about the Ravenfin.

"Follow," said Boomer, and she did.

They headed east toward the strait. The clouds had cleared, and behind them the sun dipped toward the horizon. Time had passed too fast. When Mothersong felt better they picked up the pace, hoping to find the Ravenfin before nightfall.

"I heard the same as before," said Boomer. "Calls about surface-dwellers hunting, and cries of alarm and pain. What did you learn?"

"Much — and it's deathly news," she answered. "Not just our kind is being hunted but dolphins, deep-whales, white-whales, and other species."

Mothersong described the languages she'd heard, and her theory: deep-whales had heard the anguished orca calls, mimicked them, and put them into their song — then boomed into the sound channel for all to hear.

"Fascinating," said Boomer. "Where are the singing-whales? How far away?"

"I do not know," said Mothersong. She considered the wisdom of the tales from her elders. "The lore states that deep-whales always mark location in their songs. But I can't tell. At least not yet."

She was certain the message contained the coding for *where*, but hadn't been able to pick out the words or images. When she slept tonight, and dreamed, the sounds imprinted in her mind might emerge and make sense — as had happened before. Aural memories were foundational to understanding the ways of the world.

Deep-whales roamed much further than orcas, and the ones she'd encountered in her travels had spent their winters far away. They always came back in the summers, and sang about the places they'd visited. Most of it she couldn't understand, but some words such as *cold, warm, clear-water, food,* and *hungry* had seeped into her consciousness over time.

When Boomer and Mothersong entered familiar territory, they began calling. Their voices couldn't carry nearly as far as the transmissions within the sound channel, of course, but by repeating the call as they travelled, they hoped to catch a return signal from the Ravenfin and steer toward them.

It was well past nightfall when Mothersong and Boomer found the clan, asleep.

The harbor the Ravenfin had chosen was isolated, and had been a safe haven for them in troubled times before.

Aware that each orca had one eye open and were half-listening,

Mothersong murmured soothing sounds as she approached, to signal that all was well.

Spyhopper and Flukethumper stirred awake, and turned toward Boomer and Mothersong.

"We will speak in the morning," she whispered in response to their quiet probes. "Now is the time for rest."

BUBBLES. Fire.

In the dream world, Mothersong flinched away from the scorching heat of a vent erupting on the seafloor. Thundering cracks created an impenetrable wall of hot bubbles, obscuring everything behind it.

Mothersong stirred, and rose to breathe. Seeing the clan was safe within the harbor, she sank below the surface and into the dream again.

Her semiconscious mind probed the whale's song as it replayed. Memories from the echoes of voices heard throughout her lifetime sifted through the trills, squeals, and bellows. Images formed, then words.

Like a calf learning its first vocabulary, Mothersong experienced the thrill of discovery as she linked an image to a sound. Though one-half of her mind remained asleep, the other half churned through simulacra. Meanings emerged, and attached themselves to the three-dimensional models her dreaming mind constructed.

The song had originated on the far side of the ocean and, for the deep-whales, was thirty-days of travel. It was a place where fire could erupt to boil the waters.

The dream shifted.

She witnessed Shin naked, helpless, and near death. Mothersong swam toward him, and carried him to the shore.

The dream jumped and blurred.

Shin hovered in the water next to her, covered in black and attached to a machine that bubbled. He spoke to her with cold clarity: *I will hunt those surface-dwellers and make them stop.*

A buzzing built in Mothersong's mind.

She shuddered and woke up.

The clan were still serenely half-asleep... but the buzzing continued and grew in volume and pitch as it streaked toward them.

"Alarm," Mothersong screamed. "Dive!"

Around her, orcas jerked awake. Thrashing into action, they repeated her cry, and body-checked slumbering neighbors slow to respond. Soon the whole clan was in motion, and dove to avoid the surface-vessel powering inbound.

Oddpatches squeaked, "Air," and headed upward.

"No," said Melody, and spun to chase after her calf. "Stop! Dive!"

Mothersong scanned. A V-shape rippled the surface and zipped toward the area the calf was rising to.

"No!" she screamed.

From beneath, Pouncer streaked upward.

Time slowed.

Pouncer struck the vessel, and for a brief moment Mothersong lost track of it.

A crunch, like a giant-whale landing after breaching, shook the water as the vessel slammed back down. Shrieking, it splintered apart.

And fell silent.

Oddpatches dove to his mother. He appeared unharmed, but he'd been a dorsal-fin away from being struck and killed.

Pouncer hung limp on the surface, grunting in pain.

Mothersong sped toward her. Blood seeped from a gash on her side. Pouncer had rammed the vessel to save the calf.

"Breathe slowly, and hold still," she said. "I must look."

In the bright moonlight, she inspected Pouncer. The slice in the skin was nearly the length of her pectoral fin, but narrow, and the bleeding slow. The surrounding tissue, however, was puffed and swollen.

In addition to the cut, she's broken ribs, thought Mothersong. *Or worse.*

She then realized that there was far too much crimson in the water for it to be due to Pouncer's wound.

Mothersong spun, clicked out instructions for all to check in, and scanned the clan. Though she was near the surface, pressure squeezed her chest with the intensity of the depths of the sound channel.

Chatter rose and fell as everyone called out their name and their health.

Mothersong breathed easier. No one else had been injured.

Rhymehealer approached, and clicked that she would attend to Pouncer.

Mothersong glided the short distance to the maroon stains in the silvery moonlight. Debris bobbed on the surface. Other parts of the vessel settled downward, releasing bubbles of foul, viscous oils.

Death.

She didn't know how many surface-dwellers had been on the fast-vessel, but as she interrogated the water, Mothersong found three — not moving. One was ripped in half.

Mothersong returned to Pouncer.

"It hurts to breathe, move, or laugh," Pouncer said. "But I will live to fight another day."

Pouncer's ribs were bent and misshapen, and the next several days would see the truth of whether she survived or not. Mothersong thanked Rhymehealer and drifted away.

She berated herself and cursed her failure to warn the clan soon enough. She cursed the environment that had become so hostile. The fields of fish had dwindled, and hunting in the noise and traffic of the surface-dweller's vessels had become too difficult. The Ravenfin's numbers were declining. They were slowly dying.

Mothersong sought guidance from her ancestors.

Different waters — far away, she thought. *I must lead them there.*

24

Shin's second morning in Wakkanai began better than his first. He managed to get up by 10 a.m., and the jet lag had eased to where his mind no longer felt mired in sticky mud. The dark thoughts of yesterday had lightened by several degrees, though not to a level that would be considered bright or cheery.

He shuffled into the kitchen, and fixed tea. As it was steeping, he read the note attached to the house key his cousin had left. Daichi would drop Fumi off for her 5 p.m. train and then head home. The note also contained the code for the alarm system in case Shin wanted to go for a walk.

In the pantry, Shin found a bag of cereal called Calbee. He opened the top, and then dumped some of the brown-rice granola into a porcelain bowl. After dousing the granola with milk, he sat down to eat and read the cereal package.

Like American cereals, Calbee featured the words *wholesome* and *delicious* — ubiquitous in the advertising world. It made sense. No one wanted to eat a cereal that used *noxious* and *putrid* as buzzwords. Still, it seemed artificial, as if the marketing folks had just given up and shrugged, then copied and pasted the words.

Glancing down at the bowl, Shin noted that the unperturbed brown-rice clusters had achieved varying degrees of buoyancy in the milk, which seemed to be a function of how many bubbles were sequestered within a given cluster. As Shin watched them bob, his mind drifted to the problem of finding information — any information — on the *Zheng Yi*.

After shaking off the moody contemplation, he slurped down the rest of the cereal.

He rose to pour more tea, then retrieved his laptop. *The search resumes*, he thought, and cracked his knuckles as he sat down again.

Three hours later, despite utilizing different search engines, queries, and internet databases, Shin had uncovered nothing. He thought of the Einstein quote about insanity. The internet was a black hole as far as the ship was concerned, and his continued forays fit Einstein's definition to a tee. Doing the same thing over and over, and expecting a different result, was insane.

He wasn't going to get squat from the internet. He clenched his jaw as he searched for a way through the impasse.

Shin had explained to Daichi that his reason for traveling to Wakkanai was to stop the hunting of orcas. Though he'd been keen to host him, his cousin had cautioned Shin that it was a topic not to be discussed in front of Fumi. The mixed messages puzzled Shin.

Perhaps when Daichi returned without Fumi, Shin could ask him for help. This phase of futile rod-casts into the fishless internet needed to end.

Shin plotted the specifics of the conversation. He knew enough about Japanese culture to comprehend that there were both familial and business ties that could, at times, put husband and wife at odds. Yet he had no true knowledge of how to navigate these complex codes of behavior.

Despite his fluency in the language, and the norms and behaviors he'd learned from his parents, Shin was *nisei*, and would always be a foreigner in Japan. If he asked Daichi a seemingly innocent question, which would be accepted as open and honest in the US, he risked running afoul of one of the honor codes. A minor misstep would shut down a conversation. A major one would see Shin ousted from Daichi's home and permanently ostracized.

A loud chime jarred him from his musings.

It sounded again, and he turned his head to try and locate the source. A flashing blue light near the front door caught his eye and he spotted an LCD panel, part of the home security system. He rose and went toward it.

The video screen displayed a man in blue-coveralls. "Hello, I have a delivery for Shin Takeda at this address."

Shin punched the security code into the panel, and hit the button to open the gate. "I'll be right there," he said. *It must be my scuba gear*, he thought, and his mood brightened a bit.

Outside, a Mitsubishi truck bearing the Yamato Transport logo — a black cat carrying a black kitten on a field of yellow — beeped as it backed into the driveway.

Two delivery men wearing clean blue uniforms and white gloves wrestled an enormous black box onto a hydraulic lift. Shin was startled at the size of it.

It can't possibly be for me, he thought.

Hydraulics groaned as it was being lowered. One of the men hopped off the lift and approached Shin with a clipboard. ID was needed, so Shin trotted into the house to fetch his passport.

When he returned, they'd finished off-loading the box. Shin signed each of the three forms on the clipboard: one each from Yamato Transport, Japanese Customs, and the US military base in Yokosuka.

Puzzled, Shin opened his mouth to ask about the shipment — especially since it had come via a US base — but the two deliverymen abruptly bowed, climbed into the truck, and drove off. The gate to Daichi's house rolled closed behind them.

Shin stared at the monolithic black box, which was almost the width of Daichi's Acura. It was criss-crossed with red tape from the Customs Office of Japan, with a handle at each end and a locked clasp. It was a colossal footlocker.

He'd never seen it before. *Certainly Tyler couldn't have sent this.*

Judging by the efforts of the deliverymen, it was heavy. Shin wondered how he was going to drag it toward Daichi's front door without carving deep trenches in the grass, disrupting stones, plowing over sculpted plants — or otherwise laying messy medieval siege to the immaculate Japanese garden.

Who would even own a footlocker this size?

Despite his earlier dismissal, Occam's Razor kept slicing.

Tyler.

It had to be him. No one else knew this address. *But what the hell has he sent?*

Shin had given Tyler a medium-sized cardboard box, with simple instructions. In return, Shin had received a yeti-sized trunk, which must weigh five-times more than what he'd asked to have shipped. He briefly entertained the thought that Tyler might pop out of the trunk.

As he pondered a way to get the damn thing inside the house, he wondered why the US military had been involved and how much it had cost to ship the trunk.

Shin checked his watch, fretting about getting the footlocker inside before Daichi came home.

Remembering that proper technique wins over brute force, he squatted and extended his arms to grip the footlocker by the handles. Like a Romanian deadlifter, Shin grunted and levitated the footlocker. Centimeter by centimeter, it rose.

His thighs and arms began to shake and then cramp.

Gravity and fatigue ultimately won the battle — and Shin's feet zipped out of the way as the weight came crashing down.

"Dammit," he yelled, and danced around the box, toes intact.

Open it here, he thought. *And shuttle the contents inside.*

Shin glanced at the security cameras bordering the property. He assumed they were recording everything. He hoped Tyler hadn't sent anything illegal.

It's cleared customs, Shin reassured himself. *So it can't be anything to worry about.*

He knelt next to the footlocker, slashed through the red tape with his makiri and then cut off the Customs Stamp zip-tied through the clasp lock.

Shin held the combination padlock in his hands, staring at the rotary dial. Three sets of numbers were needed to open it, but which ones would Tyler would have chosen?

He spun through the numbers for his birthday (09-01-42), Tyler's birthday (06-21-76), without success. He tried other dates like 07-1776 and 09-11-01, but got nowhere.

Shin dropped the lock in disgust and wondered if Daichi had a sledgehammer in the garage.

He stood and paced around the footlocker. There were four labels proclaiming *This side up.* He wondered what might be on the underside.

Standing at the long edge of the trunk, Shin grasped the handles and leaned back with a foot wedged against the side.

The trunk tipped over with a thud.

He scurried around it.

On the bottom, written in silver, were the words: "Death and rebirth. I believe in you." And a drawing of an orca.

'Death and rebirth' was a date Shin couldn't forget.

His suicide attempt and rescue by Mothersong — along with the hospital bills he'd accumulated thereafter — had frozen the numbers in his mind. Rushed fingers dialed 04-07-06.

The lock clicked. Shin removed it and pulled open the lid.

On top, well packed, was the original box of scuba gear and specialized comms equipment that he'd asked Tyler to send.

He lifted it out and jogged into the house.

Returning, he hefted out a black hard-shell case, a mil-spec tactical one. Shin didn't own a case like this. He saw that there were two other clam-shell cases just like it underneath. He ferried all three inside the house.

Finally, he hefted the footlocker — which still had more stuff in it — and eased it through the doorway.

In the guest room, Shin sorted through and inspected the contents of Tyler's delivery. His scuba gear and comms equipment appeared undamaged. He turned his attention to the clam-shell cases.

Inside the first one he was startled to find a state-of-the art Canon digital SLR camera, and several lenses, one of which was as long as his forearm. Everything was brand new, and the kit included SD cards, extra batteries, and cables.

The next case contained a military-grade GPS unit, a sophisticated dive watch, and Kevlar-reinforced scuba booties and gloves. There was also a desalination unit, pump, and filter, and an assortment of MREs — meals, ready to eat.

The third contained his Hush Puppy, silencer, four clips of ammo and a note from Tyler: *All the firepower I could get you. Hope you won't need it. Watch your 6 and stay safe — T.*

Holy moly, thought Shin. *What has the big, dumb giant done now? This is probably twenty thousand dollars worth of gear. And how the hell did he get all this through customs?*

His thoughts were cut short by the chime of the front door opening.

"Hello. I brought some take-away from my favorite restaurant," announced Daichi from the hallway.

Shin threw a blanket over the cases and footlocker, and rushed out to meet his cousin.

"Not as good as being there," said Daichi, unpacking the food boxes in the kitchen. "But I can take you there one night soon. Perhaps after our trip to Rishiri Island."

"Yes. That'd be great," said Shin. Then he shifted conversational gears. "There was a delivery today."

Daichi raised his eyebrows.

"It contained my scuba gear," said Shin, omitting mention of the other contents. "When we visit Rishiri tomorrow, I'd love to find a good dive spot. Before we go, though, I need to rent some air tanks. Do you know a place? I have my international diving certificate with me."

"Yes," said Daichi. "I do. At the harbor, where my boat is moored."

"Cool," said Shin.

"*Shachi* are a frequent sight around Rishiri," said Daichi. "Perhaps we'll see some tomorrow."

Shin's mouth went dry in anticipation of being underwater again and possibly encountering orcas. "That would be awesome."

"Ready for dinner?" asked Daichi.

"Yes," said Shin. His mind flew a mile a minute.

"I think I can get a baseball game on the TV, if you'd like," said Daichi.

"Sure."

Shin's thoughts, however, were consumed with the orcas in the region. *If I find them, will I be able to communicate? And if so, will they trust me, as Mothersong has done?*

One hope, which burned the brightest, was that he would learn a missing piece of the puzzle from the orcas who were being hunted.

25

In the morning, Mothersong called a council of the elders. All members of the clan were permitted to listen, of course, but only the inner circle could speak. Rhymehealer, Wisdom, Huntress, Deep-dive, and Bonecruncher formed a ring around Mothersong.

As she began to speak, rumbles chopped the air above them and penetrated the waves. It was an unnatural sound.

Spyhopper bobbed up next to Mothersong, and balanced vertically on his fluke, the upper half of his body out of the water. "Surface-dwellers in the sky," he said, after sinking below the surface.

Mothersong rose and watched them. Traveling in a V shape like birds were three of their flying machines. She had taken to calling them artificial-birds, and had observed different types: some were tiny, and left long white-scrapes in the blue sky; some thundered and streaked by the water's surface at the height of trees; and some, such as the ones above, could hang above the water.

Her thoughts soured. These days, it seemed that she saw more of the artificial ones than the natural. And like most surface-dweller machines, they emitted enough noise to stun a school of salmon. *Why must they shout all the time?* she thought as she eyed the formation flying overhead.

Recalling the other times she'd seen the artificial-birds, Mothersong wondered why the surface-dwellers rode in them. She'd seen a surface-dweller fall from a machine and die, and she'd observed artificial-birds smack the sea, and sink beneath the waves and drown. In her youth, Mothersong had explored a wreckage on the sea floor. The odd, twisted structure had a skin composed of nothing she had encountered in the natural world. And the bent wings were sharp, as she'd discovered after cutting a pectoral fin.

She watched the formation above fly away. Their rumble faded.

The council resumed, and Mothersong spelled out her angst. Hunting had become more difficult; the noise of the surface-dwellers disrupted everything. There had been several stillbirths to healthy young cows in the clan, and everyone was hungry. The waters had changed; it was no longer a safe, nurturing environment. The Ravenfin were dwindling. Her duty was to ensure their survival.

"I believe we must travel," said Mothersong, "and find a new home."

Clicks of surprise swept through the clan.

"And what of Talking-Shin?" asked Wisdom. Next to Mothersong, she was the eldest female.

Mothersong thought about the artificial-birds, then Shin's words. *Is he traveling in one of their machines?*

"I believe he will help all orcas," she said.

"How?" asked Huntress.

"Shin will find the surface-dwellers who are hunting our kind across the ocean, and make them stop. He speaks our language," said Mothersong. "Ancient stories foretell of such a stranger, who will aid the orcas and restore balance to the world."

"Perhaps it is wise to broadcast a message in the sound channel," suggested Deepdive. "Talking-Shin is coming to help."

Mothersong considered the advice, but Boomer interrupted her thoughts before she could articulate them, although he wasn't supposed to weigh in on council matters.

"I will do as the council wishes," said Boomer. "The surface-dweller Talking-Shin is a friend who is coming to help. I will deliver this message to the sound channel."

Besides speaking out of turn, her grandson's proclamation surprised Mothersong for two reasons. One, Boomer was part of the contingent that deeply mistrusted all surface-dwellers, and especially Shin. Two, the council hadn't yet reached a conclusion.

Mothersong wanted to steer the council's discussion back to the issues she had raised — starvation, noise, and declining fertility — but judging by the murmurs and mutters resounding, the topic of Talking-Shin now dominated the conversation.

The council members began encouraging Boomer to go. She added her blessing and bid her grandson a safe journey.

Mothersong had broached her concerns with the council — and would again. But a delay in further discussion, while Boomer delivered the message to the sound channel, was useful. At present the Ravenfin needed hope, and taking action provided that.

Over time, her words would sink in and the council would wish to reconvene to discuss finding a new home. The challenges were more severe than anything she had seen in her lifetime; the clan's fortune must change. Mothersong had faith that Shin held the key to their survival. However, she wasn't certain that any of the Ravenfin were prepared for the drastic course she had envisioned.

26

O n Shin's third morning in Wakkanai, the jet lag had abated and he woke up on Japanese time without feeling like crumpled origami. Rain thrummed on the roof as he joined Daichi in the kitchen. He accepted the offer of tea, sat down, and gazed out the window into the torrential downpour. The coastline and sea had vanished, and it seemed as if a cloud had swallowed the house. Thunder rumbled like *taiko* drums.

"Looks like the weather has dampened our plans for Rishiri Island today," said Daichi, looking up from the green glow of his laptop screen. "Although tomorrow is promising to be beautiful."

The news was a letdown. Shin had hoped that diving would break the hopelessness with which he was struggling.

He had plotted the milestones for this mission, and their logical order. But now that he had arrived here, he was stuck. Without actionable intel he could do nothing.

Shin needed to go underwater. Even if he didn't learn a damn thing, the physical activity might stimulate an idea.

"There's work I must attend to," said Daichi, and bowed. "Please excuse me. I must go into my home office." He slid open a shoji screen which led to stairs, stepped through, and closed it after him.

Shin sighed. He grabbed his laptop, intent on proving Einstein wrong.

Fat raindrops struck the roof and windows, hissing and sighing in phases as the storm progressed.

An hour later, Shin muttered to his laptop, "Why can't I find anything on the damn ship?"

"Perhaps," said Daichi, making Shin jump, "you don't have the right sources."

His cousin stood in the doorway. Shin had been so lost in frustration he hadn't heard the screen slide open.

"Would you like to see something I found about the *Zheng Yi*?" said Daichi, and beckoned.

Shin gasped. He'd never discussed the ship's name with his cousin. Confused, he followed Daichi up the steep stairs.

As he ascended, Shin saw the rain pounding on a skylight. At the top of the stairs, he stopped on the polished mahogany floor and stared. Daichi's home office was like a page from a high-end style magazine for tech geeks. Against one wall was a floor desk, above which were mounted three large LCD screens. Shin had initially mistaken them for windows because they were recessed into the wall and were blurry with shifting beads of water, providing the same view of the outside as the skylight and the two *true* windows. There were no wires visible and the computer displays were angled in such a way that a person seated on the floor at the desk (for there was no chair) could focus on any one of them without the need to turn their head.

In one corner of the room stood two metal-framed server racks containing black boxes with softly blinking green LEDs. Everything in the office imparted a clean, futuristic vibe. Upon a table the same height and style as the floor desk, were two rectangular objects, each the size and shape of a mini-fridge. One, Shin identified as a laser printer because it had just finished spitting out a stack of printed pages. The other, larger box had plexiglass sides and contained what appeared to be a replica of a crane used to offload shipping containers in ports like Seattle.

Shin stepped closer and cocked his head to the side to peer through the plexiglass. The 'crane' had several pistons, which allowed it to articulate in all three dimensions, and there were several spools of different colored material attached to its sides.

"Three-D printer," explained Daichi, as he grabbed the stack of pages from the adjacent laser printer.

"Three-D printer?" repeated Shin, perplexed. He'd never heard the term before.

"Yes. Instead of two-dimensional ink across pages, like these," said Daichi, holding up the papers he'd just retrieved, "one can construct physical objects, like those." He pointed to a shelf full of miniatures: buildings, statues, and geometric shapes.

Shin picked up a mini pagoda with five towers, which was the height of his hand. The tower was made of a lightweight woven material, and the details were so rich that he could count every simulated roof tile.

"It's remarkable," he said. "You created this with *that* machine?"

"Yes," said Daichi. "An indulgence at present — but the technology will continue to advance and will fulfill personal utility rather than trinkets. Industrial versions of this machine are already operational and printing with metal thread. One day, you will be able to craft all the tools you would ever need at home."

"Is this your field of work?" asked Shin, amazed by the revelation.

"This? Oh, no," laughed Daichi. "It is a hobby. I work in information — not construction."

"Who did you say you worked for?" asked Shin.

Daichi frowned.

Shin hoped he hadn't transgressed a boundary in respectful Japanese conduct. In feudal times, a guest who dishonored his host would either have his head chopped off or witness the host commit *seppuku* — it all depended upon a series of obligations to social ranks and relationships. Shin had once tried to learn those rules but had soon recognized his quest was futile.

There was a saying for *nisei* like Shin, who had grown up American: *Once a clay pot has cracked, the bound-up roots of the plant discover free soil.* His understanding of hierarchal life in Japan equaled Mothersong's comprehension of driving in Seattle.

Daichi cleared his throat. "Because of confidentiality, I haven't spoken of my employer," he said. "Regardless, these documents will provide the answers you seek." He held out the sheaf of paper. "Take a look."

Shin accepted the printed sheets. The top page was filled with a picture of a large black trawler. Stenciled in yellow on the bow was the name *Zheng Yi*.

He flinched, and his eyes darted to his cousin. "H-how," said Shin. "How'd you get this? I never—"

"Told me the name," interrupted Daichi. "I know. I browsed through your internet traffic and searches."

The admission of snooping took Shin aback. "Oh," he said.

His face must have displayed his unease. Daichi's countenance softened. "I'm sorry," he said. "I should have informed you. My information work involves a highly-secure area. As a precaution, all internet traffic into and out of this house is monitored. I hope I have not caused my guest offense."

Shin shook his head. "No," he said, though he wondered what other information his cousin might have omitted.

"I am pleased to hear that," said Daichi. "Is this the vessel you are searching for?"

Shin nodded. The hairs on his forearms tingled as he began reading through the stack of papers in his hands.

"It's an Icelandic stern trawler," said Daichi. "Purchased in 2001 for one hundred million yuan. It was retrofitted in a Shanghai dry dock and renamed the *Zheng Yi*."

Shin thumbed through the first several pages, which included schematics of the eighty-meter vessel. There were eight decks, an octagonal wheelhouse (with windows facing all compass points), a galley/bar, a gym, and crew quarters for forty.

"How did you manage to get this information?" he asked. "It's a ghost ship."

"From a database," said Daichi. "Please study it." He gestured at a shoji screen at the end of the office. "There's a comfortable chair in there, and good lighting." Daichi sat down before his desk with folded legs. "Please take advantage of the space and take your time. I have a strategy game online that needs my attention."

Shin said nothing. He nodded and strode toward the barrier.

As he slid the screen closed behind him, Shin wondered *whose* database his cousin had referred to, and what sort of permission was required to access it.

He sat down in the lounge chair, flicked on the bright LED study-light, and returned to his examination of the printout.

The ship had two diesel-electric engines, which generated two-thousand horsepower apiece and gave the vessel an impressive top speed of 25 knots, well beyond that needed for a fishing trawler. It had a range of two thousand nautical miles, depending on conditions. The hold was large enough for nearly three thousand cubic meters of cargo. It was equipped with a hydraulic stern ramp, and multiple configurations were possible, including modular crew compartments.

She could sail as a luxury power yacht, catering and entertaining to a handful of elites and their companions on a deep-sea fishing adventure, complete with a dance floor and a bar. Or she could officially be a factory ship for the harvesting of fish in a huge conical net dragged behind it, tensioned by gears and winches.

Or she could serve as a mothership for dozens of small fast boats, to hunt and capture cetacean specimens for zoos.

The more Shin read, the more he got the willies. Someone had spent a lot of money and effort to enhance the *Zheng Yi* — as well as conceal her. It confirmed his earlier supposition that the dark missions this ship was capable of extended beyond the horrendous capture of cetaceans for amusement parks.

When he'd finished reading, Shin rose and slid open the shoji screen. He stepped into the main office.

Daichi was engrossed in a game of three-dimensional chess.

Shin asked, "What kind of IT work did you say your were in?"

"What do you think of the information on the *Zheng Yi*?" said Daichi, ignoring the question. He typed on the keyboard and the monitors flipped back to the view of the outside world and the rain.

"I don't understand how you were able to gather this much data," exclaimed Shin.

"From a database," said Daichi with a shrug.

"Yes, you said that."

Daichi's expression turned to stone.

Shin realized he'd best not make any further inquiries, and politely excused himself. He retreated down the staircase and into the kitchen to fix himself a snack

He spent the rest of the day studying the data, calculating, and jotting notes.

———

UNFORTUNATELY, in the morning the weather remained poor.

And the next day was the same.

Shin used the time to complete his analysis on the *Zheng Yi*, and though he was eager to get underwater, there was nothing else to do until the weather cleared.

His irritability threatened to transform him into a caged tiger. He exercised — or exorcised — the negative energy out of his system with yoga.

Finally, on the third day, the storm moved on. The last thing Shin did before retiring that evening was to organize his scuba gear for the morning.

———

SHIN PULLED THE SMALL, wheeled cart containing his gear bags and the air tanks he'd just rented and followed Daichi along the pier. Calm, dark cobalt-blue water sparkled in the early morning sun, and rust-iron volcanic rock rimmed the coastline. As promised, there wasn't a cloud in the sky.

"Here we are," said Daichi.

For several seconds, Shin stared at the rickety skiff and its tiny outboard motor. *We're going on that?* he thought, grateful they'd chosen a tranquil day for the fifty-kilometer journey. The ferry to Rishiri took two hours; he wondered why they hadn't selected it. He estimated it would take them a half-day to reach their destination in this little craft.

"I love this boat," said Daichi, as he climbed up the aft ladder of a double-decker power yacht moored next to the skiff.

Shin stubbed his toe, and almost fell. He gawked at the luxury vessel.

"The *Tokugawa* feels like a home away from home. Fumi and I have taken some wonderful camping and fishing trips on her."

Shin gazed at the vessel's sleek lines and tinted windows. *Holy cow*, he thought.

He followed his cousin onto the ship.

"Stow your things there," said Daichi, pointing to the aft deck. "I'm going to get the engines started." He disappeared within the ship.

Shin finished shuttling his gear. A soft vibration passed through his feet as the engines purred to life.

"Come join me on the bridge," said Daichi, emerging from below deck.

Shin ascended the three steps to the wheelhouse, which was accented in cherrywood and contained an array of computer screens and gauges.

"She's powered by a pump-jet system," said Daichi. "It propels water to squirt us forward, without propellors and all that noise. The ship's wheel vectors the jets, including reverse. She's fully electric and pretty quiet." He smiled and patted the teak and brass wheel. "I can tell you more about her, but let's cast off. Do you mind getting the port lines?"

"Aye," said Shin, and suppressed a smile. *This is pretty damn cool*, he thought as he exited the bridge. *Must have cost a bundle.*

"Lines clear," he announced, then rejoined his cousin on the bridge as the 50-foot craft slid away from the slip.

"Below are berthing quarters for six, and a saloon-slash-galley," said Daichi. As they cruised toward the water-break, he inclined his head and said, "And a fly-bridge, up top."

Shin admired the bridge. The surrounding windows afforded an almost 360-degree view, and there were a lot more electronics than he was used to seeing on a power boat.

"Once we're out of port," said Daichi, "I'll pass control to you. Head up to the fly-bridge and I'll join you in a few minutes."

Shin climbed up the short ladder to the fly-bridge, which commanded a perspective that made him feel as if he were gliding on a magic carpet. The propulsion system was next to silent, without a rumble or shudder. Again, he wondered what his cousin did for a living.

"Can you take the wheel up there?" asked Daichi. The ship had just left the harbor.

Shin stepped over to the controls. "I've got her," he said raising his voice to be heard above the gentle rustle of the wind. The speed gauge read 5 knots.

"Okay," said Daichi, appearing next to him. "Take a northwest heading toward that notch on the edge of the island — see it?" He pointed.

"Got it," said Shin, and adjusted the wheel.

"Now open her up," said Daichi.

Shin complied and eased the throttle forward. The craft surged. He became familiar with the response of the wheel, and then, at his cousin's urging, he played.

Shin whooped, wind streaming in his hair. The speed gauge had jumped to 28 knots.

The *Tokugawa* struck a wave and flew into the air. Shin's stomach leapt into his chest as he went weightless. "Holy shit!"

"She'll do 34 knots," said Daichi, after they'd splashed back to the surface. "But perhaps we should slow down a bit."

Shin backed off the throttle.

The *Tokugawa* heaved into an effortless 15 knots — and the motion underfoot was almost undetectable.

"So smooth," said Shin. "She's amazing. There's no delay in response. Not even a whisker."

"Yes," agreed Daichi. "She's quite special."

The volcano island on the horizon drew closer. Ten minutes later, it dominated the ship's heading. Not knowing their exact approach and destination, Shin handed the wheel over to Daichi.

"That was fantastic," he said. "Thanks for letting me take a spin." He stared at the mountain, which seemed to float above the water. "How tall is that?" he asked. "And is it still active?"

Daichi laughed. "It's classified as dormant, but even those sometimes fool vulcanologists and blow up," he said. "And to answer your other question: a mile high. Mount Rishiri is 1700 meters. In the winter, it has some of the best powder skiing you can imagine — but don't spread that rumor in California, please. We don't want Californians moving here."

Shin laughed. "In Washington state," he said, "we don't like them either, so no worries. As long as Japanese moguls don't return to their US West Coast real-estate buying frenzy of the 90s, I think you're free and clear of Californians."

Daichi shot him a side glance, and chuckled. "Yes. Some of my compatriots got a little greedy and saw nothing but yen signs in their dreams. But that was years ago. I think Japan has other goals now."

Shin nodded but remained silent. Their conversational parry and riposte — as well as the expensive boat — told him his cousin was higher up in whatever company he worked for than Shin had suspected. Given the incredible level of detail on the *Zheng Yi* his cousin had provided, Shin wondered if Daichi worked for an intelligence agency of some sort, either governmental or private.

"There's a nice cove for swimming and diving over there," said Daichi, slowing the boat and steering to port. "If you start getting prepared, I'll find a spot to drop anchor."

Shin descended to the aft deck and his gear. His heart rate jumped. The last time he'd gone underwater, he'd had conversations with killer whales.

He had no such expectations this time.

The boat glided into a shallow harbor, which was nearly deserted. The only other craft were two sailboats anchored in the calm waters. Shin finished donning his wetsuit and then buckled on his vest and belt.

Daichi dropped anchor, then joined Shin on the aft deck. "The mouth of the harbor opens into deep waters pretty quickly, and the currents out there can be tricky," he said. "So I recommend sticking within the cove as you explore."

"Will do," said Shin. He completed his gear check, and adjusted the tank on his back. He slipped on his fins, and sat on a low railing.

"Take your time," said Daichi. "I'll be right here. There are a few emails I need to answer."

Shin toppled backward into the frigid water. The shock took his breath away. He bobbed in place as he adjusted the mask and his buoyancy. He flashed a thumbs-up to Daichi, then dove to explore the shallow waters.

The visibility was better than he was used to in Puget Sound, which gave him confidence in the unfamiliar waters. His body warmed up with the effort of powering the flippers. He bumped into a mass of bull kelp, and changed directions to circumnavigate it.

The water's chill began to release its grip and Shin relaxed as he explored. Mindful of his cousin's instructions, he approached the mouth of the harbor.

Closer to it, the swirling current sped up. Angling toward land, Shin kicked hard and headed sideways in the ebb tide dragging him out to sea.

As he continued, an odd noise drew his attention. The rising and falling notes were the warbling songs of a whale, he realized, though he'd no clue whether it was sperm, humpback, blue, or another species. He absorbed the sounds washing over him, and marveled at the complexity.

Shin stopped moving and held his breath for several seconds as he listened. The tide pulled him but he didn't resist, and drifted out. The groans and clicks of the whale song were loud and distinct. Given that he was only five meters deep and his back was to the harbor, the whales must be in front of him and quite close.

It's wonderful, he thought. There was a periodicity to the whale song, and the warbles and trills resembled a looped synthesizer track. Sadly, there were no words that he could identify. Shin had been holding out hope that he might understand all cetaceans were he to swim with them, but this sounded like the hydrophone recordings he'd listened to in the past: tantalizing in a beautiful and alien way, but unintelligible.

Still drifting, Shin allowed himself to be tugged along. The dark rocks on the harbor's bottom accelerated and then dropped off as he exited the narrow mouth into open waters. Here the current slowed. Though mindful of Daichi's warning, he remained unconcerned. As long as he stayed near the surface, didn't float too far away, and the weather stayed clear, he would have no difficulty swimming back into the harbor.

The song shifted, and Shin identified a different rhythm which had a swooshing sound to it, like the brushing of leaves off a sidewalk. *Shh. Shh. Shh.*

The sequence repeated, but morphed and there was a different syllable, and then another.

For four beats, the pattern recurred. A shock went through him when he understood the syllables formed a word: *Shin*. The pronunciation reminded him of Mothersong's diction.

My God! They're singing my name.

Intoxicated by the realization, his mind and body drifted.

The song changed, and a new sound emerged with a hiss like a snake. Gradually, another syllable was added as the sequence built and recurred like a mathematical formula or a Bach concerto. Pulled by the siren's call, Shin was so transfixed by discovering words within the whale song that he could do little other than breathe.

When the full meaning unfolded on him, he shivered. *Shin. Is. Comes. Shin. Helps.*

The whale song began anew, and it became louder and louder.

Jerking out of his trance, Shin swam up toward the surface. Popping topside, he ripped off his mask and scanned the water.

"Holy shit," he panted, as he looked for the misty plumes of whale blow, hoping to catch a glimpse of the whale, or whales, singing his name.

For a minute he bobbed and watched. His heart ached to be close enough to touch one of the creatures, and to reassure it that he was here. And that he would fix things.

Seeing no signs of whales, he resealed his mask and dove again.

Shin's breathing rasped in his ears and his heart hammered. He belatedly remembered that he could broadcast his voice. If the whales used orca words, perhaps they might understand him.

He willed his body to stillness.

The word 'helps' echoed several more times, before the whale call changed into a series of high-pitched chirps and squeaks.

"Shin is here," he said through the speakers, speaking as he would to M-pod.

He recalled the timing of the song he'd just heard, and broadcast his message again, but using the same cadence and gradual build as the whale had: *Shin. Is. Here.*

Shin repeated his new song, its volume rising with each recitation, until he began to go hoarse.

He checked his new dive watch and pressure gauge, and realized he had ten minutes of air left. He swam toward the surface.

When he reached the top, he bobbed in place. Having been over-whelmed by his experience underneath the waves, the realities of where he was on the surface only now crept in.

Crestfallen, he recalled all the cardinal scuba sins he'd just committed, which had put him over a mile from the harbor.

The good news was that the weather was clear and he could still see the central volcano. The bad news was that he would soon be overdue, and it was a long swim.

Shin aimed himself at the volcano, rolled onto his back, and dug in with long sweeps of his flippers. He stared at the sky as he tried to process what had just happened, while keeping an eye and ear out for boats.

Whales are calling my name, he repeated to himself as he swam.

If Martians had landed a flying saucer in Shin's front yard in Sequim, and invited themselves in for tea and a chat, he wouldn't have batted an eyelid. But this was off-the-charts strange.

A half hour later, Shin arrived at the *Tokugawa*. He removed his fins as he clung to the ladder. He climbed up to the aft deck, and sat down. After being underwater, the warm sunlight on his body was luxuriating.

"There you are. How was it?" asked Daichi, popping out of the cabin.

"Interesting," said Shin. To his ears, the word sounded detached and artificial, as if spoken by an automaton. The experience had rattled him, and he knew that speech on autopilot was necessary until he had time to wrap his head around it. "Let me change, and I'll tell you."

The engines started as Shin toweled off and changed clothes below deck. He came up to find his cousin hauling anchor.

"Join me up top," said Daichi.

They were soon underway, and headed to the mouth of the harbor.

"Do you have a set of binoculars?" asked Shin.

Daichi reached into a stowage compartment next to the wheel. "Here," he said, handing over a pair of Nikons.

Shin steadied himself and raised the binoculars to scan the horizon.

"What are you looking for?" asked Daichi.

"Whales." Shin drew an imaginary line to a spot offshore.

"Really?" exclaimed his cousin. "You saw them when you were

diving? Shachi?"

"No," said Shin. "But I heard whale song."

"That's incredible," said Daichi. He pushed the throttle; the *Toku-gawa* surged forward.

"Yes, it is," said Shin. He relived the moment as he continued searching with the binoculars. He shivered. *Nothing,* he thought, *will ever beat hearing whales sing about me.*

The bow of the ship kissed the tops of the swells, jostling him. Several minutes later, he stopped his search, and handed back the binoculars.

Shin went down to the aft deck, and repacked his scuba gear. He stretched out on a lounge chair in the bright sunlight, wondering how long until they reached the orca memorial. He absorbed the warmth into his chilled bones, and closed his eyes as he processed his underwater experience.

'Shin is coming to help,' is how he translated the message. But he'd no explanation as to why everything else on either side of these words in the song had been garbled. It was as if a radio dial had rotated through a wide bandwidth of foreign language stations, and he could only under- stand a sliver in the middle. And those *were* orca words.

Despite the cool breeze, the delicious heat of the sun was perfect. The hum of the boat's engines lulled Shin into a trance.

Boomer had learned of orcas being hunted in a faraway place by what he termed the 'sound channel'. Submariners called it SOFAR (Sound Fixing and Ranging) and it existed because of a reflective feature within the Earth's oceans. Temperature and pressure layers formed an acoustic roof and foundation within which a strong sound pulse could bounce up and down across the width of the ocean.

Analogous to a hundred-meter-tall ballroom with acoustic reflectors on the ceiling and floor — but stretched out over thousands of miles and curved to the Earth.

The sweet spot existed at a depth close to a thousand meters, deeper than anything a human could achieve outside of a submarine. The pres- sure was one hundredfold what it was on the surface. Even the newest atmospheric diving suits, which encased a human in a pressurized exoskeleton, which resembled a crustacean, couldn't go that deep.

Nuclear subs listened for adversaries in the SOFAR using passive sonar — and employed software filters to block out the whale noises.

Until this day, Shin had never contemplated that it was also a communication network for whales: a cetacean internet developed over millions of years of listening and speaking.

The message in the sea about me, he thought, *had to have originated from M-pod.* He'd promised Mothersong he'd help. And here he was in Japan, hearing his name.

Though it must be true, the linkage stunned him. *Why,* and *how,* had an orca message been inserted into a humpback or sperm-whale song?

Shin's internal clock roused him. He sat up, blinking in the sunshine. On the horizon, Rishiri Island had receded to a distant white pimple, and he realized they were headed back to Wakkanai. He stood and ascended to the bridge.

Daichi wore a headset and was speaking into the mic.

At Shin's approach, his cousin turned his head. "We're on our way home," he said. "There's a development of interest."

"Yeah?"

"*Zheng Yi* has left port in Shanghai."

"What!" exclaimed Shin. "When? How do you know that?"

"Sources," answered Daichi. His flat expression held the look of a parent tiring of a toddler asking the same question over and over.

Crap, thought Shin. He itched to check the AIS website, though he'd no reason to doubt the veracity of the information. Daichi had produced in-depth data on a ghost ship, and valuable intel was priceless. He needed to find a way to turn it to his advantage.

However, like being in a swift tide, Shin couldn't escape the sense that he was being pulled into something beyond his control.

"I know you wish to stop the *Zheng Yi,*" said Daichi. "I thought you might want to strategize, so I'm piloting us home. We can visit the memorial another day. "

Shin swallowed, and nodded. His mouth went dry as he thought about where the *Zheng Yi* might be going, and what Shin could do to halt her operations.

27

Sitting at the kitchen table in Daichi's home, Shin watched the blip on his laptop flicker. Though there were thousands of similar icons on the screen, it was the only one of interest. Every thirty seconds the screen auto-updated and all the green, red, and blue triangular blips shifted as they propelled themselves through the software construct representing actual ships on the sea.

The *Zheng Yi* had indeed left port, headed east. And Shin had been watching her progress for the past two hours. The blip bent north, headed to the Sea of Japan. From there, the Sōya Strait would take them to the Sea of Okhotsk. Its route would be so close to Wakkanai that Shin could almost swim out there and have a look at the vessel as it steamed past.

Shin jotted calculations in his journal. He doubted the ship would travel much faster than 10 knots, even though it could go much faster. A big trawler zipping along like a speedboat would attract attention, and would also burn a huge amount of fuel.

He guessed he had thirty-six hours to intercept the ship before it entered Russian territorial waters. Though he'd no vessel, Shin imagined cruising up alongside the *Zheng Yi* and shooting the boat and crew with his new camera, as Tyler had suggested. The fast digital SLR with its expensive 400mm zoom lens could take incredible pictures.

Shin couldn't understand where Tyler had gotten the money for the equipment, nor how he'd managed to ship it express via a US military base (along with Shin's service pistol, silencer, and ammunition tucked in for good measure). He needed to talk with that Texan, but it would have to wait.

"I don't think that further study of that blip on the screen is useful," said Daichi.

"Thanks," said Shin. He clenched his jaw. *Not helpful*, he thought as he zoomed in on the display.

"I have to go to Sapporo in the morning," said Daichi. "I will be back late. But the next several days are open. Have you thought of what you'd like to see in the area?"

"The Onsen Dome sounds amazing," said Shin, remembering Fumi's recommendation of the natural hot springs.

"The best in all of Hokkaido," said Daichi with a smile. "I recommend spending a good two or three hours to explore and relax with all that it has to offer. It's quite close. I have a bicycle you can borrow, if you'd like — as well as a guest pass."

"Yes. Thanks," said Shin. "I'd also thought about going down to the harbor and testing out the new camera equipment."

"Also a good idea," said Daichi. "The views on a clear day can be quite nice. And I believe there may be some sunshine in the afternoon."

"Cool. Can I borrow your boat?"

"No."

"I think I could snap a few pictures of the *Zheng Yi* on their way to capture orcas," said Shin. "And if I upload those photos to a few media outlets, there could be major international pressure. Greenpeace used that strategy in the seventies — and won!"

"Two problems with that approach," said Daichi. He cleared his throat. "Three, actually. First, we're no longer in the 1970s. Second, the *Zheng Yi* will be hunting in Russian waters and if you're not apprehended by them, the crew will probably shoot you. Three, your brains must be as mushy as overcooked rice if you think I will let you borrow my boat given the other points I've just made."

"That's definitely a *no*," said Shin.

Daichi groaned, and his eye-roll was as exaggerated as anything in Kabuki theatre. The only thing missing was a large tongue sticking out.

"I'm just trying to find a way to stop the *Zheng Yi*," said Shin in frustration. "Is there *any* more help you can provide?"

"I'm working on it. But in the interim, I do have some advice. For once, if you Americans could listen, and not talk all the time, then I believe you would find more of the answers you seek."

Okay, thought Shin. *I'm finding my own ride to sea.*

LATE IN THE morning of the following day, Shin emerged from the Onsen Dome feeling as if a week's worth of troubles had been scrubbed clean from his soul. Daichi's guest pass had turned out to provide VIP treatment, and Shin had taken advantage of everything the natural hot-springs spa had to offer, including shiatsu massage.

Shin's neck and arms tingled with the afterglow, and he was energized as he thought about the next item on today's agenda. He fastened his helmet, straddled Daichi's bicycle, and headed to the Wakkanai marina.

He found a rental place, and after some back and forth questions, signed the agreement and handed over his passport and credit card as collateral. The sport fishing boat he'd rented was solid, quick, and seaworthy, but the price tag for taking her out solo for two hours was steep.

Shin eased on the throttle, left the dock, and puttered through the marina toward the breakwater and open sea beyond. In the Sōya Strait, he planned to intercept the *Zheng Yi* as she navigated the narrow international waterway between the tip of Hokkaido and the southern edge of Sakhalin Island, owned by Russia.

He'd studied this passage and knew the marine traffic navigated a politically neutral, but nautically winding channel. It wasn't large in terms of cargo ships per day because the flow was restricted by the S-shape of the strait and the confines of the international lines drawn in the ocean by blood enemies.

The boat he'd rented had sufficient range and maneuverability that he should be able to guide himself to a position where capturing photos of the ship was possible. The half-dome wall, Wakkanai's symbolic guardian against the fury of the ocean, passed by on the port side as Shin left the marina.

He rechecked the calculations and looked at his GPS screen. *Seven nautical miles to go,* he thought, and adjusted his heading. The gorgeous sunny day, with its cloudless cornflower-blue sky, lifted his spirits.

Shin had memorized the silhouette of the *Zheng Yi.* He hoisted his binoculars to scan the horizon for it.

He counted the commercial vessels in the distance and noted the types in his notebook: tankers, closed-containers, bulk-carriers, and tugs. In addition, between Shin and the shipping lane, were a dozen or so recreational vessels — sailboats and small power-craft — all out enjoying the calm seas and the clear day.

"A light wind from the northeast is a sign the weather will be calm," the rental boat's owner had said, and it seemed like a lot of other people knew this adage as well.

Shin calculated the trajectories of the various craft on the sea, and adjusted his calculus for the best course through the sailboats and powerboats as he aimed toward a sharp bend in the shipping channel.

For the cargo ships, navigating the strait was a bit like driving around a huge roundabout in Europe. All the big ships' captains had to slow down, be alert, and steer. However, changing the momentum and direction of a 100,000 deadweight-tonnage vessel was glacial in response to the input. It was as if you tapped the brakes and turned the steering wheel in a car, only to have it respond ten minutes later.

All the marine traffic slowed through the turns. The *Zheng Yi* could defy these rules, and she had the speed to launch around slower traffic, but that would draw attention — something Shin knew was anathema to her mission.

She'll go with the flow, he thought. *After all, she's just a stern-traveler, out to drag a few nets and catch some delicious fish for the folks back home in Shanghai.*

Bile rose in his throat at the deception. Since he'd learned about the ship's true capabilities from Daichi, every hour that the *Zheng Yi* operated seemed an affront to both nature and humanity.

He swallowed thick saliva, and his gaze jumped along the horizon. There were two goals: see the ship at sea with his own eyes, and capture photos. Learning the schematics and performance data on the *Zheng Yi* had been an intel windfall, but nothing beat personal observation. And if he could fill the void in the internet at the same time, then it was a win-win.

Shin would triumph, and non-violent confrontation was the pathway.

Once past the last wave of recreational craft, Shin slowed the boat. He was a mile from the nearest vessel in the commercial lane. The large container ship, stacked with multicolored railway boxcars, was about two hundred meters in length and looked overloaded — as if a child had placed too many Lego blocks on a small plank floating in a pool.

Shin checked the GPS and adjusted the boat to idle. He extracted the long-lens camera from his bag, and focused on the container ship to practice.

Deciding that closer would be better, Shin piloted the boat to close half the distance. He stabilized himself against the gunwale as gentle swells pulsed the hull, steadied the crosshairs on the container ship, and snapped several frames.

He reviewed the images on the LCD screen. Some were blurry, so Shin adjusted the shutter speed and auto-focus. He wasn't much of a photographer and was glad for the brief time he'd practiced with this camera, because if you knew the right settings it could do almost anything short of making tea.

The weather remained calm, but waves from the large traffic in the strait began to rock the boat, further challenging his photography skills. As Shin spun the boat around to motor a little further out, he saw the *Zheng Yi.*

His heart hammered against his ribs. He idled the engine, and for several seconds could do nothing but gawk.

Remembering the camera slung around his neck, Shin held it up and put the crosshairs on the ship. He zoomed in on the bow and held down the shutter button. The SLR motor purred, and the auto-focus adjusted on the fly as it snapped out eight frames a second.

Shin lowered the camera from his face, and reviewed some of the photos. *Got you,* he thought. *Now for more.*

The *Zheng Yi* was on a heading opposite to Shin's and, in a minute or two, would pass by him broadside at a distance of about one hundred yards. Close enough that with this telephoto lens, he might be able to capture a face in the wheelhouse.

With shaking hands and grinning with excitement, Shin reeled off another round of shots. Then watched the *Zheng Yi* as he waited for the camera's buffer to finish downloading images to the memory card. In less than thirty seconds, the ship would be abeam and at the closest point to his position.

He exhaled a quick breath to slow his heart rate and stem the shakes.

Finally, some photos, he thought as he studied the ship's superstructure. *When all this get's out, you won't be able to find a barnacle to hide under.*

Raising the camera again, he spotted a person moving on the upper deck near the wheelhouse. The camera vibrated as it reeled out more shots.

A glint caught Shin's eye, and he pivoted the camera to look aft along the *Zheng Yi.*

Atop the stern boom platform, he found the location of the light. He zoomed in.

Bright sunlight mirrored off of a small disc. A shadowy form was crouched behind it. Shin's scalp tingled at the realization that someone with a lens was looking right back at him. He studied the figure.

A muzzle flash interrupted his thoughts—

"Shit," Shin yelled. He dropped the camera and dove.

The rifle report hit his ears right after the cockpit windows — port and starboard — exploded from the bullet passing through both. Glass shards tinkled down around him on the deck.

Assholes, he thought as he crawled through the safety glass, and punched the throttle. The engine revved and the boat leapt forward. Crouching low, Shin peeked over the bow and spun the wheel. He leaned the craft hard into a turn to keep his body out of sight, and headed back toward Wakkanai. He angled toward a container ship the size of a horizontal skyscraper, aiming to put it between him and the sniper.

I'm in international waters, he thought, *but they don't give a shit.*

Shin raced the boat toward the massive container ship. A small geyser erupted just off his bow, and a loud crack from a rifle echoed across the water.

He flipped them the bird as his craft zipped behind the cover of the cargo ship.

— — —

BACK IN THE MARINA, Shin lied and told the rental owner that the two windows in the cabin had just burst and he didn't know why. He apologized, and offered to clean up the mess, pay for new windows, and compensate the owner for any loss of rental income while the boat was being repaired.

After the man's shouting diminished, and the redness had faded from his cheeks, the grumbling man accepted Shin's offer.

Under the owner's baleful scowl, Shin swept up the broken glass. He was thankful there weren't any bullet holes in the boat. That would've involved the police, and questions he didn't feel like answering. Plus, Daichi would be mortified at the attention his guest had brought upon the household.

After returning the rental craft to shipshape, minus the windows, Shin gathered up his belongings. Missing was the Canon and its big lens; he relived the memory of the equipment disappearing overboard during the shoot-and-run event.

Shin slung his remaining gear over his shoulder and stomped off the pier, still under the withering glare of the owner. As it stood, Shin had escaped with his life, which was something he should be grateful for. The end goal of any endeavor was to come back safely.

But that victory was pyrrhic.

He'd seen her, but now the *Zheng Yi* was beyond him, and whatever data he'd captured on the camera now rested in Davy Jones's locker. The ship would soon be in waters he couldn't reach and then it would begin its hunt to capture orcas, dolphins, and Beluga whales. Shin wanted to scream at the sky and rage against the injustice.

But his angst stilled as he recalled the word he'd bellowed in anger weeks ago. That one word had harmonized the strings of his wife's koto: *Life.*

Shin unlocked Daichi's bicycle for the uphill ride home, then turned back to look at the Sōya Strait. The golden sunlight rippling off the water would have been relaxing were he not ruminating about his failure and the forthcoming crisis the orcas faced.

Tyler was right, though, every day above ground was a good day. Shin had survived. There would be other opportunities and he *would* find a way to stop the *Zheng Yi.*

He clenched his fists. They'd shot at him. Though he'd been warned of that possibility, the actual act changed the whole equation. He tried to steer away from the growing wave of hatred, but failed.

They tried to kill me.

Regardless of which tools he needed to employ to get the job done, in Tyler's vernacular, Shin was *done messing around with these assholes.*

———

"How did your day go?" asked Daichi.

"The hot baths were fantastic," answered Shin, and felt a pang of guilt at burying the lead story of the day. The baths had been luxurious and relaxing — and it *had* been a great day, until he'd been shot at.

"And the photography session?" said Daichi. "Were you able to capture the scenes you were looking for?"

"I think so," answered Shin. "But the camera went overboard." He then described the details of what had transpired, leaving nothing out.

"I see," said Daichi through clenched teeth. "That was quite foolish of you — and explains the rumors from the pier."

Shin felt his face flush. He stared at his feet.

"Wakkanai is a small town," continued Daichi. "Even before the internet, word travelled fast. But I must say, your actions are quite *unexpected.*"

In Japan, the word *unexpected* uttered in this way was an insult. It didn't mean that Shin had performed a move not anticipated on a chess board — but rather that he'd committed a deliberate violation of the glue that held society together.

The social contract that kept peace and order in Japan demanded adherence to a hierarchy and its attendant codes of honor. To step beyond that was *unexpected of an honorable person* — an affront to self, family, and community.

As *nisei*, the insult didn't affect Shin the same way as those born on the home islands. He looked up and met Daichi's gaze.

"I told you when I invited you here," said Daichi, his face red and his tone sharp, "that you must never bring shame on this household. Thankfully, no one at the pier knows that you are related to me or staying in my home. They also don't suspect that a bullet blew out the windows of the boat. You are very lucky you weren't shot dead. That would have placed me in a very uncomfortable position."

"You're *welcome*," said Shin, bristling at the lecture. "I'm glad I'm not dead, too!"

"It is said that even a fool can be good at something," said Daichi. "So maybe there is room for hope."

"I'm sorry, okay?" said Shin, his voice rising in volume. "I have no intention of bringing shame on your name but I'm in the dark here. The blueprints on the *Zheng Yi* are incredible, but you won't tell me how you got them or who you work for. Listen, I want to put that asshole ship on the bottom, for all eternity — but either help me or don't!"

Daichi's expression softened and the crimson left his cheeks. He sat down in a low chair, sighed, and pushed a hand through his jet-black hair. In a whisper, he said, "Then we are in agreement."

He folded his hands together and closed his eyes.

Caught off-guard by the abrupt change in his cousin, Shin said, "What are you talking about?"

Daichi stood. "Tonight," he said. "I'll take you to a place where my honor, and yours, may begin their restoration. There is no danger to you, but if you're paranoid, bring the smuggled pistol your friend sent."

Shin sighed, but kept his face a mask. The revelation that Daichi knew about the handgun didn't surprise him. Though Shin had been careful to keep it hidden and secure, he'd had a growing sense that his spy-cousin could ferret out whatever information he desired. Behind the gate, security cameras, and internet firewall was a man whose passion was to hoard information, yet be as invisible as a deer in a misty forest.

"If you're wondering about motivations," said Daichi with a shrug. "I'm simply showing you a pathway to your goal, and I think you'll see that it's superior to acting like a six-gun cowboy in a speedboat."

Shin nodded, ignoring the dig. "Okay," he said. "I'm game."

28

At just after 10 p.m., Shin followed Daichi up the steps toward the Shinto temple, lit in the darkness by soft lights. It was five hours past closing, and Shin wondered why Daichi had insisted upon dragging him to a temple that was shut.

The on-again, off-again routine was wearing thin. But the helpless feeling that he was being led around by his nose grated on him more than anything else.

Daichi bowed to a tall statue, and muttered something that Shin couldn't pick out. He then trotted into the darkness.

Shin stepped past the stone statue, which depicted a guardian-dragon protecting a child, and waited for his eyes to adjust. He followed his cousin down a steep boulder-studded embankment away from the temple.

He lost sight of Daichi, but then found him crouched next to a half-circle of large rocks. In the soft glow of a headlamp, his cousin pulled away some greenery to reveal a dull metal disc a meter across.

As Shin crept forward, Daichi reached, twisted and pulled — and a hatch cover swung open. In the soft glow of light, Shin saw rungs leading downward.

"You first," said Daichi.

Shin balked. *This is creepy*, he thought, and wondered where the hell his cousin was leading him. He peered over the edge. A stone tube descended five meters to an illuminated platform below.

"It's fine," said Daichi. "I assure you."

Shin's eyes met his cousin's, then he eased over the lip and headed down. The air smelled of ocean and ozone.

Above him, Daichi descended a few rungs before pausing to clang the lid shut. The echoes reverberating in the space below spoke to Shin of a large complex. When the noise had faded, he picked out the plops of dripping water. As he continued downward, Shin noted black-glass *mice* — cameras and sensors — sunk into the walls.

Shin reached a room. The bedroom-sized space had been drilled and hewn out of the bedrock and was lit by a wire-caged bulb. In each corner were more sensors. A dull metal fuse box was bolted to the wall next to another ladder leading downward, which had a circular protective enclosure of metal fencing.

Shin stepped and peered over the edge, but the view was blocked. A small droplet of water struck his head.

"Where is it we're going?" asked Shin. "You said this would help me with the *Zheng Yi*."

"Patience," answered Daichi as he arrived. "You will see." He opened the fuse box, pulled a lever, and a loud clunk sounded as a plate slid aside. Light shown upward from the tunnel below.

Staring downward was disorienting, but Shin saw that the enclosed ladder dropped about ten meters, and terminated at a platform. At Daichi's urging, he descended.

As he neared the bottom, he heard water lapping. The drips and plops became louder.

Stepping off the last rung, Shin turned and beheld a series of elevated guardrail-lined concrete platforms. It looked like a huge underground train station, but instead of tracks there was seawater. Bright lights rimmed the ceiling of the domed chamber and reflected off the ripples in the central main channel — and the hulls of several sleek, gray-metal submarines. *What the hell!*

He studied the scale of the moored boats and the guardrails on the platforms. It was off, he realized. Unlike the military submarines he was used to seeing, which were almost two football fields long and carried a crew of over a hundred, these were tiny, barely three first-downs in length.

Footsteps sounded to his left, and his mouth went dry; Daichi was still up on the ladder.

Shin spun. A dozen paces away, a uniformed individual wearing white gloves and wielding a submachine gun emerged from a corridor.

Shin slowly raised his arms.

"All is okay," said Daichi as he stepped off the ladder. "Routine security. Nothing to be concerned about."

Shin noted that the guard's stance was well-balanced and she appeared ready to use the weapon, though kept it pointed at the floor.

"Advance notice," he said, "would've been welcome."

Daichi shrugged. "It's one of those things that I can't talk about until we're here. And now that you *are* here, what do you think?"

The guard retreated several paces, and her body assumed a relaxed posture.

"A World War Two submarine pen..." began Shin, but then he stopped. He studied the modern power conduits, pumps, hoists, and controls. "But enhanced and retrofitted."

"Exactly," said Daichi with a smile. "You're very observant. Sixty years ago, this was a secret base for Imperial Japanese mini-subs. Beside being buried deep in the rock for protection, it was also too far for allied bombers. So it survived the conflict.

"As the war ended, the channels leading to the base were sealed by explosives. Time passed and what existed here was forgotten. The parts of the concrete submarine bunker jutting outside were repurposed for water breaks and harbor construction. The core of this facility, however, remained intact and hidden.

"When Japan's international waters were again denied her and the Soviets refused to relinquish the Northern Territories, our government resurrected this old space. We are not the aggressors, you understand, but we use this base to launch regional observation missions."

Shin stepped toward the closest mini-sub, his footfalls echoing in the cavern, and studied it. The curved hull bore a conning tower that was low and sleek, appearing only as a slight bulge on the top. The pointed bow-nose and tapered body resembled a dolphin's, and the stern planes called to mind a whale's fluke. Shin could find no propellor or housing for one.

His heart pounded. The submarine was more futuristic than he'd imagined possible. He turned to Daichi and said, "Is this thing stealth?"

"Yes. Part of our program to silently observe, while we plan. It carries no weapons."

"Why are you showing me this technology and this base?"

"Because," said Daichi, "I think there is mutual overlap in your desires and ours."

"Which is?"

"To sink the *Zheng Yi*."

Shin startled at the admission, but suppressed his emotions. "I don't understand," he said, and gestured at the stealth boat. "I do wish to put the *Zheng Yi* on the bottom of the sea, but I'm not here to kill anyone. Besides, you just told me your stealth machine isn't armed. Have I missed something in the translation?"

"No," said Daichi. "Your Japanese is excellent. But let me explain in a different vein. Earlier, you faced the hurdle of not having a boat with which to follow the *Zheng Yi*, correct?"

Shin nodded.

"And then when you rented one, you were shot at. Ultimately, I believe, you wish to stop her from hunting whales, but you have yet to figure out *how* to do that."

"All true," said Shin, and pondered where he was being led.

Submarines were used for blowing up ships you didn't like, launching ICBMs at cities you didn't like, or exploring undersea environments and creatures that you *did* like. Moments ago, Daichi had used the words *sink* and *Zheng Yi* in the same sentence, and then he had explained that the futuristic-looking subs were unarmed.

Shin's neck muscles tightened, heralding the onset of a headache, and he reached up to massage them.

Daichi watched him, but remained silent.

"So you want me to pilot that unarmed stealth-sub, and then do what?" asked Shin.

"Oh," said Daichi, and his eyebrows rose. "That is not the submarine." He turned and pointed. "That one is."

Shin's gaze followed the gesture. Tucked in a corner pen was something that resembled a rusty, barnacled construction-pontoon. On closer inspection he noted that the cylindrical hull bore a squarish conning tower, stubby dive planes, and two propellors.

"An old type-D midget from 1945," announced Daichi.

"What?" exclaimed Shin. "Does it even work?"

"Yes," said Daichi. "This one was commissioned just weeks before the war ended. But, like many others, it never saw service. Over the years, she has been modified and upgraded — including new torpedos."

"You can't be serious!" said Shin, his voice rising in pitch and volume. "Sending me out in that? Why don't you go out yourself and sink the damn ship?"

"Sadly, we're not allowed to," said Daichi, and sighed. "Our governing authority strictly prohibits any member of our organization from directly participating in violence."

"So you're gonna give me the keys to an ancient death-trap, look the other way, and hope I succeed," said Shin.

"You are mostly correct," said Daichi. "Though I disagree with the part about this type-D being a death trap. It's been thoroughly upgraded — better batteries, a new engine, electronics, and scanning gear."

Shin clenched his teeth. He was on the verge of storming out. But being shot at — the first time since the Vietnam war — had turned his world sideways.

The *Zheng Yi* and her flotilla were out hunting and would, if successful, rip a calf from its mother and pod.

It was past time for him to put a stop to it.

But this was nuts. "It's crazy," he said. "The survivability of a World War Two midget submarine in flippin' World War Two was next to zero. And I can't imagine the chances have edged upward in the past sixty years."

"That submarine is disguised to look like a derelict," said Daichi. "I assure you it is quite modern, and the operational parameters are impressive."

Orcas are currently being hunted, argued a voice in Shin's mind.

They are calling your name right now. The thought made his knees weak. He couldn't leave them to that fate.

"If I accept this mission," said Shin. "What kind of support can you give me?"

"Encrypted communications sharing our real-time observations from multiple platforms," answered Daichi. "But no material support."

"If I understand that correctly," said Shin, the heat building in his cheeks, "I get data, but I'm on my own. A sacrificial lamb. If it all blows up, then you can deny involvement — but I'm up the creek without a paddle. Because I'm some crazed American orca nut, who stole an old Japanese midget sub, then stalked and sank an innocent Chinese vessel in Russian waters, killing all on board. I'm sure it'll make the news, but you'll be immune because there won't be any trace-back, right?"

Daichi said nothing.

"What's the name of the agency you work for?" asked Shin.

"I can't tell you."

Great, thought Shin. *Just great.*

29

"Shin is there," said Boomer, rejoining the Ravenfin.

Mothersong asked him to repeat what he'd just said. When her grandson affirmed that she wasn't going deaf, her mind flew like a startled salmon. This was confirmation that the surface-dweller was acting as he said he would do. Her thoughts darted from hope to fear and back again.

Boomer had just returned from another trip to the sound channel. He'd taken to diving there — along with two young protégés — on every other pass of the sun, to listen.

Mothersong had been guiding the Ravenfin south, along the edge of a land mass they called *Green Above*, where the salmon-rivers emptied into the sea. Access to the deeper waters of the Pacific Ocean was a short swim away, and though she dreamed of Shin at night, her day-thoughts were consumed with finding fertile fields in which to hunt.

She tuned out the chatter of the clan as they discussed Boomer's revelation, relayed from afar, that Shin was in the water on the other side of the world

Mothersong longed to talk with him. He was the first of his kind to speak, though she didn't know how or why. Perhaps he was an outcast to the surface-dwellers, banished for a transgression. Or maybe he had chosen to abandon his clan, like a cow and her offspring who have tasted dolphin or seal flesh, and leave to never hunt fish again.

She recalled their first meeting. Mothersong had been awakened by a noise in the water as she slept. After rising to the surface to breathe, she'd heard the orca-word *beautiful* — uttered as if in the throes of a death-ceremony. Though faint, she'd located the source and sped there.

Mothersong had never seen a naked surface-dweller in the flesh before, but as she watched, he'd burbled the word *beautiful* again. He was in a place he shouldn't be, and was dying. Instinct drove her, and she'd scooped up the surface-dweller and had carried him on her head. Hoping it would be in peace with its kind, she'd flung him onto the shore, never imagining she'd ever see him again.

But the ebb and flow of the tides of the world had now placed her here, and she wondered how to use her position to aid the clan. *Can I defy the Abyss and find a way for us survive? Will Shin be able to alter the behaviors of his kind?*

There were too many questions and soon her head began to hurt.

But there were a few certainties. Like her, Shin could understand and talk with others who were not his kind. And when confronted about hunting and capturing orcas, he had said it was wrong and that he would stop it. Finally, she trusted him.

But where it would all lead wasn't something any orca could foresee.

30

"Wait, say that again," said Tyler.

Shin put his hand up to cover the cellphone, and stopped walking. The wind gusted his hair. He pivoted 360 degrees on the rocky beach, then turned his back to the foaming waves to study the hills above. There was no one with binoculars or a parabolic microphone — at least not visible.

He wouldn't put it past the unnamed Japanese government agency, though, to have a device disguised as a dead crab listening in. But a solo walk on a deserted beach seemed as isolated as he could get. Hoping the call wasn't being hacked, Shin swallowed the last remnants of moisture in his mouth, and repeated the rough outline of the plot to sink the *Zheng Yi* using a refurbished Japanese midget-sub from World War Two.

There was a harsh sound. Shin wondered if there was something wrong with the connection, until he recognized it as laughter. "Brother," said Tyler. "No way."

"I'm not going to repeat it a third time," said Shin, and put a hand up to massage his temples.

"That's awesome," said Tyler. "Are you gonna do it?"

Shin sighed. "I don't want to, but I don't have much choice. I said yes."

"What about your vow of nonviolence?" said Tyler.

"That went to shit when they shot at me."

"So you're choosing to exit this planet as a human torpedo while taking a hell of a lot of others down with you."

"I'll alert the ship before I launch the torpedo," argued Shin. "With Morse code or flares. They can abandon ship in the life rafts. No one has to get hurt, but I am going to stop these bastards—"

"Or die trying?" interrupted Tyler. "Look, you need someone with more smarts than you. I'm coming out there. Don't do anything 'til I see ya. Bye."

"Wait. Don't!" said Shin, but the line had gone dead.

"Goddamn it," he screamed at the surf, beach, seagulls, and dead crabs.

Shin hit the speed-dial button on the phone. After several seconds of clicks, the number rang.

And rang.

"Hello, you've reached Tyler — leave a message." *Beep*.

"Do not come out here," said Shin. "Don't do it! Call me back, okay?"

He stormed along the beach, toward the trail that wound upward through the black volcanic rock and green fields to Daichi's house. It had taken him an hour to reach this place of solitude on the shore. The return trip uphill would take twice as long. Daichi was taking him out to dinner tonight to celebrate the agreement, and Shin didn't want to be late. He picked up the pace.

As he stomped and huffed, he dialed Tyler's number again and again. He called so many times that when he stepped off the beach and started up the winding trail, Tyler's inbox was so full with pleadings and expletives that it wouldn't even offer the opportunity to leave a message anymore.

Shin ground his teeth.

He jogged up the trail, brooding all the way up. Maybe there was a way to pull this off — save the orcas, not kill too many people, and escape with his hide intact. But it was looking more and more like the most *fubar* thing he'd ever taken on — and that was saying something. In Vietnam, the most detested missions were those that turned out to be based upon fictitious intel, crafted to lure the SEALs into an ambush.

Here he was, decades later, waltzing into circumstances that could blow up into an international crisis. Maybe that was the ultimate goal of the shadowy agency Daichi worked for. Shin had no intention of being a sacrificial lamb.

He did possess one card hidden up his sleeve. Shin could communicate with orcas, and if he were smart he could find a way to use that to tip the scales to his advantage.

ON THE DRIVE to the restaurant, Shin learned that his submarine training would start in two days. Daichi seemed especially buoyant as they entered the Yuki Onna and he introduced Shin to the staff. The greetings were both formal and genuine, and Shin surmised that his cousin must be a well-respected and honored guest at the establishment.

"If you would like," said Daichi, "allow me to order for us. That way you can try several things."

Shin agreed.

The sake was served, then Daichi ordered. After the waitress left, Shin surveyed the restaurant. The Yuki Onna was steeped in tradition: tatami mat floors, Andon lanterns, low tables with cushions. The menu spanned a gamut of historic Hokkaido fare, all locally sourced, and his cousin described the offerings with pride.

The first course contained Wagyu beef so perfectly cooked that it dissolved in Shin's mouth like butter. The plates were taken away and the next round was served.

Shin eyed the second course: *fugu* nigiri. He deposited a morsel of the fish onto his tongue. His mouth began to tingle and then his lips went numb — and he recalled that *fugu* meant pufferfish. He also remembered that it contained a neurotoxin and had to be prepared just right. "Wow," was all he could say.

Daichi grinned at him from across the low restaurant table. "He's the best *fugu* chef in Hokkaido," he said. "None of his customers have yet died."

"Good to know," said Shin, enjoying the buzz in his oral cavity. He stared at the remaining pufferfish nigiri on the plate.

"You see, it must be in the correct proportions," said Daichi. "The right balance of meat and organs yields an unparalleled gustatory experience. Like exploring a beautiful trail along the edge of a cliff above the ocean — nature abounds and intoxicates the soul, but one wrong step and you join your ancestors." He raised his cup and drank.

Shin took a sip of sake, mouthing the rim with numb lips so as not to dribble like at the dentist's clinic. Surprisingly, his taste buds still worked. He swallowed, and was relieved that he could do that as well. "Fantastic," he said. "I'll remember that next time I mix neurotoxins for my dinner guests."

Daichi burst out laughing. "You Americans are too funny," he said, and thumped the table.

"What happens if you have too much pufferfish?" asked Shin.

"Slurred speech and staggering, like you're drunk," answered Daichi. "Trouble breathing. Seizures, coma, and death." He reached out, retrieved a nigiri morsel and popped it in his mouth.

Nerve-gas warnings, recalled Shin, all ended in those same three words: seizures, coma, death.

Daichi ordered more sake as round three of their dinner arrived: grilled *unagi* with kelp, served on a bed of rice. The food was fantastic and after round four — *onigiri* with bonito — Shin was stuffed.

As their dishes were collected, he began to wonder if there was a way to get a healthy diet of pufferfish onto the galley of the *Zheng Yi*. It would solve a lot of problems if the crew were incapacitated long enough for him to sneak on board and release any captured cetaceans. He fantasized about dumping the intoxicated crew into lifeboats and setting them adrift before blowing up the *Zheng Yi*. They would live, but the ship would settle to the bottom of the ocean and never bother any creature or human again.

The thought made him smile. An outcome that didn't involve killing a bunch of people was fast fading as a realistic probability, and he welcomed any thought of hope that steered him away from it.

"You okay?" asked Daichi.

"Sure," said Shin. "Just thinking about things."

"I hope you enjoyed your food."

"The best I've ever had," said Shin, concentrating on his words. Though the pufferfish toxin had long faded, the sake had made him a bit tipsy. "I would love to meet the *fugu* chef, if possible."

"Yes?" said Daichi. "I'll arrange it, then." He raised his hand to signal the waitress.

31

The council convened. Mothersong reiterated her concerns about the challenges that the clan faced. Given the recent injury to Pouncer while protecting the calf Oddpatches from injury or death, the council's mood was somber.

They knew she was right. Something had to change or they would continue to dwindle and die off.

"We must travel," Mothersong concluded. "We must find new waters to sustain us. We must find a new home."

Given the gravity of her announcement — an uprooting of the clan — she expected an animated discussion, but their silence told her all she needed to know. The council had reached the same conclusion. Without a drastic change, the waters could no longer nourish them. They had to go somewhere else.

Wisdom began to mourn, and Mothersong couldn't blame her for the sadness. These waters had been the Ravenfin's home for as long as any of them could remember. Though there were ancient tales of other homes for the clan in the past, these were old stories and had been told by orcas now long dead. None of the living members had had the experience of journeying and setting up in hunting-waters far away.

Mothersong wanted to mourn with Wisdom. She knew that some of the clan might not survive a long trek. Unknown challenges awaited, without any guarantee of safety on the far side.

Her thoughts of late had been obsessed with the journey. It would take every instinct and intuition the clan could muster to discover the schools of fish needed to keep them alive on the way, and to find the best new waters for their home.

"Our youngest calf, Oddpatches, is old enough to undertake the journey," said Mothersong. "And leading up to the migration, we will hone our hunting skills and fatten up as we prepare for famine and hardship."

"We will prepare," echoed Huntress. "And with your leadership, we will thrive."

"But where will we go?" asked Deepdive.

"To the places where fire has built tall-teeth from the sea," answered Mothersong. "On the far side of the ocean, where Talking-Shin has gone."

At her mention of Shin, chitters sounded from the clan.

When the murmurs had settled, Wisdom said, "You believe the lore of our ancestors."

It wasn't a question.

"I believe the fates of the Ravenfin and Talking-Shin are entwined," said Mothersong.

"But why there? Surface-dwellers are hunting our kin," said Bonecruncher.

"Shin will stop them. My trust in him is strong," answered Mothersong. She then shared a critical insight she'd gained from her nocturnal ruminations on the deep-whale song. "The waters are vast and the fish abundant. There is plenty for all."

There were clicks of approval.

"We can flourish there," agreed Huntress.

"Yes."

"We may be able to help our kin as well," said Boomer, speaking out of turn. "Shin has taught us how to harm small surface-dweller vessels."

Spyhopper and Pouncer chirped their acknowledgments.

"The place you speak of is very far from here," said Wisdom. "How will we find our way?"

"The vibrating-currents will help us across the open waters," replied Mothersong, and waited for the council to process the information.

Satisfied they'd heard, she continued: "The songs of the deep-whales are rich with markers — valleys and ridges on the sea-floor, land-masses, and strange places where fire bubbles the water. But they also contain details of the vibrating-currents to follow, and how to align, to travel from one marker to another."

Wisdom grumbled, "Though we use the vibrating-currents in our own waters, which I know like the backs of my pectoral fins, we have never attempted a journey to the far side of the ocean using them. Deep-whales are different from us. They might feel and understand the vibrating-currents in ways we cannot. Your understanding of their directions may be unreliable."

It was a valid point. Twice a year, the deep-whales travelled across the ocean. Other than in legend, orcas never did. Clans stayed along coastal waters, seldom venturing more than a day or two's journey from sight of the shore. With the vibrating-currents and echolocation, no orca would ever be truly lost in their familiar home-waters.

But they weren't contemplating travels in home waters.

"I believe," said Mothersong, "that I possess the wisdom to lead us to a place where we can once again prosper. No one can know the future, but I believe we must go — and trust in one another. The Ravenfin must survive."

32

Midget-sub bootcamp was intense, interesting, and unlike any other military-hardware training Shin had ever undergone. Similar to his prior experience in the US Navy, every day began with physical training, including martial arts, but that was where the resemblance ended. There was no classroom, chalkboard, or paper manual. Within an hour of meeting — and wrestling with — his instructor, a small, wiry woman named Mariko, he was thrust into a cramped submarine simulator and put to the test.

Mariko wanted to see what Shin already knew or could quickly figure out. The basics he understood. The dive planes, ballast tanks, and rudder controlled, in that order, the angle of attack, buoyancy, and heading. Along with the throttle, these controls guided the submarine within the three-dimensional space of the underwater realm, and were all you needed to move about.

The flip side of the coin to moving was to figure where you were in that 3D space. The displays for depth, speed, GPS, sonar, navigation, and external cameras fed the necessary information into the cockpit. There were also monitors for the batteries, air quality, pressure, engine torque, and more. The simulator was cramped — probably for the very good reason that it was designed to simulate a midget-sub — but Shin found the layout efficient and intuitive.

After two hours, he was gliding through the virtual seas abutting the coast of Hokkaido. The visual displays were so rich in information about the environment that he found it difficult to believe that the actual refurbished midget-sub that he was about to command could pull this off.

"Is this really what the sub can do?" said Shin into the microphone on his headset. "The technology is wild."

Mariko wasn't present in the simulator but her voice was always there in his headset. "Yes, it's an accurate representation," she said. "As is this."

A red light flashed, and the simulator rolled 90 degrees to port. The straps on the command chair dug into Shin's hips and shoulders as he hung sideways. *What the hell!*

"Figure it out," said Mariko. "You have roughly ten seconds."

Shin's gaze flicked around the displays. Air pressure within the port ballast tanks had plummeted. He struggled to determine how to compensate, until he found the control for the starboard ballast and blew it until the pressures equalized. The ship righted itself.

However, Shin was now sinking like a stone. He reached for the dive planes and throttle, but it was too late.

The simulator jerked and, after a huge bang, everything went dark.

"Boom," said Mariko in his ear, in English.

Over the course of his training, he heard the word several more times. It was the only English word Mariko had ever spoken to him — and a clear communication of a non-passing grade.

Shin respected that.

Boom was a submarine hull flattened like a beer can under an elephant. *Boom* was a dark, powerless sub on the bottom of the sea — air saturated with toxic-gases from damaged batteries — slowly suffocating, whilst tapping out your dying rhythm on the hull with a wrench and praying for rescue. *Boom* meant Shin had failed and wasn't coming back.

And more importantly, *Boom* was goodbye to his hope of stopping the hunting of cetaceans.

AFTER TWO DAYS in simulator school, Shin advanced to the next level. The final several days of his training were devoted to piloting the actual midget-sub, learning the specifics of the mission, and a refresher course on underwater demolition. Each evening he'd received a briefing on the whereabouts of the *Zheng Yi*, and learned there were several ports of call the ship frequented; her travels thus far matched a past pattern of smuggling runs. Sometimes more than one goal was achieved on tour, and whether the Zheng Yi would seek to capture cetaceans on her current trip was unknown.

Because the Japanese agency had the target covered, he applied his focus to the midget sub. As it turned out, the rust and dents on the old girl were all camouflage. She'd been taken apart and reconstructed with titanium pressure plates and every single bolt was new. The cockpit was as sleek and modern as the simulator had promised.

The more Shin learned, the more he realized how ideal this submarine was for stealth. Old World War Two crap turned up all the time in this region, and given that most of the islands in the Kuril chain were uninhabited, it was an excellent disguise. Hidden in plain sight and moored in a desolate harbor, she would appear, from air or satellite, to be a washed-up derelict from six decades ago. No one would bother to investigate.

The performance statistics were impressive. There was no diesel engine; the entire craft was electrical. All the old batteries had been stripped, and in their place smaller, modern units delivered more power to the counter-rotating screws than he'd have thought possible. The sub had a range of a thousand miles, a max speed of 20 knots while submerged, and an operational depth of 250 meters.

Moving quietly, the tiny sub could insert itself into Russian territory on almost any of the islands bordering the Sea of Okhotsk and be as noteworthy as a barnacle at low tide. Or the sub could 'park' outside a harbor where a target was moored, and send in an underwater demolition frogman. There were two torpedo tubes. One held a torpedo, the other had been reconfigured as a 'SEAL tube', as the US Navy called them. It was a claustrophobic fit, but the tube allowed a diver to leave, and reenter, the submarine while wearing a rebreather kit.

Sinking the *Zheng Yi* came down to two options: swim out with a limpet mine to attach the high-explosive magnetic device to the hull while the ship was in port... or torpedo her at sea.

"The mine is preferable," said Mariko. "Once attached, we'll have satellite command and can choose to detonate it at the right time."

"Right time?"

"Over deep waters, during their trip home," answered Mariko. "Far enough away from any commercial vessel as to pose no danger, and also in a position where our shadow-subs can release the decoy mines."

"Decoy mines?" said Shin, at a loss.

"Yes. Decoy mines," said Mariko. "Must you repeat everything back like a parrot or can you keep quiet and listen?"

Shin bowed his head. Point taken. "I am all ears," he said.

"After the limpet is detonated, and at *precisely* the right time, our shadow-subs will release several Soviet-era floating mines near the location. Though they are rendered inert, these will be spotted by the scans of the Russian military ships responding to the explosion and disaster of the *Zheng Yi*. Forensic analysis will confirm their authenticity. The Russians will presume that some old mines had broken free and that one of these had blown up the Chinese ship. As the proverb states, *Jigō jitoku*."

Shin smiled. The literal translation of this proverb was *one's act, one's profit*, but it was best understood as *what you sow, you reap*. He knew of the zealous, and careless, use of Soviet naval mines during the Korean and Vietnam wars. The agency's plan had rich karmic roots.

Mariko continued, "But long before the Russian warships arrive at the site of the *Zheng Yi*'s distress call, our divers will have retrieved evidence from the ship's safe."

Damn, thought Shin. *This has been in the works for a while, waiting for the right moment.*

He considered the tactics. The history of tiny submarines in warfare was not pretty. Few who'd served in the iron coffins ever came back, but this was a cool plan: a silent one-man underwater insertion and egress. His confidence rose.

"And the torpedo?" Shin asked.

"Backup," said Mariko. "It's short-range, and the timing of the ideal spot for striking the *Zheng Yi* is much harder to calculate and control, especially near a shipping lane. But we can detonate it remotely as well."

"Good to know."

"In case the sub is captured or sinks," added Mariko. "But I have every confidence that you will be successful with the mine."

"Yep," said Shin. "Me too."

Though he'd mastered the basics, he had no experience as a combat submariner. In contrast, his underwater skills, including demolition, had always been top notch. The fact that the sub could be scuttled remotely by detonating its onboard torpedo, to prevent capture or salvage, was a sober reminder of the commitment to secrecy.

He bowed to his instructor, and caught the faintest twitch of a smile on her lips.

Though Mariko didn't know of his ability to communicate with orcas, she'd correctly read his level of commitment. She knew he couldn't wait to place the mine on the hull. He hadn't told her the part about storming the ship and freeing the hostages yet, but he would.

He studied Mariko.

In her staring eyes, Shin saw his reflection.

Mariko cared about him as a human being. She had his back. A commander like that would never throw away a life, or ask you to do something they themselves would not. Mariko exuded competence and confidence — and compassion.

Shin wasn't a sacrifice. Mariko was sending him out to win and to return triumphant.

He briefly thought about, and then dismissed Tyler's counsel to wait. "I'm ready," he said.

"The day after tomorrow, at dawn," said Mariko. "We'll pick you up at your cousin's house. Be prepared."

33

S hin strolled uphill from his shopping trip in Wakkanai. He'd spent the morning stretching his legs, grateful to be outside in the fresh marine air after days of confinement and intense training. It was a warm and cloudless afternoon. He paused to shift his backpack and gaze northward over the Sōya Strait, toward Sakhalin Island.

Large cargo ships headed east, to the Sea of Japan, or west, to the Pacific Ocean. Shin shielded his eyes against the sunlight to watch their progress. Blue haze drifted upward from smokestacks and, though the ships were miles away, the deep, pulsating bass of their engines seemed as loud as if he were swimming next to their hulls.

He plugged his fingertips into his ears.

Shin thought about the *Zheng Yi*, which was out there beyond his sight, perhaps soon to capture whales and dolphins for amusement parks. Tomorrow, he'd bolt himself into a midget-submarine and go on a hunt of his own — and kill.

Not a comforting thought, but neither did it alarm him.

His pre-combat hand tremors and churning guts were as familiar as a well-worn glove. But, despite the physical signals that his body was keyed up, Shin's emotional center was as placid as a windless cove.

The horn of a distant mega-cargo ship sounded, deep and forlorn.

Shin turned his back to the sea and headed uphill. The contents within the pack weighed on both his back and mind, and there was still some assembly required. His visit to town — wharf, toy store, and hardware store — had netted him slivers of optimism. But he needed to get to Daichi's house and put it all together.

The hill was steep. Shin's heart pounded and sweat soaked through his shirt. He stopped to adjust the backpack; lumpy bags of ice shifted within. Tetrodotoxin was heat-stable — even cooking didn't inactivate it — but Shin had wanted to appear legitimate. The *fugu* chef had referred him to a fisherman, and Shin had kept up the ruse of being an apprentice chef as the pufferfish had been packed.

After a short break, Shin resumed his upward march.

———

In Daichi's garage, Shin unrolled a plastic sheet, donned rubber gloves, and then gutted all the pufferfish he'd purchased. Remembering the *fugu* chef's instructions, he separated the most toxin-laden parts — liver, muscle, and skin — into a pile.

He sliced them up into smaller pieces on a carving board, then slid them into a ceramic bowl. He added water, rice vinegar, and whisky — then stirred.

After the liquid settled into layers, he decanted the topmost one into a small mason jar. He added a dollop of wood glue to thicken it.

While it cured, Shin sorted through the other items in his backpack: a toy crossbow, rubber tubing, duct tape, epoxy, nylon thread, a box of mechanical pencils, wire, metal picture frame parts, and latex finger cots.

He checked his watch. He had two to three hours until Daichi was due.

The toy crossbow was made of plastic and metal, and was designed to fire foam-tipped darts. The baseline construction was solid but with the addition of metal strips glued onto the body, and black duct tape wound tightly around the stock, it became quite robust. Next, Shin stiffened the bow by gluing on more of the metal strips, and clamped these in place while the epoxy dried.

Now for the bolts.

He stabilized a mechanical pencil for flight by unscrewing the eraser and looping short lengths of nylon thread around the end, reattaching the eraser, then trimming the threads.

He held it up to inspect his work. It looked like a skinny artist's brush with frayed bristles. Shin felt the balance, then aimed and threw it at a cardboard box, across the garage.

The projectile thunked into the center of the box. *Perfect.*

Shin modified the remaining eleven mechanical pencils.

He'd spent well over an hour on the task so far, and needed to finish before Daichi returned home. He checked the crossbow. The epoxy had cured, so he removed the clamps. For the last step of construction, he replaced the string with a length of wire. Testing it, he cranked the wire back and it locked into place.

Shin loaded one of the modified pencils. He aimed the crossbow at the cardboard box. The wire thrummed as he depressed the trigger. The bolt struck the postage stamp he'd aimed for, went through the other side of the box and embedded itself in the garage wall. Definitely enough force to penetrate a thick fisherman's coat, and stick the flesh within.

The last part of the operation could not be rushed. Filling the conical metal tips of the pencils with toxin required a steady, slow hand. If he goofed up and poked himself, his cousin would arrive home to find him incapacitated on the garage floor.

Deciding he'd better clean up the garage first, Shin put the bolts, crossbow, and the jar of toxin — which had thickened to the consistency of honey — into a cardboard box. He set the box in his guest room, then scurried back to clean up the mess of fish guts and bones. Shin wrapped the stinking mess in newspaper, opened the garage door to air the place out, and jogged to the power composter. He scanned the pictographs, dumped the fishy remains into the correct steel orifice (or at least, so he hoped), and sprinted back.

The garage stunk. Shin picked up a folded cardboard box and began fanning.

He expected the security gate to roll open at any moment, but it remained immobile.

If Daichi had video surveillance in the garage, and if he confronted Shin later, Shin would tell him the truth. He had to make sure there were no cetaceans — whales, dolphins, orcas — or any other sentient captive on board the *Zheng Yi*. He must sneak onto and incapacitate (without killing, if possible) anyone who got in his way. He needed certainty.

If that was a deal-breaker, then so be it.

But he didn't think that would happen. Training had been a two-way street. He'd learned much about the agency.

Looking into Mariko's eyes had confirmed it. They'd found their human weapon, and weren't about to let it go to waste. The sinking of the *Zheng Yi* would add a feather to someone's cap. Exposing and sinking a critical target, would serve a warning to some powerful people in China and Russia.

Shin finished cleaning the garage.

As he retreated to the guest room, his hand touched the makiri on his hip. *Honor this blade and it will never fail you.*

He closed the screen to the guest room and started the final task of adding toxin to each dart.

Shin loaded a dap of the gooey tetrodotoxin into a conical tip and then screwed the tip onto the body of the pencil. After this was done, he wiped off any excess with a rag, then secured a latex finger-cot over the end to keep the water out.

He arranged the dozen toxin darts back into their original box, with the nylon-threads sticking out of the open end. The tips were buried in the metal-and-duct tape reinforced bottom. As he packed the box away, the words *Made in China* caused him to chuckle as he thought about shooting the modified mechanical pencils at the crew on the *Zheng Yi*, one paralyzing dart at a time.

His smile was brief. Shin hadn't tested the concoction of tetrodotoxin on a live target. Hopefully, it wasn't lethal, but worse was the prospect that it only burned like a hornet-sting and did nothing else. Slinging Nerf darts at someone armed with an AK-47 wouldn't end well.

Shin placed the box and crossbow into a watertight container and stowed it in his kit. He said a prayer to honor his ancestors and secured his makiri.

He stared at the service pistol he'd carried with him in Vietnam. His fingers found the familiar grip, its ridges worn silver with age. He picked it up. Memories returned with that contact, and Shin knew he had to take it with him.

How Tyler had managed to get the firearm, silencer, and ammunition, through customs — and then have it home delivered, along with his scuba gear, in a footlocker the size of a Subaru — was a topic Shin needed to discuss with the Texan. But Shin had been so flustered during their last phone call that he'd forgotten to bring it up.

Tonight was the eve of Shin's mission, and though he respected Tyler with his heart and soul, this was neither the place nor time for the young man to appear. He'd blend in with Japanese society, and the agency, as seamlessly as a rampaging bull from Pamplona at a tea ceremony.

Shin's pathway was clear, and he didn't want to be pushed into further justifying his reasons to Tyler. He was going on the mission. He was going solo. And he would be coming back.

Besides there was no way Tyler would fit in the midget-sub.

The gate to the compound began to roll open. Shin darted to the window, and squinted through the blinds.

Daichi was home.

34

On the thirteenth evening of the journey, the Ravenfin had full bellies after another successful hunt. Though initially the waters they travelled had been colder than back home, they'd been getting warmer, there was ample sunlight during the day, and the fish were plentiful.

Each night since they'd started this trek to the other side of the ocean, Mothersong's dreams had changed. She saw snatches of strange places. Locations and seas she'd never visited before were rendered in detail, and she had confidence she would recognize them in real life were the clan to encounter them.

More remarkable, though, were her experiences during the day.

As they journeyed, they heard the songs of the deep-whales. To Mothersong's astonishment, she'd begun to understand so much of their language that it was as if she were listening to an elder orca from her youth.

All orca calves heard their first tales from their mothers, who spoke in simple terms. But growing young calves started to hear, and grasp, the more complex adult conversations. Stories of old times, good and bad. Stories of sex, hunting, and exotic realms full of fish. And stories of pain, tragedy, and death.

Mothersong's deepening understanding of the speech of the orcas' massive whale cousins was like her trip from birth-calf to cow to matri-arch. A narrow passage had opened, and over decades of listening to, and telling, orca stories, comprehension had granted her wisdom.

Though they caught distant echo-glimpses, the clan were never close enough to see the whales with their eyes. Even Spyhopper, who'd tried to spot their plumes or tails, had failed. Deep-whales were shy and rightly mistrustful of all orcas.

Rebel orca bands who'd tasted whale flesh would hunt in groups of a half-dozen. Mothersong's clan ate only fish, and wouldn't even hurt a tiny seal, but she couldn't blame the whales for keeping far away from thirty-six orcas.

But the deep-whales, whether solo or in groups of two or three, had sung their songs and she'd heard them. Those tales had filled in the gaps of missing lore that she'd never known existed.

As darkness closed in, the clan stopped and settled down for the evening. Harbor camping was preferable to the open sea, but there were few opportunities to do that on this trek.

The apprehension within the clan at being so far from their home waters was fading with each successful hunt. The absence of the growling from the surface-dweller behemoths had been a peaceful boon to orcas fraught with uncertainty.

Everyone slept better after a good meal.

This was the journey of their lives, and that fact quelled almost all grumbling. Though Mothersong suspected a few members were harboring doubts, they kept their thoughts to themselves. A clan unified was stronger than a wavering one. Mothersong hoped that trust was not misplaced and that she was leading them toward the light and not the Abyss.

Though the open ocean had provided sufficient food to this point, it wouldn't sustain them for long. The Ravenfin must establish a new fishing range, and only rich coastal waters could provide their society with a home, security, and a life-giving regenerative cycle of fish.

Orca history was recorded in stories and, from a young age, Mother-song had always been attracted to — and frightened by — the tales that spoke of a clan's plight for survival: stories of harassment by surface-dwellers or struggles against famine. The young Mothersong had never imagined that she would one day be matriarch, leading the Ravenfin on a journey for their survival.

35

The roll of the cutter was subtle. The level of the water in the glass next to Shin's bunk barely moved, but the gentle rocking of the ship and the rumble of her engines in his bones, told him they were underway.

He closed his eyes and exhaled a long, slow breath — but the technique to center his mind failed. He was too torqued up with anticipation.

The *Zheng Yi* was now deep in the Sea of Okhotsk, probably seeking specimens. His hopes now rested on interrupting their return trip — with a big bang.

The past twenty-fours seemed a blur. In fact, the whole week had been.

Yesterday, he'd been picked up at Daichi's house by Mariko, and driven to the city of Akkeshi on the Pacific Ocean side of Hokkaido. From there, they'd been shuttled by skiff to a bright white Japan Coast Guard cutter with blue markings, moored in the harbor. The *Shikishima* was large and modern, and carried two Puma helicopters, and an array of armaments including two 20mm Gatling-style rotary cannons and a four 35mm anti-aircraft guns.

Last night he'd slept on board in the quarters assigned to him. Solo, spacious, and with a head, it probably belonged to an officer who was now bunking it up someplace else with a grudge — or maybe not.

After a nearly a month in Japan, and despite a lifetime of tutelage by his *issei* parents, his understanding of the contract that kept the Japanese society flowing was as clear as invisible ink.

Why would the military be any different? He'd have bitched and moaned if he'd been an officer displaced by an old rag-tag commando.

Perhaps later, Shin could explore the vessel, and talk with the crew of the *Shikishima*. But for now he had been politely — and firmly — encouraged to stay put. He supposed it was for operational security.

Shin picked up a copy of the *Hokkaido Shimbun* and read the headlines. He detected a shift under his feet as the ship swayed, and knew they had left the harbor and were headed into deeper waters.

A sharp knock sounded on his cabin door.

"Come in," said Shin, and dropped the newspaper.

The door opened and Mariko stepped into his quarters. She was dressed in the same black fatigues that Shin had been issued, without insignia or rank, and an attaché case was slung over her shoulder.

"Urup is your destination," Mariko said in a tone softer than Shin was accustomed to. She unfolded a map that encompassed Hokkaido, Sakhalin Island, the entire Kuril chain, and the Kamchatka Peninsula.

Urup was part of the middle third of the fifty or so Kuril Islands, and commanded a strait leading into the Sea of Okhotsk. Roughly seventy-five miles in length and twelve in width, Urup was mountainous and had a high point of almost a mile in elevation.

"There are no civilians there," said Mariko. "There might be surveillance devices, if the Russians have bothered to maintain them. Regarding actual military presence, there are some half-buried Soviet era tanks, which some idiot field marshal convinced the Kremlin to repurpose in the 1950s and 60s as a turreted-gun coastal defense system for the Kurils — apparently having not learned the lessons of the Maginot Line or Fortress Europe in the forties.

"Most of these next-to-useless weapons are clustered in the southern islands — aimed at Japan." She tapped her lip with a finger. "Perhaps, if Japan were to once again send wooden ships armed with archers and samurai, the tanks' cannons would prove useful. But as it stands, they are largely decaying buckets of rust. If needed, you could hide in one to avoid detection, but I would be careful about unexploded ordinance, which still litters many of these islands. The Russians are even more careless than the Americans and Chinese with respect to old bombs and shells."

Shin smiled at Mariko's dig.

He admired her no-nonsense approach to instruction. He'd had commanding officers like this in his past life in the Navy. Once you found a gem like Mariko, you didn't want to let them go, because they worked miracles to keep their charges alive.

Mariko reached into her attaché case, and unfolded another map. It was a tactical one, and Shin was familiar with the topographical format system which used one kilometer squares. It was centered on the south-western tip of Urup.

"Tonight," said Mariko, "small patrol boats will guide you and the sub to a cove, here." The narrow harbor on Urup faced east toward the Pacific Ocean.

Mariko returned to the strategic map overview. "The *Zheng Yi*, when she returns from her activities, will refuel either here at Korsakov on Sakhalin Island, or here at Petropavlovsk-Kamchatsky. The latter is a Cold-War-era port on the Kamchatka Peninsula, which still has a sizable Russian naval base. You will be informed which port and the timetable for your interdiction when that information is available. Let's hope for Korsakov. It's closer to Hokkaido and will be a lot easier to get in and out of."

In the excitement of studying maps and listening to Mariko's briefing, Shin had almost forgotten about the midget-sub. "By the way," he said. "Where is my submarine?"

"The craft you reference," said Mariko, "is tucked in an amphibious deck below the aft helipad, along with the patrol boats. Also, the sub is *not* yours."

"Cool. I'll be happy to return her when I am done," said Shin. "But as her first captain, I'd like to name her and assign a call sign."

"You test dangerous waters," said Mariko, frowning. The double entendre wasn't lost on Shin. Mariko brooked no talk-back, and he was on the cusp of being inserted into the Russian-controlled sea.

"*Orcas' Hammer*," said Shin, charging ahead. "That's her name."

"Hmm," said Mariko. After a moment, she smiled, which was both rare and beautiful. "Okay. *Orcas' Hammer* it is."

Shin grinned.

Mariko continued, "The islands are mountainous, and vessels passing within sight are unlikely, but the *Shikishima* must stay outside of Russian territorial waters, so we must use stealth for the last leg to the island. It will be dark. The radar and sonar profiles of the submarine and the small escort craft are minuscule, and we're far enough away from Russian military bases that risk of detection is minimal.

"Once we're certain that our penetration has been unobserved, we'll off-load the supplies, and secure the sub. The patrol boats will then leave, and you'll be alone.

"This satellite phone," she said, and slid a black object across the table, "is how we will communicate. Questions?"

"None at present," said Shin. "But I do have a confession."

"Is this about the crossbow and tetrodotoxin darts in your bag, and the silenced Smith and Wesson 9mm pistol with three clips of ammo?"

Shin flinched. He sucked in a breath, and relived the memory of Mariko slamming him to the mat during judo training. Though he had her beat on height and weight, she'd always moved faster. Despite everything he'd tried, he'd quickly found himself off-balance and thrown onto his back, gaping in wonderment.

Just like now.

"Yes," he sighed.

"Well?" said Mariko. "Out with it."

Shin struggled for a moment, then said, "I can't blow them up, or put a torpedo up their aft, unless I know there are no hostages aboard — nor any danger to the sea."

"The only people onboard the *Zheng Yi*," said Mariko, "are ones who smuggle, or hunt *shachi* and *iruka*." A brief frown crossed her face before she resumed, "You know the other missions it can conduct, of course, but their current profit-making run does not involve the transfer of chemical or nuclear materials, nor human trafficking."

"That's not what I'm talking about," said Shin. "If there is a captive orca or dolphin in the hold, I cannot blow up the ship."

Mariko's face betrayed no clue as to her thoughts.

Shin waited.

"I see," she said. "You want to sneak onboard while it's moored in a Russian port — paralyze the crew with tetrodotoxin, or shoot them with a silenced pistol — and then free any captured whales?"

"Yes."

"No!" said Mariko, her nostrils flaring. "The plan is to put the ship on the bottom of the sea."

"And I... we will," said Shin.

"You are intelligent," said Mariko. "My advice is to follow your training and the mission as outlined. You have been given sufficient guidance, equipment, and support to succeed and return safely. But you if you go *cowboy* on us, you jeopardize everything."

"I will slit every human throat on the *Zheng Yi* with my makiri if needed," said Shin. "But I won't sink the damn ship until I'm sure that there are no captives on board."

Mariko glared at him. "You understand that the second phase of the operation hinges upon the success of the first. That means stealth. You attach a limpet mine, undetected, and get out. *Undetected.*"

"We sink the *Zheng Yi* where and when we wish. If you go running around, shooting the crew, whilst searching for a whale or two, it blows the entire stealth part of phase one out of the water. It risks the whole operation."

"I'll attach the limpet first," said Shin. "You can blow up the *Zheng Yi* whenever — but you have to give me this chance."

"Even if you're aboard?"

"Yes."

"No," said Mariko. "This is unacceptable. The ruse of floating mines fails if we blow up the ship in harbor. And we won't have access to the data trove and gold within the safe. So, sorry, no!"

Shin said nothing. He'd set his anchor. He wasn't going forward.

Mariko frowned and repeated her entire message in fluent English — far beyond the one word, *boom*, she'd tended to utter during training.

"I understand you perfectly," said Shin. "And I say, it's my way or the highway."

"Shit," continued Mariko in English. "You're kidding me, right?"

"No," said Shin. "I am not kidding."

Mariko stood, stepped out into the hallway, and slammed the door behind her.

Shin could hear her yelling in the corridor as she stomped away, but it was difficult to pick out the words.

Shin sat in silence and stared at the walls in his cabin. Perhaps he'd pushed too hard. However, a line in the sand had to be drawn: every whale or dolphin held hostage had to be freed.

Thirty minutes later, there was a sharp knock on the door. A millisecond later, Mariko stormed into Shin's cabin and sat down, glaring at him.

She cleared her throat. "After you plant the mine, and *only* after you plant the mine, you are permitted to free any captives aboard while incapacitating the crew in the process. We now have a cover story for the outcome that it all goes to crap, you are captured, and we have to blow it up in port. But you must first plant the mine. Only after it's attached may you go forward."

"Yes. I agree," said Shin.

"Good luck, cowboy," said Mariko. "If the Russians try to capture you — you have your pistol. I would advise using it right here." She opened her mouth and pointed a finger at the back of her throat.

Though he'd never been a POW, Shin knew from Vietnam some of the tortures that were possible. He had no intention of being captured by the Russians or Chinese.

"I understand," he said. "Thank you."

"My honor is a stake," said Mariko. "Make sure you win."

36

The Ravenfin suffered. They hadn't eaten in days, and Mothersong despaired that none of the best scouts had picked up a sizable school of fish for the clan to hunt. Beneath the gnawing hunger lurked the fear that she had led them astray.

But the tickle on the right side of her scalp aligned with the deepwhale's song-navigation, and in her heart she was certain that they were going the right way. The discomfort and pain in the clan, though, were as plain as the towering dorsal-fin on Boomer's back. They were nearing a limit. The young calves had done well, but she worried about the elders, Deepdive and Bloodbull.

Mothersong clicked a signal to slow the pace, hoping that Sounder and Huntress on the advance wings would locate something to eat. Even a small school would be welcome.

She considered how to take their minds away from their suffering. "Who's for a story?" she asked.

"Me," squeaked Oddpatches. The youngest of the Ravenfin had grown during the journey. As had Chirpy, a girl-calf only a year his senior. Cared for by Melody, Flukethumper, Pouncer, and others, they'd both received extra portions of fish during the arduous trip.

"Then you shall have it," said Mothersong, and chuckled. "A story that the youngest have never heard before. The ancient legend of why we are the Ravenfin — a story from long before I was born."

Approving murmurs echoed around. Most had heard the story before, and it was a favorite. As they swam, Mothersong recounted the tale.

"In old times, before surface-dwellers appeared on the waters, our clan faced starvation. The Matron guided them over a long route to a place where she hoped to find food.

"Arriving at unfamiliar shores, after a fishless journey, the clan searched. Though they spy-hopped and sounded, they could find nothing to eat. The Matron floated on the surface, eyed the trees and lush rivers of the land, and puzzled. There should be food here.

"A black bird swept down to land on her dorsal-fin. The raven perched there, called to her, and flew away. Then it came back, and landed again. After a while the Matron realized the raven was pointing out a direction, and she and the clan followed.

"The raven flew onward, calling to them in the strange language of birds. On and on it led them, sometimes coming back to rest on the Matron's fin again — until the famished clan struck riches of fish beyond your imagination. The glorious feast saved them all from starvation.

"You see, the raven could fly high and see further than the eyes and scans of the orcas. But ravens aren't eagles, and they can't dive underwater to catch food — so the strength of the orcas' flukes to pummel and stun the fish was needed. During the orcas' feast, many fish floated to the surface and were easy prey for the raven and his friends who flew in from the trees.

"Together, the orcas and ravens shared in the bounty. And that is why we are called Ravenfin."

37

On Urup Island, within a shallow clover-leafed harbor, Shin set the mushroom anchor of the midget-sub. During the trip from the *Shikishima*, he'd sat in the command chair of the inert sub watching the navigation system, while the two RIB boats, to starboard and port, had quietly guided him to this spot.

He opened the hatch, and poked his head out into the blackness of the cold, dank night.

High above the clouds, a crescent moon was shining — at least that's what the tide-log indicated. But from his spot atop *Orcas' Hammer*, the thick cloud layer had sponged up all the moonlight and turned the world into grainy charcoal outlines on black paper.

As his eyes adjusted, he noticed someone waving at him from the port escort-boat.

"Time to help us cache the supplies," said Mariko. Then she switched to English. "Move, *cowboy*."

Shin suppressed a laugh, swung his legs out of the midget-sub, and stepped aboard the RIB. Two crewmen freed the lines attaching it to the sub, and the engine purred as Mariko piloted them to shore.

He assisted with offloading the watertight cases, then securing and camouflaging them well above the high-tide mark. They contained extra rations, batteries, an antennae and comms gear — and explosives to torch it all remotely.

Each of Shin's footprints in Russian territory would be erased, regardless of outcome. If everything really hit the crapper, and Shin sparked an international incident, he imagined that his footprints in the digital realm would be removed as well. If he were killed or captured, the agency would clean any record of him ever visiting Japan.

Mariko sloshed through calf-depth water to the RIB, and hauled herself aboard.

Shin shook off his musing and followed.

Two minutes later, back atop the hatch of his sub, he watched the two escort ships preparing to leave. The dark sky wearied of its burden, and hurled a volley of stinging rain like a medieval arrow storm. Shin shrugged on a black waterproof shell and, amid the pings and pops, watched the boats untie.

He waved goodbye as the escorts ghosted off. Their quiet motors were soon lost within the waves of the ocean and the hiss of the rain.

Shin retreated within *Orcas' Hammer*, and closed the hatch. Out of paranoia, and mariner habit, he reexamined the tide tables and confirmed that she wouldn't be stranded at low tide.

He tried to settle his thoughts and focus on the immediate future, the next twelve hours, but his melancholy grew. The thought that he was alone on foreign soil and could be erased from the world tomorrow — so soon after he'd discovered a newfound purpose to his life — seemed cruel beyond comparison.

Shin didn't believe in God. He had witnessed too much suffering in the Vietnam War. Afterward, when he'd found peace within the beautiful decades of Ayumi's love — she'd been ripped away.

Tears flowed onto his cheeks. He wiped them away, and began the shut-down routine for the submarine.

I pray for a benevolent order to the universe, he thought as he sat in the command chair, flipping switches. *And that I am successful.*

Shin sat motionless, with his eyes closed. He recited a mantra for forgiveness and harmony, and tried to still his rapid heart rate. He repeated the mantra until the emotional wave receded.

Growing heavy with exhaustion, he reclined the chair into sleep-mode, grateful that, years ago, some engineer involved in the midget-sub redesign process had won an argument in a conference room.

The rain singing on the top of the hull and the gentle rocking of the sub lulled him into a deep sleep.

AT 0600, Shin turned on the satellite phone and opened the submarine hatch. It had stopped raining. He waited for the phone to find the satellite and then dialed.

"Orcas' Hammer," said Shin.

"Dolphin base says the shark is dark," said a voice. "Coords from 0500 are 148.255404E, 53.233858N. Next check in at 1200. Out."

Shin wrote down the numbers, then clicked off the sat phone.

He turned on the sub's navigation system and punched in the coordinates he'd been given. Though the *Zheng Yi* had switched off the AIS, the agency was tracking the ship from whatever spy satellite it had aimed down here.

He found the ship's location: due north, several hundred miles away, deep in the center of the Sea of Okhotsk.

NOT MUCH WAS different at the 1200 check-in, other than that the *Zheng Yi* had tracked further north. But at 1800, Shin learned that the ship had stopped moving, and had held a fixed position for the past five hours. He wrote down the numbers and checked the navigation console.

The location was just outside of an unpopulated harbor on the northern tip of Sakhalin Island, about 80 km from the nearest human settlement.

The fact that the ship was stationary could mean that she'd cornered her prey, and had engaged the small-vessel flotilla to abduct a young specimen or two for a zoo. Or maybe she was regrouping after losing sight of the prey.

Shin grasped a bulkhead and squeezed it until his knuckles went white.

There was nothing he could do but sit here and wait. He stared at his watch. Mariko had shortened the check-in time interval to four hours.

At 2200, the *Zheng Yi* was still in the same location. The news was the same at 0200 and 0600.

But at the 1000 check-in, Mariko had a significant update: the *Zheng Yi* was about half-way to Korsakov, a refueling port that was known to be a favorite.

His mouth went dry at the bigger news, though. He'd been cleared to go.

Shin signed off, and turned to the nav console.

Korsakov was on the southern end of Sakhalin, in the center of the two pincers of the island which reached toward Hokkaido like the claws of a crab. The city had a population of twenty thousand, and was a regional fishing and commercial shipping hub. Its harbor was deep, protected by the topography. There was a remote locale, which Mariko had identified in her last communication, where Shin could anchor the sub ten meters below the surface. From there, after exiting via the SEAL-tube, the *Zheng Yi* would be within swimming distance.

Shin plotted a course to Korsakov, and prepped *Orcas' Hammer* for departure. At near max speed it would take ten hours and burn through over half the battery charge, but it would put him there near midnight.

Darkness was an old friend.

38

Over the last several days the ocean had further warmed, which was a blessing because many in the clan were fatigued, and had lost insulating fat due to the dearth of good food and the long days of travel.

Though the songs of the deep-whales had long ago disappeared, Boomer could still dive down to the sound channel and catch a word or two of the distant talk. But Mothersong no longer needed the songs to guide her. She'd absorbed enough that she knew where she was, and where the Ravenfin were headed. With each island or land mass they'd encountered, another mental image had materialized into reality. Though she'd never visited these places before, the deep-whales had, and the imprinting of their song into her memory boosted Mothersong's confidence.

But the clan was suffering from the demands of the journey. These past five days, hunting had been poor, and she must guide the clan to rich waters with good food.

She crested the rough ocean to breathe. And dove.

"I saw dark land-teeth, with white tips," announced Spyhopper, appearing alongside her. "Straight ahead."

"That is a good sign," said Mothersong without emotion, though in truth she could barely contain her excitement. It was another of the deep-whale's markers — and a critical one. Here the waters became shallow and the fish plentiful. This was where the deep-whales from Mothersong's home waters travelled each year, and a place where the clan could rest and fatten up for several days.

When they were again ready, they would trek toward colder waters for the final segment (she hoped) of this journey. She worried about Bloodbull, who'd been lagging. Sounder had stayed alongside him, but the old bull was suffering and was a half-day behind. Mothersong hated the thought that uprooting the clan and the ensuing sojourn had accelerated his aging, but perhaps rest would restore some of his strength.

As matriarch, she carried a heavy burden. Mothersong had discussed her fears with the members of the council and they knew that the Ravenfin would not arrive at their destination without loss. But staying at home in failing waters would also mean loss.

Mothersong believed in her bones that this great migration was their salvation. There were too many portents for it to be false. From her comprehension of Shin, and the ways of the surface-dwellers, to the complex language of the deep-whales, there had to be some meaning behind this tidal-wave compelling her forward.

Though she feared for the Ravenfin, Mothersong knew she must never let go of the hope guiding her. If she faltered, the clan would flounder in these unfamiliar waters. They must believe in her view of the future, and strive together toward that goal.

The ocean floor began to rise. Mothersong heard several orcas on the wings of the formation start to scan.

"Oh my," announced Huntress, from the right side. "A large school of yummies."

"Very large," agreed Wavedancer.

"Wow," said Jumper.

Mothersong clicked her approval for Huntress to organize the hunt. She had spotted the prey first, and it was her privilege. Both cows and bulls had roles in a hunt — from scouting to hunting and killing — but there were few who could see the field and command it clearly. Huntress, Sounder, and Pouncer were in that group.

Huntress called for a seven-formation. Four fast orcas would circle, two by two in a crab-pincers, and drive the fish-school toward three huge, fluke-thumpers charging up the middle. The massive thrashing of the bulls' tails would stun or kill thousands of fish.

It was a beautiful plan suiting the size of the school and the slope of the rising seafloor. The fish couldn't dive deep enough to escape. And the follow-through with the rest of the clan would be delicious.

Mothersong held pride at the way the younger ones had learned and grown enough to command a hunt — especially in unfamiliar waters.

Huntress called the names of the seven, and they fluked into action.

BLOODBULL AND SOUNDER rejoined the clan, and had a big fill of the hunt leftovers. "We've reached the paradise of warmth and fish," said Bloodbull. "Mothersong, I am grateful for your guidance."

But Mothersong knew Bloodbull was not long for the ocean, and would soon greet the Abyss. His wheezing breath and pale lassitude spoke the truth. He knew it as well.

Bloodbull was younger than she, but old bulls died earlier than old cows who had stopped their birthing-cycle. It was the way of things.

Drifting, breathing, belching, and half-sleeping, the Ravenfin spent the night in the warm waters underneath a bright moon. But Mothersong's rest was fitful.

"Beautiful."

The word woke her and she scanned the clan.

"Beautiful," said Bloodbull. "My life has been beautiful."

Mothersong roused the clan, though some were already awake. They gathered at Bloodbull's side. He wouldn't rise and breathe.

Rhymehealer nudged Bloodbull, trying to rouse him.

Unlike a calf in distress, he was too big for one orca to carry, but several of the Ravenfin lifted him to the surface. They kept Bloodbull upright but he hung limp, unmoving and not breathing.

Abruptly, he shuddered and inhaled.

Rhymehealer went underneath Bloodbull, and gently pressed the top of her head into his chest. Mothersong waited for the pronouncement... but she knew.

"His heart no longer beats," said Rhymehealer.

Singfin, his life-partner, began the death-cry. The clan joined her. They released Bloodbull.

Bubbles leaked upward as he drifted downward. The Ravenfin were powerless to alter his death and descent to the Abyss, where life would spring anew. *Beautiful* was the last word a dying orca said.

After the death-cry faded, the Ravenfin began their tributes to Bloodbull.

Singfin told the history of his life and all the names he had earned.

As a calf, he was first named Sillyflipper, for having one pec-fin shorter than the other. Later, he became a strong young adult named Flukekiller, who could stun a hundred fish with a single tail swipe. After fathering two children, Soulnurture and Brokenfin, he aged into the battle-scared Bloodbull who'd defended the clan many times. His wounds weeping into the water were legendary.

Mothersong's instincts had warned her that a long trip would risk the most vulnerable of them. The Ravenfin had done their best as a clan to protect and feed the youngest, but there wasn't much to do for the eldest. All orcas died. One day it would be her turn to feed the Abyss.

The wish, challenge, and ultimate blessing, she reflected, was to have pursued a life enriching the clan. Some were born fast and strong. Others could scan a long distance. But the clan's nucleus rested on its ability to grow through change. The birth and development of new lives meant their survival.

Times of famine and stress halted pregnancy, and Mothersong hoped she could guide them all to fertile fields. There were old stories about clans who'd ceased to exist, and these tales terrified her more than anything else in the world.

39

At just after 0300, Shin rose to the surface. The central part of Korsakov harbor was a good two to three kilometers away, and the water droplets on his mask refracted its distant industrial lights. His immediate surroundings, by contrast, were dimly lit. But Shin was right where he wanted to be.

He slid up his mask and hung stationary in the soft swells. Stars and a quarter-moon were bright in the cloudless indigo sky.

Shin stared at the bow of the *Zheng Yi* a hundred meters away.

A handful of its windows were lit pale yellow, and a soft blue glow emanated from the wheelhouse, but he could detect no movement. He held his breath and listened. An auxiliary engine growled deep within the vessel, but Shin heard no voices or footfalls.

Getting here had been easy — at least, the last kilometer of swimming had been. The preceding part, the half-day journey from Urup to Korsakov in the submersible iron coffin, was something he never wished to repeat again.

Shin had taken to marking the interior of the sub's hull with a black Sharpie, like a prisoner in solitary confinement, using a short vertical line for every half-hour that passed. Despite being state of the art, a sub remained a prison.

Because the mission was now a *go*, he'd been in constant communication with someone (not Mariko) at Dolphin Base the entire trip. At one point, after maneuvering to avoid a tugboat-towed barge, the chattering in his headset had driven him batty, and he'd told them all to *STFU*. Later, after he'd avoided a Russian Coast Guard light patrol, Shin had lost the last remaining gossamer thread of composure and begun raving about *armchair quarterbacks* to Dolphin Command until Mariko had come on the mic and calmed him down.

The one upside to all the stress of the past week was that he'd burned through enough calories to wiggle out of the SEAL-tube in the modern rebreather kit without difficulty. Afterward, the exertion of the swim to the *Zheng Yi* with his gear had restored several levels of sanity that he'd lost within the claustrophobic sub.

Shin pushed all of that from his mind, and stared at his target as he floated in the cold harbor.

The *Zheng Yi* was moored at an L-shaped pier. Just beyond the dock complex, sat a three-story concrete building exhibiting the unbridled architectural charm of a Soviet brick factory.

Both the length of the pier and the perimeter of the building were lit with dim incandescent bulbs, spaced at distances so far apart that twenty Shins could have stood in the shadows between them and been invisible.

Were it not for the *Zheng Yi* docked there, he would have assumed it was an abandoned fishery. However, the cover and concealment seemed perfect for pirates, and he knew there must be fuel lines and power conduits. And guards, though he couldn't see any.

Shin picked a solitary light on the bow of the *Zheng Yi*. He replaced his mask and submerged to a shallow depth. He swam toward the amber glare rippling the surface above until he located the anchor chain, and then surfaced.

As he sculled toward the bow in the darkness, he retrieved the limpet mine from his belly pouch. Dropping below and feeling his way along the hull, he hovered and eased the mine toward the steel. The magnets pulled, and he heard a thunk as it attached itself to the hull.

First task over, he thought, and resurfaced.

From this point onward, if he failed — if he was shot, killed, or captured — a shaped charge of TNT would punch a piano-sized hole in the *Zheng Yi*'s hull. The agency could detonate it any time they wished. The limpet mine also had an anti-removal device and would explode if anyone tried coaxing it away from the hull — a bit like an anti-theft tag in a retail store but with more severe consequences.

Shin swam sidestroke toward the stern. He kept his gaze locked on the gunwale above, alert for the presence of crew. As he neared the widest part of the ship, he stopped and stared at a group of small boats moored in the darkness along the *Zheng Yi*'s stern.

What the hell?

These were the light speedboats used to herd and corral orcas. But they should be stowed on the aft deck if the *Zheng Yi* was headed back to open water and then Shanghai with captives. The presence of the craft lent him hope that they'd been unsuccessful.

Regardless, his goals were set: search the *Zheng Yi*, free any hostages.

He glided toward the first of the boats, an inflatable with twin outboard motors. There were no lights, and it was unoccupied — as was the next boat.

Passing through the cluster of watercraft, ranging from RIBs to fiberglass-hulled speedboats to jet-skis, all bobbing in the gentle swells, he continued toward the stern of the *Zheng Yi*.

Shin removed his fins and mask and stowed them in the belly pouch the mine had occupied. The stern ramp was in the up (closed) position, so he ducked under a series of mooring lines until he arrived at the aft starboard ladder. He grabbed the first rung and began climbing upward. At the top, he loosened the buckle securing the silenced pistol in his shoulder holster. He peered over the lip. The railed walkway was empty.

Shin eased himself over the edge and stepped down. His rubber booties were both grippy and silent.

He paused to listen and scan, but detected nothing other than the hum of the auxiliary power unit. Shin had memorized the blueprints, but being onboard an actual ship was always a different kettle of fish. Crouching down, he extracted the crossbow from its watertight container, pulled the wire back until the trigger locked it in place, and loaded a pufferfish dart.

The aft deck below, rimmed with safety lights, was deep, expansive, and empty. There was no cargo, only coils of rope, tarps, chock-blocks, and tie-down hooks. It was like peering into an enormous, empty orchestra pit — but in this instance, all the major instruments were bobbing just outside.

Huge hydraulic pistons flanked the stern ramp. The metal door was five meters across and could swing down beyond 90 degrees, like a drawbridge, to open up the back end of the ship.

Towering above it all, rising taller than the wheelhouse near the bow, was a rectangular boom. It arched across the aft deck like a support tower on a suspension bridge, and provided an important arm to the structural triangle that enabled a big commercial stern trawler to drag a conical fishnet the size of the Eiffel Tower behind it.

A pivoting crane atop the boom aided in moving cargo, as well as speedboat deployment and extraction.

Shin clenched his jaw and padded along the corridor. The staircase down to the aft deck was just ahead.

He descended and found that the wide deck-hatches leading to the hold below were closed. Any hostages would be down there.

Shin stalked toward a watertight door, opened it, and crept down the ladder steps, crossbow in hand. With each step downward, the thrum of the auxiliary engine grew louder.

He heard a voice and froze. Someone was singing in Chinese.

Shin knew little Mandarin, but he was certain the singer was drunk.

He stepped off the end of the ladder and crept toward the sound. The corridor he occupied was on the port side of the ship and its gentle curve matched the hull, to which it abutted. Electrical conduits ran overhead, and several vertical pipes passed through the floor and ceiling. Ahead, there should be another set of ladder steps which would take him down to the storage hold and engineering.

Despite the acuity of Shin's hearing, the echoes and hum in the passageway made it difficult to discern the proximity or location of the drunk warbler. He could be just around the next set of pipes, or within a hatchway hidden by the curve of the corridor, or maybe down in the storage hold.

Shin held the crossbow at the ready, and stepped forward.

Seeing a black wool cap rising from the decking at the end of the corridor, Shin ducked behind a thick vertical pipe. He waited for the crewman to finish ascending the ladder, then leaned out, lined up the shot three meters away, and pulled the trigger.

The twang of the crossbow was followed by a slap as the dart hit the crewman on the chest of his dirty-blue coveralls.

The man's eyes rounded in surprise. He bellowed a stream of Mandarin curses loud enough to wake the dead.

Shit!

The yelling crewman took two steps toward Shin, and raised a fist—

—and then spun around, and retreated back the way he had come, still shouting.

Shin pursued.

The crewman vanished down the ladder.

The shouting stopped. Shin realized he must have escaped. The ship's alarm would erupt at any second.

He arrived at the top of the ladder — and found the crewman immobile on the decking below.

Shin descended and knelt next to the crewman. His breathing was ragged, he reeked of alcohol, and there was a fair amount of blood welling up from a deep head wound.

It didn't look like he'd be getting up any time soon, if ever. Whether he'd stumbled and fallen from tetrodotoxin, alcohol, or both, was anyone's guess.

What was known was that the crewman had made a shit-ton of noise, and that anyone on the ship not deaf or wearing hearing-protection in engineering had been alerted. It was also apparent that the toxin darts he'd created didn't work like they did in movies featuring spies or blowpipe-toting aborigines.

Shin hadn't expected his target to collapse instantaneously — though that would've been nice — but he also hadn't imagined that there'd be a minute of the man screaming like a banshee. Maybe a couple of silenced pistol shots would've been better.

So much for your ideals of non-lethality, harped a cynical voice in his mind.

He rose and listened for footfalls. Both the passageway and deck above remained silent.

The crew must be on shore leave, he thought. *And have probably drained Korsakov of a substantial quantity of its vodka stock.*

He checked his watch: 0322. He needed to be off the ship and in the water before dawn.

Shin approached the door that led to the storage hold, and eased it open. The dark space smelled of diesel and fish. In the dim glow of the emergency exit lights, he found the light panel. He withdrew his pistol before flipping on the toggle switches.

Fluorescent lights some eight meters above flickered and lit.

In the center of the hold was a rectangular metal container, roughly five meters in length and three meters in height and width. Bolts and welds were visible at the joints, and a plexiglass cover was clamped to the top. A step ladder was perched at one end.

As Shin approached it, he heard a *whoosh* sound of air escaping. He ascended the ladder, first seeing the black tip of a dorsal fin, and then the white saddle patch on the back of a young orca.

The cruelty robbed him of breath, as if he'd been punched in the gut. *How could anyone do this to a sentient creature!*

The killer whale was a calf, and must be frightened near to death at being imprisoned in a tank only half-full of water, separated from its mother and family.

Shin's blast-furnace of anger kicked in. He was going to hunt down every single one of the torturers on this ship — and he hoped that each of them screamed as much as the first one he'd shot. After he'd rendered them all inert, he'd return here and set the poor creature loose into the harbor.

He evaluated the prison. There were large eye hooks at each corner of the tank: the crane on the boom high above the hold was how they'd lowered it down here. At sea, with the smaller boats, they'd probably manhandled the orca into the prison tank with slings under its torso, then pulled up alongside the *Zheng Yi* where the crane had taken over.

If Shin could raise, pivot, and then lower the prison (minus the plexiglass top) into the sea, the orca would be free to swim away. But before he did anything else, he wanted to let the hostage know that he or she was about to be rescued.

He undid the clamps securing the plexiglass top, and grunted and heaved until it teetered on the edge and fell to the deck with a loud thud. He paused for a count of thirty to listen for sounds of the crew.

Hearing nothing, he climbed back up the ladder and donned his scuba mask. The orca watched him with one eye as he lowered himself slowly into the tank.

Stroking its head, Shin submersed himself. Though young, the orca was over ten feet long and must weigh a thousand pounds. If it spooked and thrashed, Shin would be crushed.

But other than the one eye blinking as it watched him, the orca remained motionless. Shin put his head under the surface and said, "I am Shin. I will set you free."

"Help me!" cried the young killer whale with such force that it felt as if a hundred hammers had struck Shin's body. The terror in its voice reverberated in the marrow of his bones, and he wanted to scream.

"I will free you," repeated Shin. "But you must remain still. What is your name?"

"Piper," said the orca, and Shin realized from the vocal tone that it was a female calf. "Where is Mother and friends?"

"I will set you free, soon," said Shin. "But you must stay still, Piper. As still as if you are sleeping. I will return."

Shin was shaking as he left the tank. He removed his mask and his tears joined the wash of the tank's salt water streaming down his face.

He crossed the hold to the control panel, and located the switch for the huge overhead deck hatches. After several unsuccessful attempts to get them to open, he figured out that the panel was locked.

None of the controls for the big hydraulic gear worked. From his studies of the ship's systems, Shin knew the controls wouldn't function until unlocked by the bridge and engineering. Known as an *idiot lockout*, it prevented the inadvertent use of heavy equipment at inopportune times. Other than lighting, the entire aft deck was offline.

But to rescue Piper, Shin would need to open the hatches, and then use the crane high above to haul up the tank.

He crossed the hold toward the exit. "Time to help a few assholes overboard," he muttered as he loaded a dart into the crossbow. "Engineering first, and then the wheelhouse."

THE ENGINEERING DECK was so loud that the crewman in the oil-stained coveralls who was bent over a pump, tugging at it with a large spanner wrench, didn't hear him enter. In other circumstances Shin would have felt guilty about shooting a man in the back.

The crossbow vibrated in his hand, and the dart hit the engineer between the shoulder blades. Shin's target dropped the wrench and he twisted his arm up behind his back in an attempt to reach whatever had stung him.

He rose and spun toward Shin, his mouth wide open, apparently screaming but Shin couldn't hear a word amid the ear-piercing cacophony of the machinery.

The man's eyes locked on Shin. He took two steps — and then sank to his knees. The engineer struggled, tried to stand again, then fell over face first.

Shin's hands shook and his heart pounded as he bent over to examine the engineer. The man's chest rose and fell, but he seemed unconscious. Shin dug his elbow into the man's ribs to see if pain would rouse him, but it didn't.

He found the switches for the hydraulics to the aft-deck, and turned them to the *on* position. Red indicator lights showed the bridge command circuits' lockout was still active.

The wheelhouse was his next destination.

He ran up the stairwell to the deck above, and stopped. Anger had flooded his veins with adrenaline and unless he slowed down, he risked blundering into a situation that would get him shot. He'd been lucky so far, but sooner or later his luck was bound to run out. If he encountered a guard wearing body armor, his darts wouldn't do crap. Only a head shot with his pistol would work.

And there was at least one guy with a high-powered rifle, though Shin had no idea if the sniper was currently aboard or drinking ashore. If he had the chance, Shin would settle the score, but his focus was on freeing Piper. If he failed, the Japanese would blow up the ship, and the terrified calf would die.

When his heart had stopped trying to jackhammer through his chest, Shin resumed his march upward.

Three decks higher, he mounted the final staircase to the wheelhouse.

A blue glow radiated from the small round window in the door. Shin approached it by hugging the stairwell wall, out of sight of whoever might be within. He was certain there must be someone minding the ship.

He focused on his tactics: stealth in, incapacitate those inside, and free the controls for the aft deck.

Shin turned the latch, and eased the door open.

Head on a swivel, he crept onto the bridge — then halted.

Two meters away, a tall, fat man wearing blue coveralls with epaulets on the shoulders faced Shin. He had a gun in his hand.

Shin raised his hands. The crossbow clattered to the deck. The dart fell out, and the weapon thrummed harmlessly.

"And your pistol," said the man. "Slowly!"

Shin carefully extracted his pistol with his fingertips, and set it down.

Shit, thought Shin. His gaze flickered across the bridge, searching for a way out of his predicament. It didn't look good.

40

Mothersong's scalp tingled. The waters had turned colder, and Spyhopper had returned with the news that he'd sighted a long row of white-teeth on the land far in the distance.

It was the final whale-marker of their journey — but it was still a day away.

The ocean thundered, and the Ravenfin halted.

Mothersong scanned, and she sensed the echo-probes of those around her as they tried to ascertain the potential threat to the clan. Was it a surface-behemoth?

The waters abruptly warmed. Confused, Mothersong directed her focus straight down.

A wall — an immense mass of hot-bubbles — streamed upward.

From my dreams, she realized. *Warnings from the deep-whales.*

"Scatter!" Mothersong cried.

The seafloor had split and fire scorched within its cracks. The Ravenfin fled, swimming hard to avoid the burbling eruption below.

It boiled the surface as they dispersed.

Dead fish rose. But in their desire to escape the eye-burning sulfurous waters, no orca had an appetite.

"This way," clicked Mothersong. "Spyhopper has seen our goal."

The Ravenfin gathered.

They followed her, and she led them away from the eruption and into colder waters. The call of Mothersong the Matriarch had never steered them wrong, and she hoped to continue that for as long as she breathed on this ocean planet.

41

"Your only chance at living," said the captain in Chinese-accented English, "is to tell me who you work for. Do you understand?"

Shin kept his hands raised and nodded. "Yes," he said.

"You're clearly Japanese," said the captain.

Shin shrugged but said nothing.

The captain cocked the revolver's hammer and took a step. From a meter away, the gun was aimed at Shin's chest.

Shin kept quiet. His thoughts raced for a way out.

Stepping closer, the captain pressed the muzzle of the barrel against Shin's forehead. "What do you have to say?" he demanded. "Talk."

It was a foolish move; the captain was too close. Between stimulus and response, human reaction consumed eleven-hundredths of a second. By the time the captain registered Shin's motion, it would be too late.

Shin smiled.

"Grinning like a Japanese fool—"

Shin dropped into a squat.

The gun fired into the space where his head had been. Shin grasped the weapon with both hands.

The captain pulled the trigger again, and the gun fired, but Shin held the barrel above his head as he stood. He swung the gun around and down, keeping it pointed away from his body, and put his weight onto it. He rolled his hips, twisting the gun and the captain's hand.

The pistol fired a third time. Shin felt the bones in the captain's trigger finger snap as he rotated the weapon 180 degrees.

The captain screamed. Shin torqued the leverage further, and more bones fractured.

Shin yanked the weapon free.

The captain collapsed onto the deck. "Get away from me!" he shouted. "What do you want?" Holding his shattered right hand, he slid backward toward the consoles.

Shin glanced at the array of screens. All high-tech, military-grade displays.

"Whatever you want," said the captain. He twitched his lips into a trembling attempt at a smile. "Tell me. Yes?"

Shin picked up his crossbow. He pulled the wire back until it locked into place.

"There's gold. You can have it all," said the captain. "It's in the safe. I will open."

"Have you ever heard a kidnapped child scream for their mother?" said Shin as he loaded a toxin dart.

The captain shook his head.

Whether or not the man truly understood the question, Shin didn't know.

He thwacked a dart into the captain's calf, wanting him to feel the burn of the painful sting while Shin gathered more information about *Zheng Yi*'s owners. The large captain was the mass of the first two crewmen combined. A leg shot should have made him scream and talk. But it didn't.

The captain convulsed and foamed at the mouth. Twenty seconds later, he stopped breathing entirely.

Damnit, thought Shin. The quality control on the tetrodotoxin needed work.

Remembering the slim camera the agency had given him, he extracted it and began snapping photos. He darted around the bridge to study the various displays and their status: helm, comms, sonar, engine room, navigation, and aft deck.

Shin evaluated the console commanding the aft deck. Grayed-out pictographs occupied the bulk of the display and depicted the aft ramp, crane, winch, tensions, and hydraulic pressures. A large padlock icon dominated the top right of the screen.

Unlocking everything was as simple as holding his finger on the padlock and waiting ten seconds until the console beeped and the icon changed.

He stepped over the dead captain, then glanced at his watch: 0419.

Dawn would arrive soon and, with it, some of the shore crew. The window of time to free Piper was expiring.

Shin loaded another dart. In vindictiveness, he shot the dead captain again.

He left the bridge, and sprinted downward. He chucked his crossbow into the harbor, but kept his Hush Puppy in hand, aimed ahead.

When he arrived down in the hold, Shin went to the control panel and cycled open the hatches. He trotted over to the tank. He laid a reassuring hand on Piper, who blinked and watched Shin as he attached hoist chains to the corners of the tank.

After ascending from the hold, Shin scurried up a ladder to the top of the high aft-boom, and then scampered across it. He entered the control cubby of the crane, and studied the controls.

Grasping a joystick, he adjusted the crane to position the load-block directly over the now open hold hatches. He spooled out cable until the block rested on the bottom, next to the tank.

Shin raced back down, and connected the block to the hoist chains on the corners of the tank. Then he climbed back up to the crane.

His muscles burned as he entered the control cubby, and his heart pounded. Shaking hands reached for the controls—

He halted, closed his eyes, and recited a mantra to center his focus, blunt the adrenaline, and channel the steady aim of a marksman.

Shin looked down onto the tank as he reeled in the slack at a snail's pace. When the engine groaned, and the load moment indicator display spiked, he knew the crane held the full weight of the tank.

The hydraulics hummed as Shin raised the load. He glanced at the tank emerging from the hold, and continued cranking it upward until it was high enough to clear the gunwales.

He needed to rotate the crane's boom to position the tank outside of the ship and above the waters of the harbor, but there was a problem. There was no ground crew with tag lines to prevent the load from swaying.

An unstable load could smash into the ship, or break the crane, and would kill the hostage he was trying to rescue.

Shin held his breath, and applied light finger pressure to the joystick. The boom pivoted and, after a second's delay, the tank began its horizontal journey toward the edge of the ship.

It began to rotate and spin around the block, but Shin dared not stop.

The weight must be free and clear of the ship before he halted the crane's rotation. The built up momentum in the tank would make it oscillate like a pendulum after the boom stopped moving. Shin wanted it over the water when that happened.

This was a one-pass attempt. Shin kept the crane's rotation to a crawl, aiming for a gentle swing of the forty-five-ton tank when it stopped — and not a wrecking ball. Killing Piper because he was in a rush would be tragic.

When the tank was outside the hull and directly over the water, Shin eased off the joystick; the crane's rotation stopped. The tank swung out and then headed back toward the ship, but the oscillations were as calm as Shin had hoped for.

After two swings, the pendulum dampened, and he lowered the prison-tank. A few seconds later, he lost visual contact as it disappeared behind the gunwales. He sighed, grateful that despite the urgency to free Piper, he'd paused to consider physics.

Shin slowed the descent and watched the LMI screen.

When the value plunged to zero, he knew the tank was in the water.

Shin spooled out ten more meters of cable.

A sharp metallic clang reverberated in the crane's cab, followed by another. He scanned the readouts on the dashboard to see what was wrong, but they were all green. Had a cable snapped? The tank should be sinking.

A titanium spark flashed and cracked on the metal boom, a meter from his face.

Crap! Someone's shooting at me.

The crane's displays went dead.

Shin crouched low and tried to determine the direction of the incoming rounds. Shore-leave was over, and the whale kidnappers were pissed off.

He crawled out of the cab, and scooted down the ladder.

Though he was blocked from the gunman's line of sight by the structure of the aft boom, he was sure that wasn't the only threat to worry about.

Abandon ship ASAP, he thought, *and check on Piper.*

As Shin stepped down onto the aft deck, automatic gunfire burst from the shadows. He dove behind a winch.

The firing continued. Flashes and sparks kicked off the deck and the winch housing.

Though Shin hadn't been on the receiving end of AK-47 rounds in four decades, the sound of the weapon was unmistakable. He'd always had a healthy respect for the Kalashnikov, because it could take a limb off. However, this second gunman shooting at him had attended the spray-and-pray school, and kept the trigger down despite the gun bucking all over the place.

Bullets and ricochets clanged, and sparks danced.

The muzzle flashes in the darkness marked the man's location as clearly as a casino sign in Las Vegas. Shin cradled his Hush Puppy, and waited.

The AK went silent. Shin heard the clink of the banana clip hitting the deck.

He rose, braced his pistol, and from ten meters away put a silent round through the man's forehead.

Though he wanted to hunt down and kill every one of these bastards — especially the sniper — it was time to go.

Shin grabbed a coil of rope. He tied off one end to the winch housing, then looped a section around his waist. He ran up the stairs to the aft deck walkway.

A shot rang as he leapt off the ship.

The rope dug into his waist and swung Shin back toward the hull. He slammed into it, and lost his breath.

After he had recovered, Shin lowered himself toward the water. His thigh burned; he looked down to find shredded neoprene. He'd been hit.

Shin uncoiled the rope from his waist and dropped into the harbor. The saltwater stung his wound like a thousand needles.

Five meters away, the crane's cable snaked into the water. He needed to be certain that Piper had escaped, and wasn't tangled up and drowning.

Shin applied his mask, connected the rebreather, and sank below the surface.

Grimacing in pain, he swam toward the cable attached to Piper's tank below. He pulled himself downward, and called out, "Piper! Are you free?"

When he arrived at the prison tank, Shin found it empty.

"Piper," he called again. "Piper."

A zipping sound interrupted his search. Shin glanced up to see bullets streaking into the water. He sank further, interposing the tank between himself and the shooters. The AK rounds lost energy rapidly underwater, turning inert within a meter, but Shin knew these assholes had grenades and would probably soon begin dropping them. It was how they drove off or stunned orcas.

He was likely invisible to those on the railing above, but wanting to take no chances, he dove deeper. He put on his right fin, then stifled a scream as he secured the left.

Using his good leg, Shin powered deeper and then angled toward the stern of the ship, where all the powerboats were clustered.

A blast wave ripped through the water, but he was far enough away that the grenade did little more than create a ringing in his ears.

The rebreather left no bubble trail, and it would be hard for the on-deck gunners to trace his path under the water. He circled behind the stern and the moored boats. Even if the crew figured out where he was, they wouldn't drop grenades onto their own speedboats (and gasoline).

Upon reaching a boat far astern, Shin hauled himself over the edge and crawled into the middle of the 20-foot craft. He held his breath, and listened to the shouts aboard the *Zheng Yi*. Boots thundered along the gangway.

More angry yells, futile grenades, and gunfire were cast into the water.

Shin withdrew his makiri and cut the lines mooring the speedboat. A light wind eased him away from the other boats and out into the harbor.

He huddled down and inspected his leg wound.

It was ugly.

There was no way he'd be able to swim back to where the *Orcas' Hammer* was hidden. The brisk flow of crimson welling from the wetsuit meant his wound needed immediate attention.

Shin scoured the storage compartments of the drifting boat, and found a rag and a roll of duct tape. He grimaced as he fashioned a pressure-dressing and rolled layers of tape around his thigh.

The gunfire from the *Zheng Yi* stopped. Commands were yelled.

From a hundred meters away, Shin heard the deep rumble of her engines. Dead captain be damned, the *Zheng Yi* was preparing to steam out of port.

He wished he could've seen the faces of the crewmen when they'd discovered that the entire prison tank had been spirited away, along with the captive. Shin lamented that he hadn't been able to kill more of the crew before going overboard.

The Japanese would, at some point, detonate the mine stuck on the hull. The game plan called for the *Zheng Yi* to be sunk in waters which favored the recovery of the ship's safe whilst covering the area with dummy Soviet-era naval mines.

But Shin's immediate problem was that the *Zheng Yi* had become a platform for a lot of angry people with guns. Plan A had crapped out.

Searchlights, bow and stern, lit up aboard the *Zheng Yi* and played across the harbor. Outboard engines amongst the small boat flotilla coughed to life. Sirens blared.

He'd kicked the hornets' nest for sure. The queen and her hive were coming for him and the lost prey. Shin hoped Piper had gotten a good head start and was hauling it out of the harbor, back to her pod.

A searchlight beam flicked over his boat and moved on.

Ten seconds later, it doubled back and hovered. Shin smiled and waved, hoping against the odds that they would take him for one of their own.

The muzzle flash and bark of a Kalashnikov punctured his fantasy like a pit-bull on a rag doll. Shin cranked the engine and jetted it out of there.

More automatic-weapon fire and roaring engines followed him. The chase was on.

Another searchlight joined in. Shin was transfixed by the intersecting beams.

His stolen boat had some serious horsepower, so he kept his head down and the throttle wide open.

The lights of Korsakov harbor receded, and he lost one of the searchlights.

His craft hammered the crests of the shallow waves, jarring his fillings. If he could make it to the edge of the harbor, he could duct tape the throttle and wheel, and ditch himself overboard. He had enough oxygen left in the tank to dive, and he'd jumped out of plenty of fast-rides in his SEAL days. Success, and future attempts, existed in the proper body roll.

These assholes can chase an empty speedboat all the way to freaking Hokkaido.

A red dawn stroked angry black clouds to his port. He steered toward the gathering storm. He imagined the *Zheng Yi* was in full-fledged retreat, and would provide good hunting for Mariko. All in all, it was looking promising...

Incoming rounds punched holes in the fiberglass bow, ten feet in front of Shin's head. He flinched, and flipped a glance over his shoulder.

Despite pegging the twin outboards to their maximum, he'd failed to escape the two chasers. One of them bore a spotlight wielded by a magician; no matter what Shin did to evade it, the beam always came back.

"Just a little further, baby," he said to his stolen craft. He pulled her hard to starboard, then over the next swell, dodged to port.

Shin shot a glance over his shoulder.

He'd lost the searchlight again — but this game of hide and seek couldn't go on for much longer. The pursuing craft had the edge in both speed and size. The rising wind from the storm brought chop, and conferred further advantage to the larger boats behind him. He was running out of room to pull off the invisible bailout trick.

He turned to look—

—and was flung forward, hard against the wheel, as his boat plowed into a wave.

Recovering, Shin spun the wheel, while keeping the throttle full on.

A blast from behind shook him. His stolen ride slowed; one of the engines was on fire.

Game over, he thought, and prepared to bail.

A bright orange flame shot from the magician's boat, and Shin leapt overboard as a rocket-propelled grenade streaked in.

42

The cries were faint.

Mothersong couldn't tell the distance, but as they grew louder, she knew she was closing in. And it was the unmistakable call of a calf for its mother.

"Do you hear?" said Boomer.

"Yes," answered Mothersong. "Ahead, I think."

She picked up her pace, and the clan followed and scanned to try to locate the young one. Jumper and Spyhopper went airborne to see what could be seen above the water.

Mothersong called out, "We hear you and are coming."

A dozen heartbeats later, she echo-located the young orca, and changed her direction to swim toward it.

"Don't be frightened, young one," she said. "I am Mothersong."

"Help me. Chased."

Though its dialect was strange, the female calf's call of distress was recognizable by any mother. She was terrified and fleeing from whatever was behind her. As the Ravenfin closed in, Mothersong broadcast reassuring sounds to coax the young one over.

When they did meet up, the frightened calf babbled in such a torrent that it was difficult for Mothersong to understand what she was saying. The clan gathered and the security of their presence calmed the calf.

"What is your name?" asked Mothersong.

"Piper," said the calf.

"Know that you are not alone, Piper," said Mothersong. "We will protect you. Tell me what happened."

Piper whimpered, slid closer to Mothersong, and began telling her tale.

As the edge of terror receded from the calf's voice, her words became more intelligible — at least to Mothersong. Later, she would relay the information to her clan, but for now she listened and cooed reassuringly. Melody and Oddpatches came closer and echoed her soothing noises, welcoming the calf to the Ravenfin.

The more Mothersong listened to the calf's words, the angrier she became. Piper had been beaten during her capture, two orcas in her clan had been severely injured — perhaps killed — trying to protect her, and she didn't know where her family was.

Mothersong's heart wanted to wail, but she held silent.

"Surface-dweller. Prison," said Piper. "Shin. Freed me."

Mothersong flinched and she heard gasps amongst the clan: "Shin!"

It was a word that spanned dialects and species. *Shin is here!*

Mothersong was so invigorated by the news, she wanted to play *skytime* with the adolescents. They'd located Shin, but the waters were troubled. She stilled the clan to silence, and focused on each and every syllable that Piper uttered: "Danger. Fast. Thunder. Nets. Pain."

The calf didn't possess sufficient language to express words for the surface-dweller's vessels or weapons, but when she mimicked their noises, Mothersong experienced the painful memories of her own youth as viscerally as if they'd happened yesterday.

Shin has freed Piper, but where is he? she wondered.

"We should find Shin," Mothersong announced to the Ravenfin. "But we must be wary of the orca-hunters."

She called for a triangle formation, with Pouncer and Sounder leading the wings, and Spyhopper in the center-front. Calves were to be protected in the center, and Mothersong said, "Piper, stay by me."

She heard a sound. She ordered the clan to silence.

With concentration, Mothersong detected a faint keening. Far off, but growing louder.

Voices.

"Incoming," she whispered. Then she commanded, "See!"

The seventeen orcas forming the wings and center-front opened up their scans to interrogate the approaching creatures.

Orca-kin, realized Mothersong from the echo signatures. At least forty that she could perceive.

The foreign clan scanned the Ravenfin.

In Mothersong's waters, clans avoided each other. Beyond the survival concerns of direct competition for fish schools lurked a darker prospect for conflict. There were old stories of terrible battles between clans, sometimes driven by bulls who thought with their penises. Aggression could be difficult to manage, and to avoid the prospect of bloodshed, wise cows and matriarchs coaxed their clans in opposite directions.

But this group was charging right in.

Mothersong said, "No fighting!"

Moments later, the two clans collided.

Amidst the orcas swirling in confusion and anger, Mothersong asserted herself. "Stop!" she commanded in the root-tongue.

"Stop!" boomed a voice in the foreign clan, also speaking in root.

To Mothersong's relief, the posturing and threatening behavior on both sides ceased.

Piper bolted from her side, calling, "Momma,"and darted toward a cow in the other clan.

Judging by the call-and-response, it was indeed her mother.

Piper arrived at her mother's side and began to recite everything that had happened since they'd been separated. Although Mothersong knew the Ravenfin could follow few of the words, the emotion was as clear as a cold sea. A mother and child reunion is a powerful thing to witness.

Both clans hung motionless, listening.

At the end of the story, Piper started again — as all calves were trained to do, until an adult told them to stop. There was talk amongst the other clan, and more words popped into Mothersong's understanding of their language.

"I am Tidematron," said a voice, "of the Whiteteeth."

"And I am Mothersong of the Ravenfin."

"You can understand me?"

"Yes."

"How? You are not of the Whiteteeth," said Tidematron. "Clans can't communicate. We are the only clan in our sea, but I believe the stories of my elders."

Mothersong clicked her agreement, and said, "Your elders are wise and true. There are three other clans in our sea, and we share just a few words in the root-tongue. But I have been granted the gift of a hundred years of listening and learning."

"That is noble," said Tidematron, and clicked her respect. "Please help me understand calf Piper's words, because they make no sense. She was freed by a surface-dweller named Shin, who speaks our tongue?"

"Shin hunts those who hunt you," said Mothersong. "He is the first of their kind to speak— and the Ravenfin trust him."

"You know this *Shin*?"

"Yes," said Mothersong. "He is from the far side of the ocean — the same sea that we of the Ravenfin came from."

"Why did you travel here?" asked Tidematron. "The fish are bountiful, but we are hunted. I've been matriarch for seven years, and in that time ten of our youth have been captured by surface-dwellers."

"The Ravenfin are hungry and each year we number fewer," said Mothersong. "The deep-whales told of these waters, and your troubles. Shin promised to stop the hunting. And he is here."

"Piper is the first of the ten to return to us," said Tidematron. "We trust Shin. He is now protected by the Whiteteeth." Every orca in her clan repeated the guardian phrase.

Their ways are ours, thought Mothersong.

"We will show the Ravenfin the hunting-fields in our sea," said Tidematron. "There is much to—"

The sea rumbled.

A series of shock waves passed through the orcas, the tempo quickening with each pulse.

Piper whimpered, "They're coming."

"Or the hunters are attacking Shin," said Mothersong. She scanned and counted. Including the Whiteteeth, there were over eighty orcas. If the clans combined, they could leave a small group to protect the young, and send a mighty force to investigate the disturbance that was coming ever closer.

43

The bright flash above the water, and the blast of sound below, certified the conflagration of Shin's stolen boat.

The engines of approaching speedboats thundered in his ears. Shin secured his mask, connected the rebreather, and turned on the air flow. He cleared the water from the mask, adjusted his ballast, and sank.

The engines throttled back, and the boats circled overhead.

The glow from Shin's burning boat faded as he went deeper. He calmed his breathing, and tried to ignore the wound in his thigh, burning like fire in the saltwater.

He knew the crew had fish-scanners, which were used to hunt cetaceans, but Shin prayed they were too consumed with trying to find his body amongst the wreckage above — or too pissed-off in general — to think about using them here.

Shin remained motionless and drifted down into the darkness.

Suddenly, a blast tumbled him in the water, and he was as helpless as a wiped-out surfer in the Banzai Pipeline. Deaf, and unable to tell up from down, he struggled.

Fear of drowning in the darkness began nibbling the edges of his mind like rats.

"Stop it," Shin screamed as the panic possessed him. "Stop. Help me!"

Another explosion rocked him.

As Shin hung limp in the water, unable to move, his mind registered flickering gray and thunderous ringing.

His world narrowed further to jumbled snatches of sound and vision as his consciousness faded.

"Help me," he gasped.

44

The surface of the water shimmered red with the dawn. Mothersong was one of sixty-three orcas powering toward the booms in the water. The rest hung back to protect the young. She listened as Tidematron described the vessels that had hunted the Whiteteeth. Mothersong formed images in her mind, and relayed the information to the Ravenfin.

Spyhopper breached, and after he splashed back down he said, "I saw seven surface-dweller vessels. One is on fire."

"Got them on scan," said Sounder.

"Almost there," said Boomer.

Pouncer growled in anticipation.

A noise distracted Mothersong.

"Help me," said a faint voice.

Shin!

"War-time," said Boomer. "For Shin!"

The orcas accelerated and Mothersong soon found herself at the rear of the formation. "Tidematron," she said. "I will find Shin. Have your strongest Whiteteeth watch and learn from Boomer and Pouncer. They know ways to hurt the vessels."

"I hear you," said Tidematron. "Let the Abyss claim the surface-dwellers." She called battle plans to her clan and advised them as Mothersong had recommended.

The booms of the surface-dwellers had stopped, and their vessels were moving away slowly.

Pouncer dove and was followed by Boomer and Flukethumper, and over half of the twin-clan formation. The attacking bulls and cows of the Ravenfin began to chant a rhyme steeped in bloodlust.

Mothersong scanned a sinking object.

Shin, she realized, and sped toward him. She called but received no answer.

As she reached his body, the war chant grew louder. The Whiteteeth had joined the chorus.

Shin wasn't moving and blew no bubbles. Pressure squeezed Mothersong's chest as she nudged him. "Please come alive, Shin!"

There was no response.

He is drowned, thought Mothersong, and moaned.

She balanced Shin's tiny form on her head and, just as she'd done moons ago, carried him toward the surface. The maternal instinct to resuscitate a distressed newborn was strong. She refused to give up hope.

Mothersong heard Pouncer and Boomer signal how they would attack, followed by the root-tongue response from the Whiteteeth.

She crested the surface, and lay still. Shin was draped over her head, but thankfully wasn't obstructing her breathing. Mothersong spun her gaze upward, but all she could see of him were his two fake-fins.

Mothersong listened with her head, the most sensitive part of her body. She sensed his breathing, and heartbeat: though it was as rapid and weak as a newborn, he was alive.

Shin stirred.

SHIN WOKE from the drowning dream.

He was face down on a black tube. His eyes told him he was at sea, but he couldn't figure out where or why. Air hissed just in front of his head, and he watched the spray drift in the cold air. *Engineering should look into that leak,* he thought.

He pushed his torso upright with his hands, and let his legs swing down over the tube—

Pain skewered his thigh, jolting him further awake.

He remembered being shot. He studied the silver duct-tape wound around his thigh. Memory blobs began to assemble themselves into a semblance of a picture, and with each heartbeat, the fuzzy Monet painting sharpened in clarity: he'd piloted a midget-sub; fought a battle on a ship (and killed people); freed an orca calf named Piper, then escaped on a stolen boat, which had exploded.

What the hell have I done?

Shin looked down in confusion, and realized he was sitting astride an orca. Upon seeing the white saddle and eye patches, he was startled that he recognized them.

Mothersong?

But it couldn't be her. The matriarch and M-pod lived around Puget Sound. He was in Japan... or Russia.

He'd lost his mask, but maybe he could still communicate.

Shin rolled forward and pressed his head against the sleek black skin. In his loudest voice he said, "Mothersong!"

"Shin, I feared you'd gone to the Abyss," she said, the words vibrating directly into his skull. "Are you hurt?"

"Yes," he answered. "But how... why are you here?"

"It is a long tale. And now is not the time."

He wondered what was going on, and then worried about how the hell he was going to get back to Hokkaido. He'd hidden the sub someplace nearby, but egress in that machine was no longer an option. Shin hoped Mariko and crew were tracking him, because he needed rescue.

A fast moving squall line smothered the dawn like curtains of black felt. Titanium bolts flickered under towering cumulonimbus clouds, and strobed the steely sea.

He didn't know where Mothersong was headed, but his mind begged for a coherent answer to one question — because she shouldn't be in the Sea of Okhotsk.

"Mothersong," he said. "Please tell me why you are here."

"Hush," said Mothersong. She turned 180 degrees. "A battle begins. I must attend to it."

She swam on the surface, plowing through the wind-whipped waves with powerful sweeps of her fluke. Shin slid backward and clutched her dorsal fin to avoid being washed off her back.

Mothersong slowed. Shin spied the running lights of several boats, one hundred meters distant. The same assholes who'd shot at him and dropped grenades. They were headed away, probably retreating back to the *Zheng Yi* after failing to find his body. Shin wondered when Mariko would set off the limpet mine and sink the sucker.

The sky darkened. The storm crashed down with icy rain and hail.

MOTHERSONG FELT Shin's weight shift on her head, as she fluked toward the echoes of the orcas assembling beneath the waves. Though she'd have felt more secure underneath, Mothersong couldn't dive with an injured Shin clinging to her fin.

All she could do was observe and call out the dangers as the two clans fought the surface-dwellers.

She coasted, having placed herself as close as she dared.

The call was given, and the battle began.

One of the Whiteteeth rammed a small vessel from below, dumping it over.

A series of loud pops startled her, and she raised her head.

In the darkness, bright streaks leapt from another vessel. The spectacle brought forth the terror of her youth. It was too late to stop the orca attack, and her chest constricted at the thought. None of the Ravenfin knew the surface-dweller weapons like she.

But the Whiteteeth did. She prayed her clan would learn their avoidance techniques and hide from the surface-dweller weapons — and that both clans would use the tactics that Shin had taught the Ravenfin.

Another vessel was rammed, but did not dump over. She heard the shouts of surface-dwellers: and more weapon-pops.

Mothersong put her head down to scan and listen. The spirited, warring orcas discussed tactics. Thankfully, there were no reports of injuries.

Abruptly, Boomer accelerated upward in a spiral. Faster and faster he went until he breached near a vessel, and she lost contact.

SHIN GASPED as a bright pulse of lightning froze a large orca in the air above one of the RIBs.

From over fifty meters away, Shin heard the crash as it landed on the boat. Humans screamed as the bow and stern lights folded up like a taco. Thunder rumbled over the waves.

The sound of staccato bursts of automatic-weapon fire spun his head; muzzle-flashes from a large craft pierced the gloom. It was the magician's power-boat that Shin hadn't been able to shake, and which had fired the RPG at him. The half-deck yacht was too large for an orca to sink. Though one might damage the rudder, the risk from the propellers and Kalashnikovs was extreme. Shin's gut clenched.

If it weren't for the black tempest, the orcas would be easy targets. He prayed that none had been hurt.

Shin wished he had his sound helmet and could go underwater and scream at the orcas to avoid it and leave the area. Though he didn't know the current location of the *Zheng Yi*, the ship couldn't be far and her demolition was imminent. The orcas needed to be free and clear, away from both the blast radius and the ensuing search and rescue scramble conducted by navies that hated each other.

He bent over to lay his head on Mothersong to communicate his message and its urgency, but a storm powered wave crashed in.

Shin lost his grip. He was almost swept off, but re-grasped her fin.

He choked on the seawater he'd inhaled; then sputtered, gasping for air.

Shin retched, wheezed, and drew in a ragged breath.

AK-47s strafed the sea. He expected to hear the explosions of grenades at any moment.

MOTHERSONG WATCHED two orcas probe the bottom of the largest of the vessels as it moved slowly in a circle. The two left and descended to join twenty Whiteteeth and Ravenfin gathered below.

She listened as the massed group conversed in terse root-speak. After an exchange, they agreed on a plan: *hold, push-roll.*

A dozen kin rose toward the bottom of the vessel, all on one edge. Another group went to the nose — the opposite side from the whirling-blades.

The orcas stayed a body length below the circling vessel, out of sight of the surface-dwellers on top.

As one, they rose and made gentle contact. Flukethumper grasped the *rudder*, as Shin called it, and snapped it off.

The blades roared and screamed, but the vessel was held fast. Fiery streaks leapt from their banging weapons. The orcas fluked hard; each was lifting a great weight.

Mothersong peeked above the surface to see that the vessel had rotated like an adolescent trying to show its belly to the sky.

ENGINE SOUNDS from the magician's yacht surged to a full-throated roar, but to Shin's astonishment the craft remained in place as if stuck on a sandbar. The crew darted about the deck, firing their AKs.

The yacht rolled to starboard. Shin tried to figure out what was happening as the roll increased.

Before he could take his next breath, it hung on the brink, balancing on its side.

Interminable seconds later, the yacht capsized, silencing all the Kalashnikovs on board.

Motion attracted his focus. A third boat exploded from within, and its guns, too, went silent.

At that point, the crewmen of the remaining few speed-craft seemed to have decided that shooting aimlessly into inky waters at fast moving black sea monsters, during a squall, was a fool's errand. They fled the field of battle, seeking safe harbors.

One almost made it.

A GUTTURAL VICTORY CRY SOUNDED. Mothersong scanned.

One of the Whiteteeth grasped a bobbing surface-dweller, dragged it down, and held it until it stopped moving.

Jumper bit the rudder of another, smaller vessel — it roared, sped away, and rammed a companion like a mad bull. There was a bang, and both flared like the sun before dimming to midnight.

Along with the hail, pieces of surface-dweller debris fell from the sky, striking the water around Mothersong. Shin squeezed her chest, and she felt his firm grip on her fin. She hoped he was okay, and rolled her eyes up to look up at him.

The two fake-fins were still there, attached to his legs. He waved an arm, like a crab. He seemed to be trying to communicate something, but she had no idea what it might be.

The last surface-dweller vessel skipped away.

Mothersong heard the clans chanting below. *Pound. Pound.*

She caught movement, and focused her scan on it.

A huge bull from the Whiteteeth streaked upward, at a speed that seemed impossible.

The vessel was almost out of Mothersong's sight, when the bull caught it at a place where the seafloor rose into the shallows. He breached, and came down on the nose of the vessel. In a flash, Mother-song saw the underside before it shattered apart like a crushed shell.

45

Shin shivered due to both the cold, and the display he'd just witnessed. Some twenty-odd men had met a watery grave. But any sense of guilt was absolved by the sober realization that, more than any other deaths he'd ever witnessed, these assholes had deserved it.

And despite their attempts to kill him, it wasn't personal. They should have known right from wrong.

He released his grip on Mothersong's dorsal fin and rolled forward to place his head on hers. Any human who tortured these beautiful, intelligent creatures earned themselves a spot in hell — and the sooner they arrived there the better. That orcas had been responsible for doing so seemed poetic.

"Mothersong," he said. "I freed a calf named Piper. Do you—"

"Piper is safe with her mother and her clan," answered Mothersong. "It is they who joined with the Ravenfin to destroy the surface-dweller vessels. The Whiteteeth have pledged to protect you, Shin. And none of our kin have gone to the Abyss."

The words were difficult to process. Shin's emotions surged and carried him like a raft in white water. He squeezed his eyes shut but was unable to dam the warm tears streaming out.

"Shin?

"Mothersong," he said. "I need to go..." His voice trailed off as his head swum.

"I will carry you to shore," said Mothersong, and turned toward land. "To your kind."

"No, not there," said Shin, looking at Sakhalin Island. *I'll get arrested, and tortured*, he thought. "It's not safe for me."

"Then where? You are hurt. You don't live in the sea, and I can't carry you for the rest of my life."

Despite the cold, and his weakness, and the gunshot wound, Shin chuckled at Mothersong's brutal honesty. He hoped Mariko and crew were still tracking him. 'Take me to Japan,' wasn't a request that Mothersong would understand.

Sunlight filtered through the fleeing clouds; the storm was moving on. Shin shifted his position so that Mothersong could see, and extended his arm to point west. Pain jolted his thigh. "That way," he said, and grimaced.

Mothersong changed her heading and swam in that direction.

The sky brightened further, and the sunlight reflected off the water. Shin noticed that scores of orcas flanked Mothersong. Black dorsal fins pierced the surface like swords as they crested and blew out white mist. The spectacle of his escort made the hairs on Shin's neck tingle. He leaned forward to place his head on Mothersong's and hugged her.

Mothersong slowed, and called, "Yes, Sounder. I see it."

Shin lifted his head. Steaming toward them was the white bow of the *Shikishima*.

He put his head back down to Mothersong's. "Drop me. My people will pick me up," he said, worried that sharp eyes on the cutter had already seen his ride and posse. Thinking of the state of the *Zheng Yi* and the limpet-mine, he added, "Leave this area, and make sure the clans follow. I will return, one day, to find you."

"And I will listen for you," said Mothersong. "Shin of the Ravenfin."

———

THE STORM HAD VANISHED and the bright morning sun sparkled on turquoise waves. Shin limped to the railing, wearing the large coastguard coat a crewman had given him. When he'd learned that Mariko was on board, he'd insisted on being brought up here to see her: two crewmen had obliged and escorted him.

Mariko lowered her binoculars, smiled, and said, "You're just in time." She put the binoculars back up to her eyes.

Shin was handed another pair by a crewman, and he adjusted the optics as he scanned the horizon. "Shit," he said, as he spied the unforgettable black ship.

"Boom," said Mariko.

Shin glanced at her from the corner of his eyes, then returned to studying the *Zheng Yi*. The stern ramp was closed so he couldn't see the aft deck, but he imagined it was a bit roomier without seven of its powerboats.

As he continued to watch, the bow struck a wave and kicked up a plume of white spray — or so Shin thought, until the *crump* of the explosion reached his ears and he realized it was the detonation of the limpet mine and not a wave.

Smoke rose and partially obscured the bow and midships. The *Zheng Yi* slowed, then began to list to starboard.

"Follow me to the bridge," said Mariko. Shin limped after her.

The bridge was warm, well lit, and bustling with activity. Overhead speakers crackled with voices. Shin understood the communications channel was monitoring traffic in the Sōya Strait.

"Mayday, mayday," cried a voice through the static.

"Copy, mayday." said an officer into a mic. "Identify yourself. What is your emergency?"

"This is the *Zheng Yi*... there's been an explosion... we're sinking. Mayday. Mayday."

"This is Japan Coast Guard," replied the officer. "What is your location?"

There followed a crackling string of numbers. The officer scribbled notes on a pad. "Copy," he said. "JCG *Shikishima* is headed to your position. ETA three minutes."

The command for *full ahead* was given. The engines vibrated the deck as the cutter surged forward.

"This is the part where we get to be the white knight," said Mariko, and winked at Shin. "Swoop in, and rescue crewmen from the sea."

An officer, peering through the bridge windows with binoculars, announced, "I count two emergency rafts deployed. Three, now."

The captain of the *Shikishima* turned to look at Mariko, and gestured toward the door with his chin. From the speakers a high-pitched whistle sounded, followed by the call, "General quarters. General quarters. All hands, man your battle stations. Emergency crews prepare for search and rescue." An urgent chime began pulsing.

"Time for us to go below deck," said Mariko. She grasped Shin's arm, placed it around her neck, and helped him limp toward the exit.

The stairs were tricky, but Shin managed to one-leg it down by bracing his weight on Mariko's shoulder.

At the bottom, Mariko glanced at the duct tape wrapped around his thigh. "Let's get you taken care of," she said. "Sick bay is just around the corner."

The general quarters chime continued blaring.

Shin resisted Mariko's gentle pull. He wanted to see what was happening.

The corridor swam and he stumbled.

Shin was picked up and carried.

He landed on a soft surface. A bright light glared into his face, and his beloved wetsuit was sliced open by bandage scissors. Something was jabbed into his arm.

A HAND SQUEEZED his and Shin opened his eyes.

"You're awake, cowboy," said Mariko. "You'll be happy to hear that everything went well."

"Well?" he said. "That's great. So I'm not going to die?"

The corpsman attending him smiled. He pulled the IV from Shin's arm, and applied a bandage. Then he pointed to the large dressing on Shin's thigh, and said, "That will need further attention when we reach shore."

The corpsman bowed to Mariko, and left.

Mariko scowled and said, "To answer your question. Yes, you will die. That will happen to all of us. What I meant was, your wounds will heal and the *Zheng Yi* is no more. The mission was a success."

Shin grinned.

The pain vanished. Between the morphine he'd been given, and the grave truth of what he'd accomplished, Shin found inner peace.

"However," said Mariko, in a stern tone that shattered his meditation. "*You* are now anonymously famous."

"What?"

"Oh, definitely," said Mariko. She paced about the sick bay. "You conducted an operation which will be taught as a warning lesson in espionage schools for decades to come. *Shin's Explosive Spy-Guide on How to Attract Unwanted Attention.* Or perhaps this title: *The Big Bang Theory of Stealth.* Seriously: I warned you. Sentimentality is an emotion that kills. What a disaster I now have to deal with!"

"It's good to see you, too," said Shin.

"I'm grateful you're okay," said Mariko. She planted her fists on her hips. "But I need a plausible explanation for how you destroyed seven power-boats in Russian waters. Our infrared sat picked out a variety of heat signatures, but it makes no sense."

Shin shrugged.

"I vouched for you," said Mariko. "My honor is at stake. A lot of heavy international pressure is cascading in, and I need an answer that I can write into a report."

Shin contemplated his response. The full truth would accomplish nothing, but perhaps half of it would work.

"After I freed the orca calf," he said, "I stole one of *Zheng Yi's* powerboats. The whale hunters figured it out, and a half-dozen boats chased me. As hard as I tried, I couldn't lose the power-yacht on my tail. A squall closed in, and I headed for it.

"Incoming rounds blew up one of my engines. Then the gunman lost control of his weapon and shot up the boat next to him. I thought I was free, but the power-yacht launched an RPG at me and the next thing I saw, after I dove overboard, was two boats colliding.

"A gun battle erupted between the remaining boats — over what, I'm not sure. Perhaps the whale-hunters thought I was still on one of their boats. Anyway, it was a messy shootout. Kalashnikovs were spraying everywhere, and boats were blowing up. I put my mask on and got below the surface. The next thing I know, the *Shikishima* came sailing in."

"I see," said Mariko, staring at him. "That fits some of the satellite thermal imagery. But what about the *shachi*?"

"Hmm?"

"The enormous herd of killer whales nearby, just before we plucked you from the sea. Remember them?"

"Vaguely," said Shin. "I was a little out of it. Legend says they help those in need. You know there's Ainu mythology about an orca-god named Rep-un—"

"Stop!" interrupted Mariko. "I've heard it."

She gripped a pen and scribbled in a notebook. Tendons and veins bulged on her forearms. Shin's acute hearing conveyed to him each of Mariko's pen strokes, and muttered curses.

Abruptly, Mariko snapped the notebook closed.

"Were you able to get the safe?" asked Shin.

"Yes," said Mariko. "Several vessels responded to the Zheng Yi's distress call as she sank. Two patrol boats from the Russian Coast Guard were already in the area hunting for a gang of terrorists." She opened her notebook and flipped to a page, then continued, "According to the news agency TASS, 'terrorists infiltrated peaceful Russian waters and shot-up innocent crabbers, pulling up pots.' Quite the story! If they only knew it was just you, a chestnut mare, and a six-gun." She laughed.

"Huh?"

"Sorry," said Mariko. "I love Westerns. I want to go to Texas one day."

Shin was befuddled, but didn't think it was the morphine.

Mariko cleared her throat. "In any event, the dummy mines our subs released spooked the RCG, and they withdrew. We rescued ten crew members clinging to emergency rafts, and our divers recovered the contents of the ship's safe. Currently, the *Shikishima* is headed back to port. The Russians have claimed jurisdiction and will return with a minesweeper and a salvage team. With such a high-value ship going down, they're scrambling to recover the incriminating evidence onboard as well as the gold — though it's too late, of course.

"We've helicoptered the surviving crew to Kushiro Air Base, where they'll receive medical attention — and a screening for any outstanding international criminal warrants — before being repatriated to China."

"Awesome," said Shin.

He wondered about the sniper that had pegged him. Shin hoped he'd been aboard one of the chasing power-craft the orcas had sunk, and that he would never again trouble these waters. Shin was frustrated by the thought that he hadn't been able to settle the score personally, and would probably never learn whether the man was dead or alive.

AT THE PORT OF KUSHIRO, Shin limped along the gangway to shore. Brilliant sunlight sliced through the lightly misting precipitation. A rainbow glistened in the sky.

Shin watched his footing on the wet gangplank.

Mariko stated she needed to write up her report and hand deliver it to the agency's director. She'd instructed Shin to go to the base hospital, and two JCG seamen hovered at his shoulders to make sure he made it there safely.

When Shin reached the end of the metal walkway, he spotted a large figure draped in a hooded poncho, who dwarfed those around him. The man turned and Shin saw protruding from the hood a long red-beard that glistened in the sunshine.

"Whisky tango foxtrot," exclaimed Shin. "Tyler?"

Tyler pulled his hood back and stormed over. One of Shin's escorts stepped forward to intercept him.

"No, it's okay," said Shin to the sailor. "He's a friend."

Shin imagined his eyeballs bulged slightly at Tyler's fierce squeeze, but thankfully the Texas yeti avoided contact with his wounded thigh.

Tyler released the bear hug and said, "I gotta hear all about this."

"Sir, we must get you to the medical facility," interjected one of Shin's escorts.

Shin nodded, then gimped along with them. He whispered in English to Tyler, "What the hell are you doing here?"

"Seems like I'm picking you up again," said Tyler.

"But this is a military base," said Shin. "How did you get in?"

"Credentials, little brother."

<hr>

DESPITE SHIN'S insistence that it was unnecessary, Tyler hovered over him while the medical crew checked him out. It was like being followed about by an enormous puppy, and he chuckled at the arched eyebrows of the clinic staff as they gaped upward at Tyler. The distraction helped Shin handle the painful prodding as he was attended to.

Thankfully, Shin's uncomfortable time in the clinic was brief, and the news was good.

"Let's drive you home," said Tyler, once they were out in the hallway. "I've got your cousin's address written down somewhere."

Shin limped behind Tyler to the lobby. As they left the building, warm late-summer sunshine enveloped them.

The driveway in front of the clinic was empty. Tyler stopped. He scratched his head as he looked along the drive. "Hmm," he grunted.

"Forget something? said Shin. "Like a vehicle, perhaps?"

"There's supposed to be a ride here."

"Typical Marine, charge in with your heart, and leave your brains behind."

"Relax, brother," said Tyler. "I'm sure it'll be here."

As if on cue, a Mitsubishi military-truck pulled up in front of the building. A driver wearing black fatigues stepped out and saluted Tyler, which seemed odd given that Tyler was wearing blue jeans and a surfing shirt.

Tyler returned the salute. The man, having delivered the vehicle, jogged back along the driveway.

Tyler turned to Shin. "See," he said. "Now hop aboard and let's get you home."

Shin sat in the passenger seat. Tyler muttered something about short people, slid the driver's seat all the way back, then adjusted the mirrors.

"Thanks for driving," said Shin.

"You bet," answered Tyler. He shifted the truck into gear. "One problem, though. They drive on the wrong side of the road here, and this is my first time."

"Great."

Despite Shin's apprehension, Tyler stayed on the correct side of the road as he drove them to the main gate, then off the base.

"You never told me what you're actually doing here in Japan," said Shin.

"Intelligence," said Tyler. "Once you told me about your plan to sink those bastards, I ran it through my boss and he decided it was a worthy goal."

"The freight company you work for thought it was a good idea?"

"Ha!" said Tyler, "That's part-time work. My other job is in intelligence. I'm here to function as a liaison for Uncle Sam with the Japanese. Turns out the *Zheng Yi* was into some really bad stuff."

Stunned by Tyler's revelation, Shin rode in silence for several miles as he processed the information.

"How long have you been here?" he asked.

"A week," said Tyler. "I was at Dolphin Base, observing the entire operation while you were out there in the Sea of Okhotsk playing hide and seek."

"Knock me over with a feather," mumbled Shin.

Almost two hours later, they pulled in front of Daichi's house, and the gate rolled open. A military truck identical to the one Tyler drove was parked in the driveway next to the Acura.

The front door opened, and Daichi couldn't stop smiling as he welcomed them into the house. "Join us, Shin and Tyler," he said in English. "We are celebrating."

As they walked inside, Shin realized that there hadn't been an introduction: Daichi and Tyler knew each other. He was about to ask when he saw Mariko waving from the kitchen. He halted mid-limp.

"Hey there, cowboy," she said. "You made it."

"Yes," said Shin, confused. "Mariko, why are you here? You were on your way to turn in your report to the director of the agency."

"That's what I'm doing," said Mariko. "Daichi is the director. I thought you knew that."

Shin glanced at his cousin. "He doesn't tell me much."

"Welcome to the inner circle," said Mariko.

Tyler smirked.

Daichi cleared his throat. "Let me get you something to drink, and let's all sit and chat."

When they'd convened to the living room, Daichi raised his glass. "A toast," he said. "Bottoms up. May the *Zheng Yi* stay on the bottom." He giggled.

They clinked glasses and drank. Shin noticed that Mariko's eyes lingered on Tyler.

Daichi continued, "I've just finished a phone call with the Minister of Defense. What a magnificent success!" He waved his hand in the air with the flourish of a stage actor bathing in applause.

"I'm glad, sir," said Mariko.

"Oh, you have no idea how fantastic this is," said Daichi. "The Chinese are furious with the Russians, and there is a multinational diplomatic tsunami brewing. It's beautiful. The minister is so tickled that he stated his intent to award me a defense-service medal.

"However, more importantly is the fact that my honor has been restored and you have come back safely. This flawless operation has avenged my failed attempt at stopping the *Zheng Yi* abomination four years ago. And it is with the utmost gratitude that I thank all of you."

Mariko, Tyler, and Shin bowed.

Daichi rose. "Food and more sake. Be right back."

Shin's mind was still playing catch up when he saw Tyler wink at Mariko.

"Wait... you two know each other?" whispered Shin.

"Yeah, brother. We've talked on the phone for a while, but we only just met last week."

Mariko smiled.

Daichi returned with a large *tokkuri* of sake, and then a feast: takeout from Yuki Onna.

Shin launched into the first proper food he'd had in days. Everyone else must have been hungry as well because there wasn't much conversation beyond Mariko identifying food items for Tyler, and Tyler trying to pronounce them in Japanese.

After dinner, fatigue claimed Shin. Though he longed to catch up with Tyler, that would have to wait. He bid everyone goodnight and limped to the guest room.

Shin eased his battered body onto the futon, then snuggled under the bedding. *I'm too old for fighting*, he thought.

The burble of conversation and occasional laughter from the adjacent room lulled him to sleep.

46

Several days later, Shin had recovered enough strength to travel to Kushiro. After having breakfast with Tyler, who had quarters at the base, the two of them walked along the streets of the city. They made quite the pair, and attracted a number of curious stares, though Shin would have been nearly invisible without the Texan towering over people.

Shin was still wrapping his head around the fact that his cousin directed a spy agency — and Tyler had a covert life. Shin didn't know much about that line of work, but the common man's wisdom suggested that an operative should blend in as much as possible with the local environment. His yeti friend represented the opposite scenario, and perhaps that was by design: make someone so glaringly obvious that only a fool would suspect them of being surreptitious.

"So what's next?" asked Tyler.

"I was going to ask you the same question," said Shin.

"I've got another two weeks on my assignment," said Tyler. "Mariko and I are going out to dinner tonight. My boss is pretty fired up about what I've learned here so far, and I'm angling for a longer-term arrangement with the agency."

"Good for you," said Shin. "As for me, I want to heal up, then see if I can find Mothersong and the pod. After that, I don't know. I don't really fit in here."

"Brother, I don't think you can ever fit in anywhere," said Tyler, and laughed. "And I think that's the point. You talk to orcas."

"Shhh," said Shin. Though they spoke English, he scanned to see who on the street may be listening. His neck muscles tightened.

"Don't worry, your secret's safe with me," said Tyler. "The only thing I told them is that you have a special affinity for killer whales — which is the God's honest truth."

Shin let out the breath he'd been holding. "Thank you, my friend," he said, and bit his lip. "I... don't know what would happen if people believed I could communicate with orcas — but I suspect it would be bad for the orcas and me."

"I reckon you're right," said Tyler. "People might try to exploit killer whales, maybe even try to use them as weapons, and God knows what the scientists would do to you."

Truth, thought Shin. His knees weakened at what he'd done: he had taught killer whales how to fight back against humans. He was grateful that none of the orcas had died in the battle.

Tyler continued, "Mariko told me of a rumor going round the base that you were observed riding an orca, leading a pod of fifty. But few worth their salt think it's factual."

"Shit."

Tyler guffawed, then leaned toward Shin and whispered, "I knew it was true. One day soon, we'll sit down and you can tell me how it all went down. However, my advice applies here in Hokkaido just as surely as it did in Sequim. Follow your heart. Go find Mothersong and her pod."

Tyler clamped a big paw on Shin's shoulder, and added, "It'd be cool if we both ended up here, eh? I might even open up a Texas barbecue joint on the side."

47

Every day at noon, barring severe weather, Shin descended into the Sea of Japan off of Rishiri Island and called for Mothersong and the Ravenfin. Summer had turned to fall, and it had become colder. The first snows had graced the upper slopes of Mount Rishiri.

With Daichi's help, Shin had received the honor of Japanese citizenship and the generous gift of ten 1-kg gold bars from the *Zheng Yi's* safe. *A pirate's one-tenth share of the spoils*, Daichi had said in jest.

Shin had purchased a full set of cold underwater gear, and had built a new comms system. He'd secured a small house on the shore of the tiny island, close enough that he could wade into the sea in his scuba gear. There weren't any Japanese social media groups tracking orcas in this region, and Russia maintained a firewall — so he'd adopted the regular habit of swimming out into the sea and broadcasting.

Though he'd boosted the power, there was only so far the sound could travel. Shin hoped that with repetition, he might catch one of the pods passing by, or perhaps his voice might resonate with a sympathetic whale. His first whale contact in Japan had been near here. That occurrence, and the orca memorial on the island, had leant him the perseverance to perform this daily ritual for the past two months.

When Shin had parted from the Ravenfin, they'd been in the Sea of Okhotsk a hundred miles from here, but that territory was Russian and off-limits. Rishiri Island was twenty miles from the Sōya Strait and though he didn't know the ranging habits of the regional orcas, the ancient memorial and geography suggested that they used the narrow channel to access larger seas.

Today, a cloudless blue reflected in the calm water as Shin swam to the marker buoy, then followed the line below to the mooring-anchor.

Each week, it had become colder, and soon, the winter would bring ice floes.

He checked his watch: thirty minutes of air time. Shin drew in a breath and broadcast: "Mothersong. Ravenfin. Whiteteeth. This is Shin. I am here."

He listened and waited five minutes before repeating the message.

Shin swam in a circle around the mooring anchor to warm up.

"We seek Shin of the Ravenfin," said a voice. "Where are you?"

"Here!" exclaimed Shin. *My God.*

His heart thundered. He held his breath and waited.

A half-minute later, Shin's skin tingled with the scans of orcas.

A set of white eye-patches appeared in the clear water.

Followed by more.

Orcas surrounded him and called, "Shin."

He startled when he recognized Mothersong as she drifted in and hovered next to him.

"Shin, my heart sings to see you," she said. "The sea is fertile! Both clans have new pregnancies. We are thriving. The old stories were true. I was right to believe in you."

Shin trembled, floated closer to her, and grasped a pec-fin. He put his head on hers, and said, "Mothersong, you gave my life new meaning."

"Shin of the Ravenfin," said Mothersong, "may our souls forever dance together in the waves."

THANK YOU

Thank you for reading Shin of the Ravenfin. Now that you have finished the story, I would love for you to leave a review.

Connect with Mark. Please visit his website **MarkJenkinsBooks.com** and check out some interesting tidbits from this novel and his other works. Be sure to sign up for his newsletter, **Pen & Puget Sound** for original content, updates, nature photography, and works from other authors.

ABOUT THE AUTHOR

Mark Jenkins is a British-American author of speculative fiction. He is an outdoor enthusiast, swimmer, bass player, and philomath. His love of nature and adventure is woven into his sci-fi and fantasy tales.

He and his wife chase their dreams together in the Pacific Northwest.